Summer

ali smith
Summer

PANTHEON BOOKS

NEW YORK

All rights reserved. Published in the United States by Pantheon Books, a division of Penguin Random House LLC, New York. Originally published in hardcover in Great Britain by Hamish Hamilton, an imprint of Penguin Books Ltd., a division of Penguin Random House Ltd., London, in 2020.

Pantheon Books and colophon are registered trademarks of Penguin Random House LLC.

Grateful acknowledgment is made to Carcanet Press Ltd. for permission to reprint an excerpt from "Fires" from *New Collected Poems* by Edwin Morgan. Copyright © the Estate of Edwin Morgan. Reprinted by kind permission of Carcanet Press Ltd., Manchester.

Library of Congress Cataloging-in-Publication Data
Name: Smith, Ali, [date] author.
Title: Summer : a novel / Ali Smith.
Description: First United States edition. New York : Pantheon Books, 2020.
Series: Seasonal quartet.
Identifiers: LCCN 2020027016 (print). LCCN 2020027017 (ebook).
ISBN 9781101870792 (hardcover). ISBN 9781101870808 (ebook).
Subjects: LCSH: Domestic fiction.
Classification: LCC PR6069.M4213 S86 2020 (print) | LCC PR6069.M4213 (ebook) |
DDC 823/.914--dc23
LC record available at lccn.loc.gov/2020027016
LC ebook record available at lccn.loc.gov/2020027017

www.pantheonbooks.com

Artwork on rear endpaper: *Lorenza Mazzetti, Self Portrait, 2010,* acrylic on canvas (100 x 60 cm). Copyright © Lorenza Mazzetti, courtesy Paola Mazzetti. Photo credit: Eva Krampen Kosloski.

Jacket image: *English Landscape with Cottage and Stream* (detail), by Edward Charles Williams. The Print Collector/Alamy

Jacket design by Oliver Munday

Printed in the United States of America
First United States Edition
9 8 7 6 5 4 3 2 1

for my sisters
Maree Morrison
Anne MacLeod

my friends
Paul Bailey
Bridget Hannigan

to keep in mind
my friend
Sarah Daniel

and for
my huckleberry friend
Sarah Wood

It was a summer's night and they were
talking, in the big room with the windows
open to the garden, about the cesspool.
Virginia Woolf

Lord keep my memory green!
Charles Dickens

However vast the darkness
we must supply our own light.
Stanley Kubrick

I thought of that person,
him or her, as taking me to a country
far high sunny where I knew to be happy
was only a moment, a puttering flame in the fireplace
but burning all the misery to cinders
if it could, a sift of dross like what we mourn for
as caskets sink with horrifying blandness
into a roar, into smoke, into light, into almost nothing.
The not quite nothing I praise it and I write it.
Edwin Morgan

O, she's warm!
William Shakespeare

1

Everybody said: *so?*

As in *so what?* As in *shoulder shrug*, or *what do you expect me to do about it?* or *I so don't really give a fuck*, or *actually I approve of it, it's fine by me.*

Okay, not everybody said it. I'm speaking colloquially, like in that phrase *everybody's doing it.* What I mean is, it was a clear marker, just then, of that particular time; a kind of litmus, this dismissive note. It got fashionable around then to act like you didn't care. It got fashionable, too, to insist the people who did care, or said they cared, were either hopeless losers or were just showing off.

It's like a lifetime ago.

But it isn't – it's literally only a few months since a time when people who'd lived in this country all their lives or most of their lives started to get arrested and threatened with deportation or deported: *so?*

And when a government shut down its own parliament because it couldn't get the result it wanted: *so?*

When so many people voted people into power who looked them straight in the eye and lied to them: *so?*

When a continent burned and another melted: *so?*

When people in power across the world started picking off groups of people by religion, ethnicity, sexuality, intellectual or political dissent: *so?*

But no. True. Not everybody said it.

Not by a country mile.

Millions of people didn't say it.

Millions and millions, all across the country and all across the world, saw the lying, and the mistreatments of people and the planet, and were vocal about it, on marches, in protests, by writing, by voting, by talking, by activism, on the radio, on TV, via social media, tweet after tweet, page after page.

To which the people who knew the power of saying *so?* said, on the radio, on TV, via social media, tweet after tweet, page after page: *so?*

I mean, I could spend my whole life listing things about, and talking about, and demonstrating with sources and graphs and examples and statistics, what history's made it clear happens when we're indifferent, and what the consequences are of the political cultivation of indifference, which whoever wants to disavow will dismiss in an instant with their own punchy little

so?

So.

Instead, here's something I once saw.

It's an image from a film made in the UK roughly seventy years ago, not long after the end of the Second World War.

The film was made in London by a young artist who arrived in the city from Italy when London was one of the many places having to rebuild themselves in those years nearly a lifetime ago, after the tens of millions of people of all ages all across the world had died before their time.

It's an image of a man carrying two suitcases.

He's a slight man, a young man, a distracted and tentative kind of a man, dapper in a hat and jacket, light on his feet but at the same time burdened; it's clear he'd be burdened even if he wasn't carrying two suitcases. He is grave, slim, preoccupied, terribly keen, and he is silhouetted against the sky because he's balanced on a very narrow brick ledge which runs round the edge of a high building, along the length of which he's doing a joyous and frantic dance with the beaten-up rooftops of London behind him; no: more precisely, those roofs are way below him.

How can he be going so fast and not fall off the edge of the building?

How can what he's doing be so wild and still so graceful, so urgent and blithe both at once?

How can he be swinging those cases around in the air like that and still keep his balance? How can he be moving at such speed next to the sheer drop?

Why is he risking everything?

There'd be no point in showing you a still or a photo of this. It's very much a moving image.

For several seconds he does a crazed but merry high-wire dance above the city going far too fast along the zigzagging path of a ledge that's the width of a single brick.

So:

Whether I shall turn out to be the heroine of my own life, Sacha's mother says.

Then she says, Sacha, what *is* that? Where's it from?

Sacha is having breakfast reading her phone in the front room. The TV is on with the volume turned up several notches too high and her mother is shouting over the top of it.

Don't know, Sacha says.

She says this at normal volume so it's perfectly possible her mother didn't hear her say anything. Not that it makes a difference either way.

Heroine of my own life, her mother is walking up and down the room and saying it over and over. Heroine of my own life, then it's something about a station, a station shall be held. What's it from?

Like it matters.

Sacha shakes her head without shaking it enough to be noticed shaking it.

Her mother has no idea.

An example of this is what happened last night about the quote Sacha found online for the essay about forgiveness she had to write for Merchiston's class later today. To mark one week since Brexit they've all been made to write an essay on the subject of 'Forgiveness'. Sacha is deeply suspicious of forgiveness. The act of saying *I forgive you*, it's like saying *you are less than me and I have the moral or superior upper hand.*

But that's the kind of truth-spirit that'll get you a B instead of an A from Merchiston, to whom the whole class now knows exactly how to respond in the way that gets the required marks.

So, late last night, because it has to be handed in today, she looked up some quotes on the net.

As a writer from the last century so devoutly said, <u>Forgiveness is the only way to reverse the irreversible flow of history</u>.

Her mother had come into her bedroom without knocking, again, and was standing reading the screen over Sacha's shoulder.

Oh, that's good, that quote, her mother said, I like that.

I like it too, Sacha said.

Is devoutly the right word? her mother said. It

sounds more philosophical than devotional. Is it a devotional writer? Who wrote it?

Yes, it's a devotional writer, Sacha said though she'd no idea, didn't know who wrote it and had written the word devoutly because devoutly sounded good in the sentence. But now with her mother breathing down her neck and holding forth about who, she brought up Startpage and typed in the words irreversible, flow, history. The quote came up.

Someone european-sounding, she said.

Ah. It's Arendt, Hannah Arendt, her mother said. I'd like to read Arendt on forgiveness, I'd like that a lot right now.

Ironic, Sacha thought, given that neither her father nor her mother looked likely to forgive each other anything any time soon.

Though I don't know that I'd call her a devotional, her mother said. What's the source?

Brainyquote, Sacha said.

That's not a source, her mother said. Does it give the original source? Look. It doesn't. That's terrible.

The source *is* Brainyquote, Sacha said. That's where I found the quote.

You can't just put down Brainyquote as your source, her mother said.

Yes I can, Sacha said.

You need better source reference than that, her

mother said. Otherwise you don't know where what Hannah Arendt said comes from.

Sacha held the screen up. She turned it towards her mother.

Brainyquote. Quotepark. Quotehd. Azquotes. Facebook. Goodreads. Picturequotes. Quotefancy. Askideas. Birthdaywishes.expert, she said. All these places come up when you type in bits of this quote. Those are just the top sources. There are masses of sites quoting her saying it.

No, because if these sites are just *saying* they're quoting her, that's not good enough, her mother said. You'd have to go through all those sites until you find what it is they're actually quoting from. Context. It matters.

Yeah, but I don't need to know that, Sacha said.

Yeah but you do, her mother said. Check and see if any of those sites mentions a primary source.

The internet *is* a primary source, Sacha said.

Her mother went away.

Everything went quiet for about ten minutes.

Sacha began to breathe normally again.

Then her mother who'd clearly been on the kitchen laptop looking up Brainyquote Quotepark and so on shouted up the stairs as if she'd been personally insulted by Brainyquote Quotepark and so on:

None of these sites, not a single one, gives a

primary source, Sach. I can't find where Arendt wrote this. So you shouldn't use the quote. You can't.

Right, thanks, Sacha shouted back from her bedroom.

Then she continued doing what she was doing regardless of her mother.

It might not even have been said by Arendt, her mother who'd come halfway up the stairs now was shouting.

She was shouting like nobody could hear her.

It's not trustworthy, her mother shouted.

Who needs a school homework assignment to be trustworthy? Sacha said.

I do, her mother shouted. You do. All human beings who use sources do.

Worrying about stuff like this was what her mother's generation did as displacement activity from worrying about the real things happening in the world. Still, just in case her mother had a point –

How about if I note at the end of it that the internet says it's by Hannah, uh, Sacha said.

She looked online again to get the second name of the person who said it.

Not good enough, her mother shouted coming into the room unasked again. Because there's no proof Hannah Arendt ever said it. What if it was someone else, someone who isn't getting the credit?

Or. What if *nobody* said it in *any* original source and someone somewhere just *made up* that Hannah Arendt said it, typed it into the net and then it spread through all these sites?

Then Hannah Arendt, whoever she is, would be pleased, Sacha said (at normal volume so her mother would realize her own loudness). It's a good thing to have said.

You can't speak for Hannah Arendt, her mother said (yes, less shoutily, good). How would you like it if the internet quoted something or other then said that Sacha Greenlaw said it?

I wouldn't mind. I'd be pleased that someone somewhere thought I'd said something good, Sacha said.

Oh I see. Approbation's what it's about. You're acting like you're Robert's age, her mother said.

No I'm not, Sacha said. If I *was* still only thirteen, or happened to be Robert, please God no, I'd have said: return yourself forthwith to the age of pointless educational pedantry.

Come on, Sach, her mother said. Source. It matters. Think why.

What I think, Sacha said turning to face her mother. Is that I'm working at the correct acceptable level.

The level of attention I'm talking about is necessary for *everything*, her mother said getting louder again (like louder meant she was more right). And what you call the correct acceptable level is nothing but a social stratagem.

Now her mother was waving her arms about so much in the air in Sacha's room that she actually knocked the lampshade swinging.

What if you woke up one day and found that it said all over the net that *you'd* said something you'd never say in a million years? her mother said.

I'd just simply tell everybody that I never said it, Sacha said.

But what if you went online and found thousands of people angry at you regardless? her mother said. What if something like what's happened to your little brother happened to you?

You can't do anything about that kind of pile-up, Sacha said. So I don't care who thinks what. *I'd* know I was telling the truth. And I am the source of me. Go and bother him. I don't have time for this.

I would. But he's out, her mother said.

It's ten o clock, Sacha said. He's thirteen. What kind of a parent are you?

One that's doing her best for both her children against insurmountable odds, her mother said.

This has to be handed in first thing, Sacha said.

What if your reputation was ruined and you couldn't go anywhere because everybody was calling you a disgrace and a liar? her mother said.

I'd forgive them, Sacha said.

You'd what? her mother said.

Forgiveness, Sacha said, is the only way to reverse the irreversible flow of history.

There was a short pause, almost like when people pause in a play at the theatre. Then her mother laughed out loud.

Then Sacha laughed too.

Her mother came and gave Sacha a hug at her desk.

My bright girl, her mother said.

Sacha's chest filled with the kind of warmth that once when she was really small she'd asked her mother about because it felt so nice and her mother'd said *that's your inner summer.*

But you'll have to be brighter even than that, her mother said now still hugging her tight. Bright girls have to be brighter than the, the.

Correct acceptable level of brightness, Sacha said into her mother's side.

That was last night. This is next morning. Sacha's come through here to try to have her breakfast in peace while checking the news and everybody's posts on Facebook on her phone. But there is no peace. Her mother is maundering round the front room shouting words and waving a cup of coffee whose contents sometimes spill over and hit the parquet; Sacha has had to move her bag a couple of times.

The TV is turned up too high and the news

announcers in the studio and out in the world are maundering on too in their usual surreal way. Since Sacha watched that TV show where celebrities dress up in costumes with huge masked heads and sing a song, and a panel and an audience try to guess who's behind the mask, it has struck Sacha that actually everyone and everything on TV is like someone wearing a mask. After you've seen it, you can't not see it.

Take it off! Take it off! the panel and the audience shout at the celebrity who loses and has to unmask, so that people can see at last who's been in there all along.

Take it off! Sacha once saw a gang of men shouting it at a girl down near the pier.

Whether I shall turn out to be, her mother says. Heroine of my own life. Whether that station, that station, shall be held by anybody else. Will be held.

Just look it up, Sacha says.

No, her mother says.

I'll look it up for you, Sacha says.

No. Don't, her mother says.

The don't is said with all her mother's fierceness in it; these days her mother is constantly forgetting things and constantly trying not to look up online the things she's forgotten. *I'm so menopausal. It's the menopause.* Like you can defy the inevitable by shouting its name at it. She is trying to make herself remember things rather than look them up. In real terms, what this means is her mother annoys everybody for half an hour *then* goes online and looks up whatever it is she can't remember.

Will be held by anybody else, she says, whether that station will be held by anybody else. For God sake, Sach. Turn that down so I can hear myself think. So I can hear myself *not* think.

Can't. He's put it somewhere, Sacha says.

Robert has already left for school. One of his more recent japes is to turn the TV volume up several notches too high then hide the remote, because the remote is the only way they've got of getting the TV to do anything. The on/off button on top doesn't work any more (this TV is quite old; their father took the new one next door when he went). If you unplug it you risk not getting it to turn on again. So they don't.

The too-loud thing on the screen right now is a news report about an evangelical rally that has something to do with the American president.

Call him, her mother says. See if he's with your dad.

Next door dad. Like a TV sitcom from her mother's generation.

He won't be, Sacha says.

Just in case, her mother says.

Sacha calls Robert's mobile. It goes straight to voicemail.

Off, Sacha says.

Course it is, her mother says. I'll knock on the wall.

He won't be there, Sacha says.

Ashley won't let Robert in any more since he 1. stole her little harp thing she plays her welsh tunes on, 2. sold it in Cash Converters then gave her the money for it in an envelope like he was doing her a favour, and 3. told her (even though she's Welsh which is actually also British) she wasn't welcome in this country as anything but a tourist now.

And Mercy is taking the bible belt by dollar-storm, the TV reporter says. They're calling her the great white hope.

It's true, Sacha can't see a single person who's not white in any of the footage of the Mercy Bucks Church of the Spirit.

He told me to tell you. He tells me direct. He's telling me now. I can hear his holy voice, the holy voice of the great God almighty speaking to me from his own holy mouth, he's here, he's saying it right now, mercy, mercy (mercy, mercy! the people in the church are shouting back at her, or maybe Mercy, Mercy, since Mercy's her name).

Who *is* that? her mother says as she passes through the room again and stops in front of the TV.

It's a great white hope, Sacha says. God speaks to her direct in his holy voice from his holy mouth into her earhole.

17

Mercy Bucks, her mother says. That's a made-up name. And that's a terrible accent. She looks really, really like Claire Dunn. If Claire Dunn were thirty years older. Which, let's face it, she will be now.

You always think people on TV are someone you know, Sacha says.

No, I recognize her. I worked with her. If it's Claire she's had a nose job, her mother says. The nose is different.

The nose is different because it's not anyone you know, Sacha says.

She gives her mother a sidelong look. Usually when her mother brings up her acting past it's a signal that she's in a fragile way. Sacha's mother was in acting once, back before she met their father and before she did something in advertising that she gave up when she had Sacha and her brother. It is all also connected to things that can't be said out loud by anyone in the family about her mother's mother, who died when their mother was only Robert's age, by swallowing too many tablets, which their mother says was by mistake and everybody including her mother knows probably wasn't really by mistake but never says it. (Not even Robert.)

But her mother doesn't look fragile. She just looks a bit tired.

The report ends with a camera shot on the back projection behind Mercy Bucks of a clicker showing the amount of money being donated rising hundreds of dollars a second.

The next news item is about the wildfires in Australia.

They've had a hot January, her mother says.

The hottest since data began, Sacha says. And it's February now and those fires are still going.

Get the news up on catch-up for me, her mother says. Let's get another look at Claire.

Sacha holds her hands up and out.

Can't, she says.

Her mother feels down the sides of the couch for the remote. She checks behind the things on the shelves. Then she stands in the middle of the room at a loss.

Sacha hates it when her mother is at a loss.

Probably in his room, Sacha says.

Or he's taken it to school with him, her mother says.

Sacha goes into the hall and pulls her coat on. She checks herself in the mirror.

I can't get catch-up to work, her mother shouts through from the kitchen.

I've got to go, Sacha calls back through.

But she goes through to the kitchen at the note of panic in her mother's voice.

It's true; BBC iPlayer isn't working; it's not just her mother's uselessness. But Sacha can save the day for her mother and still get off to school, because Pastor Mercy Bucks has her own YouTube channel.

MERCY BUCKS SAVES

All the titles of Mercy Bucks's videos have the word white in them.

White on the skin of his body.

Behold a white cloud.

The branches have become white.

Sacha clicks on the most recent video, uploaded yesterday. *A great white throne.* 44.4k views.

In a high-ceilinged modern church the words Gain From The Gospel are haloed in fluorescent light behind the figure of Mercy Bucks.

Add Kings 21.2 to Matthew 6.33, Mercy says. *And I Will Give Thee The Worth Of It In Money* plus *But Seek First His Kingdom.* It's the only way anything will ever truly add up in life because God is the boss of our corporation. God is the ultimate accountant. And God knows everything. God knows you. God knows what you have and what you have not. Don't think God the father can't see into even the most encrypted bank account. God can reckon to the dime, to the cent. Exactly how much you're willing to shortchange God. Exactly how much you're willing to sacrifice in God's name to become a person of spiritual property. Because God smiles on those who sacrifice savings. God rewards those who render unto God what belongs to God. God windfalls those who prove themselves

worthy. God showers in benefits those who are
benefactors to God's good church.

Mercy Bucks says it all in her singsong way and
the congregation sways and rocks in the broadcast
light like they're at a rock concert, punching the
air with their phones, breaking into singing,
Mercy Mercy Hallelujah, to the old tune of Glory
Glory.

Mercy holds her hand up to quieten them.

And God says that nobody, nobody who truly
believes, could ever say anything bad or denigratory
or damaging about our president, she says.

Sacha starts laughing.

God says anybody who says such things is
speaking evil with tongues, Mercy says. God knows
the impeachment trial was evil. God cleared our
president's name with every breath our president
takes! I know God. God knows me. Believe me.
Believe me. I'm a woman hotlined to God, God's
got me on direct dial and God told me to tell you to
support our great great president who's here on
earth to do a great great work, the great great work
that God the father and Jesus the saviour have
personally entrusted him with –

Sacha is laughing so much now that she nearly
topples the chair she's on. Her mother is shaking
her head.

I suppose the fact that we're all a lot more
accustomed to blatancy these days means that

blatancy itself has to get even more blatant, her mother says.

Yeah. But what a fraud, Sacha says.

T'was ever so, her mother says. Since summer first was leafy.

Now her mother's saying lines from when she was an actress. But the only thing her mother was apparently ever really in was a washing-up liquid advert on TV back before everything. Sacha was shown the advert when she was little, there's a video of it in a cupboard, now unwatchable because there are no video players left alive. In it a young woman, a slim and coiffed stranger, unbelievable but it really is her mother, way back then, bends down in a kitchen to take a dish from a small boy who is wearing a policeman's hat and explaining to this woman who's meant to be *his* mother that in not getting these dishes clean enough she's committing a crime.

– so donate, donate, donate and do right, to help me prepare me the way of the Lord, because oh dear Lord day by day three things I pray, see me clearly, love me dearly, follow me on social media and donate day by day by day by day –

Now she's just quoting bits out of Godspell, her mother says.

What's Godspell? Sacha says.

Old musical, her mother says. We did Godspell together. We did Much Ado. Then we did the

Shakespeare / Dickens summer tour of the eastern counties.

Meanwhile the camera is doing close-ups on the people in Mercy's audience. Some look proud. Some look broken. Some look desperate. Some look lit with hope. They all look poor. Most are holding their phones in the air and waving them. The others are using their phones to donate. The screen soft-focuses close up on Mercy's face.

Yep, her mother says. Definitely.

Will I sleep it or do you want to keep watching it? Sacha says.

– are you sad? I see you, are you lonely? I see you, are you anxious? are you wired? are you mired in sin? I see you, are you tired? can't you get hired? has life made you a shadow of yourself? are you more dead than alive? are you a ghost of yourself, a wraith? then listen because, God sayeth through me, it is required, it is required –

Sacha moves the cursor arrow to click the page away.

It is required you do awake your faith, her mother says.

– awake your faith, Mercy Bucks says a split second after her mother does, a split second before Mercy Bucks disappears off the screen.

Her mother nods.

Winter's Tale, summer 89. I was Hermione. She was Understudy. Sacha, you're going to be really late. Do you need a lift? Oh no, silly me. Ms Car Embargo 2020. I forgot.

You didn't forget, Sacha says. You're just unable to allow for other people's attempts at heroism.

I don't know that I'd call a refusal to travel in anything petrol-based an attempt at heroism, her mother says. A principle, maybe. But heroism?

What's Winter's Tale Summer 89? Sacha says.

The Winter's Tale is a Shakespeare play, her mother says.

I know *that*, Sacha says (though in reality she didn't or at least wasn't completely sure).

And summer 89 is long gone. Antediluvian now, her mother says.

Anti what? Sacha says.

Ante. Before. Diluvian. The deluge, her mother says. Twenty past. You'd best run.

Sacha picks her coat up off the floor, shoulders it back on and kisses her mother on the cheek.

God bless, her mother says.

Did God just tell you to say that by speaking direct into your ear in his holy voice? Sacha says.

He did if you pay me a fiver, her mother says.

Car embargo. Like it's a joke, a fad.

Anti diluvian.

Sacha quite likes words. She doesn't really get to, though, at home, because Robert's meant to be the one who likes words.

24

On her way to school she looks up anti diluvian on her phone.

Spelt slightly differently it means before the Flood capital F.

Yeah. As if the Flood capital F belongs to the past. We're all antediluvian *right now.*

Not even when they see the pictures of Australia burning do they admit it. Not even when half a billion dead creatures – meaning 500000000 individual living things dead – is only the death toll from one single area. Not even when they see the photo of Australian people with no summer daylight standing breathing red dust air on a beach under a red sky, sort of hanging like puppets nobody can work the strings of, and a chestnut horse just standing there in the middle of them, bewildered, grave, like proof of blamelessness itself, while the ball of fire spread on the horizon behind them like a melting butter sun.

5 0 0 0 0 0 0 0 0. Sacha tries to imagine, and to respect, each dead creature individually. She lays out across a blasted plain the dead animals two by two by two by two by two million, further than any eye can see, kangaroo cinder with kangaroo cinder, wallaby ash with wallaby ash, charcoaled koala, charcoaled koala.

Her imagination isn't big enough.

She already knows she is *never* going to have

children. Why would you bring a child into a catastrophe? It would be like giving birth to a child in a prison cell. And Brighton's a good place, one of the best in the country for green things, the only place in the whole UK with a green MP, and even so people here too on the local news are saying *global warming's a hoax stop trying to frighten me stop frightening my children with rubbish so they can't sleep it's fine I'd actually like some warmer weather the globe could be doing with it summer all year round would be great*. Her own mother is one of those cracked people. It is like her mother's more freaked out by what the menopause is doing to her than she is by real things happening in and to the world.

Menopause is real too, Sacha's mother says now in Sacha's head.

Whoa.

But wait.

Is that – what just happened in her head – the same as God speaking into Mercy Bucks's ear?

Yeah, but Sacha's mother didn't *actually* speak in her ear or her head there. It's just that Sacha knows what she'd say if she were *here*. Because she knows her mother so *well*.

But God isn't real. Sacha is pretty sure about that.

God is a figment of human need and imagination.

Her mother, though.

Definitely real.

But. Wait.

Because: God *is* several kinds of real, 1. in being 'real' to the people there at those religious shows who believe in God, 2. in being made 'real' to them because he apparently physically 'speaks into someone's ear', and 3. in being a 'real' figment of Mercy Bucks's imagination with very real lucrative consequences for Mercy Bucks.

So. What does that make Sacha's mother?

Or, more precisely, what does that make Sacha's *imagining* of her mother?

Imagine you are a flower in water but that your time of taking in water as a plant is over because you're naturally starting to dry up, and the water – though you can't understand it, being a flower and everything – no longer goes up your stem in the same old way.

That's the kind of thing her mother's taken to saying. It is driven by a Freudian envy of young people, especially her daughter.

I wonder if flowers feel like this, like I do, when it happens to them. Do flowers feel like they lose their dexterity? do they bump into things all the time? do they forget things constantly? do they think that Simon Cowell's name is Simon Callow even though they know full well it's Cowell but they just can't get to the name through their neural paths for some reason any more?

Sacha blows air through her teeth out of her mouth in disdain.

Getting old is pathetic if you use it as an excuse for no longer being responsible.

Her mother could make more of an effort.

Sacha is never going to be like that.

Given what's happening planetarily, Sacha is unlikely to get to an age when it'll happen anyway.

Her mother's lucky she got to live so long.

You're the one talking imaginary rubbish, her mother says in her head. It's all going to be fine.

Her mother, real or 'real'. Both are deluded.

Still, she feels a bit guilty for feeling irritation at her and for being this rude inside her head about her.

What was that thing, about heroines holding up a station? She will look it up and text her mother what its source is. This will both annoy her mother *and* please her. Two birds one stone.

Horrible proverb.

The horror images fill her head. Something that had once been a bird in a sky, a wingframe broken and wayward, jutting out of stripped scorched ribcage.

A bird in the hand is worth.

No. A bird in the hand is unnatural unless that bird's actually chosen unforced to sit on your hand of its own free will.

Bit long for a proverb, though.

Two birds in the hand?

St Francis.

She thinks about the film in Italian they watched back when her parents were still living in the same house and watched the things with the subtitles that her mother didn't like and her father liked, back when she was Robert's age. It was about St F. trying to do his morning prayers under the trees but the birds love him so much that they crowd into the branches all round him and sing and cheep their love so loud that he has to ask them to be quiet because he can't hear himself pray.

Then all his monks crowded round him too to ask him where he wanted them to go and do their God spiel in the world. He told them all to turn round and round and round on the spot and keep spinning till they fell over from dizziness. One by one they all fell over. Then he stood above them and said, okay, so whatever direction you ended up facing when you fell over, you go that way my brothers and spread the word.

She passes Tesco. There's a guy in the doorway but it isn't Steve.

She hopes he's all right wherever he is. There are a lot of homeless people out today; it's bright and dry. The last time she saw Steve he told her about the sixteen busloads brought down from Nottingham and the northeast.

Free trip to the south coast, he said. One way

trip. They dump them wherever the MP's not a
Tory. Town's full of them. Sent them to the seaside.
May as well all be on our holidays I tell you, cause
nobody's making any fucking money now they're
all here.

She gave him what change she had in her pocket
that day. Someone had stolen his boots.

Thanks, love, he said.

Keep warm, she said.

Do my best, he said. You too.

She imagines Steve on a screen and a clicker
showing the donations behind him like the one
behind Mercy Bucks, except Steve's is going up
really slowly in increments of 10p. She imagines
Mercy Bucks spinning and spinning on the altar of
the Mercy Bucks Church of the Spirit like a break
dancer who can't stop or a needle gone mad on a
compass, Mercy demonstrating to her audience
how to spin round and round till they all fall
down. Then Mercy Bucks going round all the
fallen-over dizzy people like on a battlefield,
tending to them tenderly and pickpocketing them
while she does.

She imagines her mother now nipping out the
front door in the winter sunny glare and through
the gates and up the steps with all her invisible
blades out – a bit like a Swiss army knife display
unit in an army and navy stores, a giant red
penknife that revolves on a stand with all its

attachments splayed – and knocking at her father and Ashley's front door to see if the remote's in there.

Her mother never uses the key her father gave her. She always knocks.

She imagines Ashley opening the door to her many-bladed mother and standing there blank. Can't hear. Doesn't understand. Saying the nothing and shaking her head and closing the door again.

Her mother won't get any work done with the TV left on so loud.

Not that there's much administrating to do any more, for a business that's been brex-fucked.

She thinks of her mother this morning wandering round the front room shouting the words whether and heroine over the TV noise.

Oh yeah. Station thing.

Find the source, send it in unspoken obeisance to the Source Queen.

She types the words whether and heroine into the search bar on the phone.

Up comes drugs. Drugs, drugs, drugs, then quite far down, something about Jane Austen and Victorians.

She clears the search bar.

She types in the words station, held, and life.

Stuff comes up about how long people can live in space stations.

She adds the word heroine.

Stuff comes up about drug addicts.

She scrolls and scrolls – then there's a single visual of Greta Thunberg, the photo with her hood up in the yellow coat that looks like a fisherman's coat, the one where she looks like she won't be fobbed off by anybody or anything.

Heroine of my own life!

Only the mighty Greta can upend the internet's determination to make the word heroine refer not to a female hero but to a misspelling of a Class A drug.

As if whoever was typing it in was *bound* to have meant heroin not heroine, heroine being such a little-used notion.

Sacha thinks of Brighton station with the little slip-through entrance, the taxi rank and the place for bikes, the people in Pret and M&S. She imagines it all, all of the above, held in the palm of a giant hand. But whose hand?

No one's hand.

Sacha's own hand, now that she's imagined it.

No point in asking anyone else to hold your world.

She stands at the school gate, wipes her phonescreen clean of prints on the underarm of her coat. As she does, the phone flashes up a text.

It's from Robert.

think am about to do somer thing stupid ;-\ down

on beach opp shit st pls come rght now if you can i
need a hand for 3 mins

It's the *pls* rather than the *rght now* that does it. It
signals real urgency, given that any politeness her
brother used to have is well gone.

It might be a trick.

It might be real.

By shit st he means Ship Street.

Sacha steps back from the gate before anyone sees
her who might ask her why she's loitering and not
coming into school like she should be.

She texts Mel who will be in registration already.

Melaneeee can u pass on apology & message ive
a home emergency & will be in in 1 hrs time thanx
mel (heart emoji heart emoji) sachxxx

If it's a trick? She'll kill him.

She loves him, but. He's her little brother. But.
He is clever, like really clever. But. It is as if since he
turned thirteen a dark visor has come down over
his eyes and he is looking out at everyone and
everything through a metalled slit. From being the
kind of boy who used to say brainy but random
things like *watermelons are 92% water and 8 per
cent everything else, which means the water
quantity = 92% and the rest is melon, so melon
actually only = 8%, and the really exciting thing is
that you can make a maths equation out of
anything, even a fruit or a vegetable,* he has become

the kind of boy who gets sent home for saying things in class like *why is there anything wrong anyway with saying a black person has a watermelon smile?*

Did you really say the things they're saying you did? Out loud? To a whole class? And a teacher? his mother said looking up from the email that came from the school asking her and their father to attend a meeting about their son.

Robert, you can't say things like that, Ashley said.

This was back when Ashley was still speaking.

Yes I can, he said. Anyone can say anything. It's called freedom of speech. It's a human right. It's my human right.

It's not a joke, Robert. It's depraved, Ashley said. These are depraved things to say, and not in any way funny. How can you say such things?

Easy, he said. I also explained to them why people hate women for being girly swots and only useful for sex and having children, especially children that you don't admit to having, because being a man is all about spreading our seed.

Robert! (chorus of voices.)

And basically everybody, including quite a lot of women, think that women should shut up, he said. You're always saying we should listen more to history and what it tells us about ourselves. I say history gave us the scold's bridle for a reason.

In the email the school had told them that Robert had reduced a class to laughing anarchy by standing up and saying these things.

You're quite the satirist, Robert, their father said.

No, I'm quite the pragmatist, Robert said.

I won't have him in the house if he continues to say things like this, Ashley said.

It's one of the last things Sacha remembers her saying before she stopped speaking altogether.

You don't have to resort to bigotry to fit in, his father said.

Are you calling our prime minister and other political leaders bigots? Robert said. Stop talking down our great country. We should be standing up for Britain. Anything less is treason and reveals you to be a doomster and a gloomster.

Just tell your father, Robert, the thing you said about education, the one that particularly angered your teachers, his mother said.

I simply noted, like our prime minister's chief adviser wrote in his blog, that children who come from poverty or grow up in it aren't worth educating because they're just not up to it, Robert said, they're never going to be able to learn anything so there's no point in the state paying for them to have an education they're always going to be congenitally unable to use. And in this I'm only repeating what our own prime minister's chief adviser thinks. And our prime minister, because his

chief adviser's so good at what he does, was
recently elected with a huge majority. So what does
that teach <u>you</u>?

It made Sacha laugh.

Till Robert began to be foul about *her*, like when
Jamie and Jane, who her father had had to lay off,
came round for (apologetic no hard feelings) drinks
at Christmas and Robert stood at the door and
announced to the whole room,

my sister is an idiot. She actually thinks she can
change the world, that with a bit of a nudge from
her and her woke friends anything will change. It's
St Sacha's most recent way of getting attention,

and Jane, who's from New Zealand, said to him,
so you're a bit of a sceptic then, Robert, is that *your*
way of getting attention?

and he told her she was foreign and made fun of
the way she spoke.

Sciptic.

Then the police came to the door when they
caught him cutting nicks into the seats of a bike-
stand of parked bikes. They said he'll be liable for
a youth caution and he's not too old to be arrested
and charged with criminal damage or to find
himself at a Secure Training Centre for a six-year-
stretch. The police who brought him home were
kindly even as they said the stern stuff. Their
kindliness clearly annoyed Robert, who
announced to the police that it would be worth

being charged or whatever just to think of all those cyclists getting home with wet patches up their anuses.

He is what her mother calls intransigent, what her father calls acting like a bloody moron and what Ashley, if Ashley were to speak out loud, would call something so expletive that their father would literally *have* to leave her and move back home again.

It's because he's been so bullied, Sacha said when Robert wasn't in the room. It's because you moved him to a new school. He has to alter who he is to survive.

They don't know what to do about the stuff on social media, the stuff that followed him, like social media didn't even have to draw breath, from the old school into all the phones of all the kids at the new school.

Her mother is worried about him.

Her father is angry about him.

Sacha knows he is brilliant.

She remembers the day he took the Alexa out and down to the beach hidden in his jacket then dropped it casually over the side of the pier into the sea shouting down after it, *Alexa, tell us how to do the breast stroke*. She remembers the day he actually started wearing the trainers that had been, until then, exhibits in the Robert Greenlaw Gallery Trainer Exhibition on the shelves in his room. She remembers the film he made on his phone, and this was in the old days before it was so easy to make films on your phone, of the disconnected way that people look when they're listening to music on their headphones on the train or on a bike or walking along a street; the film he made showed their eyes, and the way they sat moving without even knowing they were to a beat that was nothing to do with what was happening round them in outer reality, and as the soundtrack to the film Robert, who was only nine when he made it, recorded himself following headphoned people around the town asking them questions about themselves which of course they couldn't hear.

That film he made had so shaken Sacha when she saw it that she'd stopped wearing her own phones, except in private, for quite a long time.

But this last while it is as if Robert has attached a dimmer switch to his own brilliance and like he is randomly turning it down as low and dark as it can go then thunking it up to dazzling, and vice versa, meanwhile the person she knows has become trapped in there. He flickers and flashes like one of the arcade machines on the pier.

He's her brilliant brother.

She also resents that she has to be the sister always aware of her brilliant brother. Like it's her lot. For life.

He's the kid who – when he'd taken to doing all

those personality quizzes online one afternoon, and
Sacha'd sat and watched him for a while before
saying, you know they use those quizzes for data
collection and sampling? and he replied, *but I am a*
data-anarchist and am consciously lying in my
answers, I always make up a person who's
answering them so as to ruin all their culled data,
and Sacha said, yeah but you know, Rob, even
those made-up people, because it's you who's
making them up, are all still *you* – looked up at her
with such dismay in his face that it nearly made her
cry to see him so defeated and she had to leave the
room to stop herself feeling it.

Now.

Where is he?

She scans the beach.

Just nine in the morning but there's always
someone on it; she can see a few people, a young
couple down by the water's edge, some old people
pointing out to sea, someone with a kid and a dog.

She can't see Robert yet.

But her phone goes.

It's not from Robert. It's a text from Mel.

Hey not in tday sach (frowny face emoji) woman
in Waitros told my mum 'not to breathe near her
children' then a guy said she should be wearing
facemask my dad went apeshit punched him
(frowny face frowny face) meltdown big time
(frowny face emoji with x x eyes) curtains closed on

our windows blinds down today don know what else to do. Doc who was whistlblower Dr Li just died think am losing my mind sach 'healthy society cannot have just one voice' he is my hero told them in dec it was bad but they dint listn thority made hm shut it & now he is gon RIP i keep cryin i cant stop xxx

Melanie's grandmother is Chinese.

Sacha thinks of the pictures of the virus online, the drawings people have created to approximate the virus. They all look a bit like little planets with trumpets coming out of their surface, or little worlds covered in spikes of growth, a little world that's been shot all over its surface by those fairground darts with tuft tails from the old-fashioned rifle ranges, or like mines in the sea in films about WW2.

The net is all photos of people in other countries with masks over their mouths and noses.

According to the net people got it from eating snakes. Other places say bats and pangolins. Stuff has gone viral online about Chinese people eating little yellow snakes on skewers.

Why would anyone want to eat a snake? Or a bat? Or a pangolin?

Unless the eating snakes thing is a racist way to link the virus to racism and being used as a slur against Chinese people.

Anyway it came from eating wild animals.

But why would *anyone* anyway *ever* eat *any* creature that has to be killed just so that someone can eat it, when there's so much you can eat in the world without killing anything?

The longer Sacha lives the more insane she realizes the species she belongs to is.

She texts Mel back.

Heart emoji. Kiss emoji. Kiss emoji. Boxing glove emoji. POW emoji. Knight in shining armour emoji. Muscly arm emoji. Heart emoji. Heart emoji.

There is no emoji she can think of that's an anti-racist emoji.

There are probably loads of racist emojis, and nothing obvious to send someone who's been racistly done over.

Why is that?

She leans on the rail and looks out over the beach.

The sea is grey even in the sun.

She exchanges a look with a seagull.

Winter for a while yet, then?

Afraid so.

Oh well.

The seagull, bright yellow at the beak and feet, settles its wing feathers and looks away.

Its beak sticks out like the masks people wore centuries ago in Venice in the plague.

She thinks of those little cotton facemasks of

now. They're like nothing at all, dead leaves, blowaway litter, compared to the real masks, the ones on the faces of the planet's liars.

All manner of virulent things are happening.

She turns and looks at the facades of the buildings behind her.

One Thursday when she was down here quite late she looked up at that building and saw cleaners cleaning it at eleven at night.

It felt like she was meant to see it.

But it also didn't mean anything. It was just coincidence.

Maybe coincidence never means the way you want it to. Because if it did it wouldn't be coincidence, would it?

She turns back, looks out to sea again.

Some people say you can see France on a clear day with the naked eye, if you're at the top of the i360.

It's not true, apparently. France is just too far for the naked eye.

(The sigh360. The why360.)

The naked eye! Can an eye ever have clothes on?

She is a person on a pavement in a city in a country on a planet, seen from above by so many satellites that aren't there so we can see how fine and beautiful our planet is from space but so the people who control the satellites can zoom in on people for all sorts of reasons that are nothing to do with what almost everybody and everything on the planet actually needs.

What are they for, then?

If seeing isn't really about seeing?

Everything is mask.

She thinks about the girl she saw on TV shouting at the prime minister in Australia. *You're an idiot. You're an idiot. You're an idiot.*

Everything needs to be unmasked, right now, like that girl unmasked that man.

No sign of Robert.

She checks the time again.

She makes sure she's got Ship Street pretty much directly behind her.

There. There's a shape slightly further along. She immediately knows it's him – even with his hood up she knows him. Those are his shoulders.

She goes down on to the beach.

Hi, she says.

He doesn't say anything.

She sits down on the wet stones beside him.

He doesn't look at her. But he says:

Can you just give me your hand, Sach, just for a minute?

He wants to hold her hand?

He sounds so small and so fragile.

So she puts her left hand out. He takes it in his, takes it right inside his (warm) jacket and dries the palm of her hand on his jumper.

Close your eyes, he says.

No, she says.

Please, he says.

Why? she says.

Just for a minute, he says.

She sighs. She closes her eyes.

He is pressing something cold and curved and glassy into her hand.

Don't look yet, he says.

What is it? she says with her eyes still closed.

Present, he says. For the future. Wait a minute.

He holds both his hands tight over and under her hand with whatever the present is in it. He keeps his hands both clasped round her hand for what feels quite a long time like that.

He lets go. But her hand feels really strange.

There's a quite large double-curved glass thing in it. It's made of two connected globes of glass. It's longer than the palm of her hand. It's smooth, the glass of it is quite thin, and it's got, what is it? bright yellow sand? inside it?

She tries to open her hand to look at it properly. Her hand won't open for some reason. Whatever it is is stuck to her. Her hand is stuck to it.

It's an eggtimer.

He holds up in front of her face, just long enough for her to see what it is, the superglue bottle.

Then he's running up the beach and she's scrambling after him on the stones, but it dawns on

her that she has to be more careful, has to *not*
scramble or scrabble because the thing he's stuck to
her hand is made of very very thin glass and she's
got to not break it or she'll cut herself open and
there'll be broken glass stuck to her hand.

She yells his name.

She watches his back disappear up under the
railings.

She stands on the slope of stones shaking her
hand as if to shake the stuck thing off. It's stuck
right across her first three fingers. She can't uncurl
them. She can move the thumb and the pinky.
They're not stuck. The other three fingers she can
only waggle the ends of.

She pulls at it. It's quite sore, to pull it.

Some people, a woman and a man, are coming
towards her going, are you all right? can we help? is
something wrong? so she must've been really
shouting.

Thanks, yeah, no, it's okay, I'm okay, she says.

Her phone goes off in her pocket.

She reaches for it with her wrong hand, awkward.

There's a new text from him:

know how worried ur about how theres no time
left so this woz best present I cud imagine from
now on u always have time on ur hands

She presses reply.

But she can't text with this hand, the
wrong hand.

She holds her phone out to the woman.

I wonder would you mind just typing in some words for me and pressing send? she says.

Sure. Of course. What would you like to say? the woman says.

Sacha thinks for a moment.

Thanks for the exceptional bonding experience, she says.

The woman laughs out loud.

The man starts looking on the internet on his own phone to see how you get superglued glass off skin.

Then the woman holds up Sacha's phone with the reply Robert has sent back:

a smiley face emoji next to a sad face emoji next to a middle finger emoji.

How did this happen to you? the woman says.

Sacha shakes her head.

Who's – the woman glances back at the phonescreen – Robert?

Sacha looks at the thing that's made a seagull claw, a birdsfoot, of her hand. She tips her claw upside down so that the sand inside the glass runs, and it does run very prettily, from the first globe into the other, a fine thread of gold through the tiny opening that connects them.

My brother, she says.

Time is dimensional. Robert Greenlaw has just demonstrated not just the curve and dimensionality of time but also its multiple nature and given himself a TOTAL HIGH by affixing irremovably a piece of curved and dimensional time into the curved dimension of a mortal hand.

Heh.

!

The song he'd sing if he could still sing would be about how time is more than one thing, time is glass and sand, time is brittle and fluid, time is fragile and tough, time is sharp and blunt, time is now and ancient, time is before and after, time is smooth and rough and if you try to remove your attachment to time, time will laugh out loud and take the skin off you.

And because time is relative and there is more

than one kind of time, today time can be *my* time and I will make it all the more mine by *not worshipping acquisitive educational success*, to quote Einstein. Given that Einstein himself was a rubbish school student. I mean, Einstein's school, when Einstein was Robert Greenlaw's age, thought Einstein was stupid. Einstein! Infra dignit catastrophe.

So today I will go home, sneak in and up the stairs, they won't know it but I'll be in and invisible and upstairs playing ABUSEHEAP till the sun goes down on me, Robert Greenlaw, lone wolf, lost boy, soul of patience in exactitude.

Had he been his younger self he'd've cocked an invisible Robin Hood cap forward on his head right now as he crosses the street past the window of the shop he stole the eggtimer out of, but he is older now and way past being some loser who wears invisible hats. What he does is he keeps his head down, face turned away, Greenlaw outlaw with his winter coat pulled round him lined with life's ironies keeping him warm. Outward 13 year old boy, inward true singer (all by ear by the way, a natural talent) of the subcurrent ballad of his time and times – because the two, time and times, are not the same thing.

Bookshop?

Yep.

Because:

there exists in the world a book he only recently found out about by scanning his mother's Sunday Times and the book is about the time/s that Einstein came to Britain and especially the time he stayed in Norfolk. Robert Greenlaw isn't completely sure where Norfolk is. He knows it's somewhere over *there*. He badly wants Einstein to have come to Brighton or anywhere in the environs of *here*. But. Nowhere on the net does it say Einstein came to Brighton.

Though anywhere in Sussex would do.

Host of other places, the net says yes, says London and Oxford and Cambridge and Nottingham and Woolsthorpe (Woolsthorpe? Because Newton, born there, understood in Woolsthorpe for the first time about the apple falling from the tree, discovered all the colours that make up light there too in 1666 when he was twenty four years old stuck at home away from college because of Yersinia pestis) and Southampton, Winchester, and Kent, Cotswolds, Surrey, Norfolk, Einstein even went to Glasgow, photo taken smoking pipe, spoke about relativity to a huge crowd, went to Manchester. But not Sussex, never Sussex, nowhere in Sussex appears ever to have been graced by the sole of the foot or the mildness of face of Einstein.

Face like an Eastertime lamb, head like a dandelion clock, but a dandelion clock holding the

hidden infrastructure not just of the world.
Universe too.

!

What weedy toughness.

And the internet's not always right, though, no, the internet doesn't know the half of it, and a new book about the time Einstein was here, on this island, might say something as yet un-net about Sussex.

And they might have this book. In that shop.

So he turns himself meek, becomes 13 year old boy again in case

why aren't you at school?

Answer ready:

physics teacher Mr Musgrave (completely made-up name, *such* a brilliant teacher, the made-up ones always are) has sent me here to see if you've got the new book about Einstein in Britain in stock,

and he slinks in through the doors of the bookshop – and nobody asks anything.

He looks.

Not in sciences.

Not in new books.

Then meek 13 year old boy goes to look on the biography shelves and

!

Boy finds book.

Boy sinks to crosslegged on bookshop floor and reads it where he opens it, about Einstein's father giving Einstein (as a boy) a compass and Einstein (just a boy himself) working out from that compass in his hand what magnetism might be.

Why have you never given me a compass (Robert Greenlaw to his father, in his head)?

Robert I've enough on my plate don't give me any more hassle (his father, to Robert Greenlaw, most days, in reality).

It's understandable. His father's business is fucked. His father's marriage is fucked. His father's girlfriend has stopped wanting to be fucked.

Back to book.

Robert Greenlaw opens it at random again: story about when Einstein gave a lecture somewhere in England and wrote his arithmetic equations on two blackboards and the two blackboards were put carefully aside after he left because they were now treasured possessions and they got sent to a museum or special place of storage where ONE OF THE BLACKBOARDS GOT CLEANED BY MISTAKE.

!

Einstein's actual handwritten figures – erased.

!

Also, accompanying story that Einstein's maths calculations on those boards had *mistakes* in them too.

Einstein = human

!

It is funny.

Robert Greenlaw knows from online how trolls from everywhere piled in on long dead Einstein after the BBC reported that in his diaries Einstein said some rude things about Chinese people and people from then Ceylon now Sri Lanka.

Racist and xenophobic!

Einstein! who the Nazis said they were going to hang soon as they got the chance because of him being so Jewish.

Einstein! who called for civil rights in the USA.

Einstein! who warned against the nuclear bomb and said if he'd known they would use what he discovered about quantum and relativity the way they used it he'd have become a cobbler and mended people's shoes all his life instead.

Well that's what you get if you read people's private diaries.

I am offended! shout all the lined-up people just before they're shot into ditches in Robert Greenlaw's imaginary computer game provisionally entitled Blood and Irony which one day soon he will properly invent and sell for a fortoon

troubled?

me?

so Robert Greenlaw checks the index at the back of the book about Einstein coming to Britain, for the word

Brighton

no

Sussex

no.

Ah.

Ah well.

He is sad, though, about it.

Why does he need to be near a place where Einstein has been, today, right now, at this point in his life?

Who knows?

It is a mystery.

He just does.

He flicks through the book again, photos of Einstein taken in the very same country that Robert Greenlaw is in right now, England.

In the photos Einstein always looks unlikely.

It is brilliant.

Dishevelled genius; because genius doesn't need to be hevelled, whatever hevelled is.

Quote at the front of this book about Einstein, written by someone who saw him with his own eyes at the time:

See him as he squats on Cromer beach doing sums, Charlie Chaplin with the brow of Shakespeare . . . So it is not an accident that the Nazi lads vent a particular fury against him. He does truly stand for what they most dislike, the opposite of the blond beast — intellectualist,

individualist, supernationalist, pacifist, inky,
plump.

Plump.

It is kind of an unpleasant word to use.

(Robert Greenlaw has been called plump in his time.

It is why he is now very, very lean.)

What / where is Cromer?

Robert Greenlaw looks it up on his phone.

Ah. *There.* Okay.

Opposite of the blond beast. If that was written nowadays blond beast = UK prime minister. Yesterday the blond beast prime minister tried, like the Americans, banning some journalists and not others from being let into Downing St. Some were told to stand on one side of the carpet and the others to stand on the other side of the carpet. On the one side they were going to be permitted. On the other they weren't. All the journalists boycotted the dividing of them into two. But that won't last. Robert Greenlaw admires above all the adviser of the prime minister, who knows how to style politics so that it doesn't look like politics any more, who knows full well that Stalin and Hitler were possible even though everyone in old-style politics looks aghast when anyone suggests it's possible to act the ways they did.

The people in charge in England right now are geniuses of manipulation.

Robert Greenlaw is in awe of their performance of callousness.

He is in awe of how they get away with talking about patriotism with all the fervour of 12 year olds – Robert Greenlaw still aspires to it a bit, though he's now 13 and recognizes its pre-adolescent ventriloquisms.

It is all just more genius.

Prime minister, consciously dishevelled. Styled.

He puts, in his mind, the two dishevelled men together on, what was it, a beach.

Hmm.

One looks dishevelled because disinterested in looks and clothes, because thinking.

The other looks like he's acting a bit drunk or acting like a boy not a man. It is a brilliant subterfuge to look like he doesn't know what he's doing and to make people like him for it.

One is his hero for bucking every trend and rewriting the universal truths to make them truer.

The other is his hero for the opposite – for the brilliant application of lies. It is impressive. And for seeing, following, cultivating, using and profiting big-time *by* the current trends, which is the best way to survive the trends.

What would they say to each other if they met? Would they talk about time? Would they talk about ethics, heroism? Robert Greenlaw knows what Einstein thinks about heroism. But the PM?

Robert Greenlaw gets his phone out and keys in 'Einstein', 'hero', 'Prime', 'Minister', 'ethics', and 'time'.

A quote comes up from – Time Magazine.

There they both are, on an English beach.

Einstein: *Heroism on command, senseless violence, and all the loathsome nonsense that goes by the name of patriotism – how passionately I hate them!*

Our PM: *My hero is the mayor in Jaws. He's a fantastic guy, and he keeps the beaches open, if you remember, even after it's demonstrated that his constituents have been eaten by this killer fish. Of course, he was proved catastrophically wrong in his judgement, but his instincts were right.*

It's not a real conversation. More like a caricature.

But that's okay because this is the dawn of a new era, a caricature kind of an era.

Robert Greenlaw's father's girlfriend comes into Robert Greenlaw's head.

Uch.

There is a trunk in his head, like a medieval trunk, in which he locks her whenever she does that unasked.

Take care, she used to say in the days when she still spoke. She said it instead of saying the word goodbye. She said it like a threat. *Take care.*

In you go. Lid down. Padlock.

Now.

Robert Greenlaw, scrolling the phone, sees again his sister's reply,

bonding experience

He smiles.

He closes the Einstein book. He is going home to play ABUSEHEAP. Ultraviolent catastrophe.

He checks, without looking like he's checking, for CCTV.

No. Do it like you have power.

He looks straight at the camera. He shows it himself tucking the book into his trousers, pulls his jumper down over it, pulls his coat closed, stands up.

No bells, no nothing, no sound of anyone coming after him,

yep, there, see,

nobody gave a fuck,

sign of the times,

nobody even saw, or if they did, cared.

What Robert Greenlaw finds most curious about playing ABUSEHEAP (subheading *die a thousand deaths*) is that it doesn't matter what era/s you're in, torture really hasn't changed much. When electricity starts to be available it gets more everyday since every room has a socket and there are so many ordinary things that can be plugged into that socket, drills and saws, and others more excitingly innocent like lamps, toasters, hair curling irons. One of the first things they did with the invention of the telephone is work out a way, by connecting it by wire to a human and turning its little crank handle, to deliver pain. They called it? The Telephone.

Riches, ironies. Robert Greenlaw is an Iron(y) Man. Just as well, since across the aeons and the global distances what all the peoples of the world really have in common is so many similar ways of doing humiliating and painful things to each other.

Dislocation, discomfort via acute ways of sitting / standing / squatting / hanging. Boiling oil / tar / wax / water. Just water. Dripping it very slowly on to someone, in exactitude. Or just filling people with too much of it. Heat, cold, roasting, freezing. Heavy stones. Iron chairs or contraptions featuring spikes and blades. Finger screws. Toe screws. A global variety of boot-like contraptions via which the foot and leg bones can be wedged till broken or crumbled.

The contraptions which hold the whole body in place are often, interestingly, designated female. Skevington's Daughter, Duke of Exeter's Daughter, Iron Maiden. There's also the claw-like metal thing called The Spider, for when Victim is itself a female.

That stuff's level 3 and 4 on ABUSEHEAP. Robert Greenlaw is way beyond that now. He is

Perp level 7, has access to early electricals and a chat room entry key so he can access Victim data and profiles and compare and discuss tortures in conference with other Perps. Plus, up until level 5 Perps have to do the tracking, chasing and capturing of Victims themselves but from level 6 on, they're presented with Victim after Victim as gifts of the game. But the twist – so to speak heh heh – is that you *have* to outwit Victim in interrogation and succeed in getting information, and if Victim dies before delivering the info you drop back to level 3 Drudge. If you get it badly wrong and Victim escapes, game profile plummets you into Victimzone.

There are a lot more Victims than Perps.

It is easy, to end up killing. Rat torture might look a sure bet to get someone to spill their guts – cut skin above the stomach of Victim into bloody strips then tie bag with rat in it round Victim and rat starts to eat – but it almost always ends in death, too-literal gut-spill. Robert Greenlaw's own favourite way of killing someone who's no longer valid (having given up all info), if he's okay for point totals and can afford it, is Torn in Two, original medieval, in which one arm and one leg are attached to one large horse, the other arm and leg to another horse, and the horses sent in different directions. For not-killing he favours Pear of Pain, which stops people speaking until you let them again, and Pitchcap, which the English did to the Irish in the c18th: pour hot tar into paper cap attached to Victim's head then rip it off taking the scalp with it. (You can also fill orifices with pitch or tar but Victim'll definitely die if you do, so use it only on Victim you don't need anything else from.)

So far he has found that the simplest abuse gets the best results.

Jetlining (ancient practice with modernized name). You don't need anything but a wall for that.

Fingernailing (ancient).

Dryboarding (ancient *and* bang up to date; if it's working right now for the CIA it'll probably work for *you*).

Level 10 gives you the latest electromagnetic torture gadgets and Robert Greenlaw is looking forward to those. Mind-altering! But only the best Perps reach level 10.

Sigh.

Only ten minutes into the game today and Robert Greenlaw is feeling the usual nothing.

He just doesn't give a shit what Victim knows or doesn't know.

Anyway the Perp room is practically empty. Everybody is at school.

He leaves Victim dangling, pauses the game.

Bit distracted now.

Bored.

There's someone downstairs, on a visit. He heard them there when he came in

(and here's what Robert Greenlaw's achieved since he arrived at the front door half an hour ago, opened it noiselessly and shut it noiselessly: furniture polish from cleaning cupboard + hinges = noiseless entry).

a). he had a good look in whoever's visiting's bag by the umbrella stand. Canvas. Heavy. No wonder. A quite large, completely round stone in it. Like a small stone football. Garden thing? Thing for top of a pillar? Old unused cannonball? He'd put it back down very very carefully. He'd climbed the stair, missed out the creaker step.

He'd heard, as he went up, people in the lounge talking.

No TV noise.

Must've unplugged it.

He'd halted on the landing to listen for a moment.

No one was talking about the eggtimer.

Nobody sounded outraged.

But he couldn't hear for definite.

They were talking about – Worthing? Or – something worthy.

Bored.

b). he'd gone up the next flight then up into the loft. He got a pair of socks out of the sock drawer, put his pods in and watched a bit of porn like any self respecting 13 year old boy is ancestrally and con-genitally bound to do. He'd felt bad again after. It always makes him think (it is so fucking annoying even to have it in his head) of the story of the hunter out hunting who sees the virgins all bathing naked and of course he sits and watches them for as long as he can, who wouldn't? so the goddess of the hunt catches him and is so furious with him for desecrating her virgins by looking at them impurely that she turns him into a stag which his own dogs not recognizing their master and seeing only a stag instead then subsequently maul to death. Robert Greenlaw, inward balladeer, soul of patience in exactitude, once wrote an essay for school based on that story and proclaiming how if you go about life seeing the pure thing when you aren't pure yourself then the dog inside you will tear you apart.

Good boy.

!

After which Robert Greenlaw, outward outlaw, tore that essay up and threw it away on his way to school, told Milton he hadn't done the homework and gave him a good insolent stare back throughout the reprimand

troubled?

me?

So he clicked away the 16 yr old (more like 35 really, hair in bunches doesn't mean you're not old)

French au pair getting done by father of family, groan, banal beyond banal, anal beyond anal, fake-moaning and stilettos in the air, and tipped his invisible hat to whoever was recording him watching it through his computer's camera since someone somewhere will have been. Given that we all live in an open prison now and ought just to admit it and stop imagining we don't.

Bored.

c). he watched on YouTube instead the clip he likes from the black and white German film where the jester does the crazy jerking Dance of Death in the inn and all the peasants go into a trance and follow him doing the dance too like automatons, shaking and jerking like sweaty zombies. It is called Paracelsus. It is something to do with Hitler even though it's set in the middle ages. The jester gets into the town bringing the plague because unscrupulous merchants who don't want to lose trade and money import their goods through the blockade. Then Robert Greenlaw stood up and did some of the jerky dance moves soundlessly round his room.

But was he the jester – or the follower?

Heh.

!

All the same:

bored.

d). he brought up the link to the live Echo feed to see if it had spoken again. One day an Echo in someone's house woke itself up unasked and said out loud to the room, with its Echo-owners staring at it amazed, this sentence:

every time I close my eyes all I see is people dying.

Of course it became a viral news story; of course some random canny Echo-owner was clever enough to set up an Echo-cam on their own Echo and since then there's been more than a million people every day watching and listening to a live 24 hour feed for the moment when this Echo, or the god who speaks through the Echo, says something else.

Which of course it never will.

It is brilliant, Robert Greenlaw thought again looking at the screen showing an Echo, any old Echo, on a sideboard, and the number of people online watching it right then, 360,746 (America is asleep). I mean. Who programmed an Echo to be so poetic? Who placed that little primed grenade at the heart of the machine? It always makes him laugh, the people out there hooked and waiting for the god, or the machine, same thing, to give them the message.

30 seconds later?

Bored.

e). he sat on his bed and tore the photograph out of the Einstein book, Einstein in an overcoat standing on a lot of cut grass in a field in England, hands in his pockets, cheery-melancholy.

He cut its edge straight with scissors, neat.

He tore out the one of Einstein with the sculptor standing outside a hut on either side of a clay head the sculptor's just made of him.

He did the same, scissors, neat edge.

He stuck them both on the wall with Blu-tak.

Albert Einstein on the wall looked past him, melancholy-cheery, into the distance in his room.

What does *soul of patience in exactitude* actually mean?

Uh-oh. When he starts to question himself – *bored*.

f). he brought up his ABUSEHEAP profile.

a + b + c + d + e + f = ?

Now. New Victim on The Donkey. No guts spilled yet. Robert Greenlaw has the lackeys tie Victim's hands behind back and suspend from the rafters.

Crack. Dislocation.

Still nothing.

Then Victim presses the button. *I'll talk.*

Uch.

Robert Greenlaw sighs the sigh of an ancient tyrant who's seen it all.

Bored.

He clicks the game off before Victim can follow through and save itself.

Almost wishes he'd gone to school after all.

Wonders if his sister still has time on her hands ha ha.

Wonders who it is, downstairs.

Robert Greenlaw silents himself out of his room and down the loft stairs again. Then silents himself down the staircases. Halfway down the last flight Robert Greenlaw sits, but with his feet well up off the next step because it's the creaker.

His mother is telling the visitor one of her stories about how proud she is of her children, how clever they are, how one of them at a very early age, maybe eight years old, had said at the dinner table that if a TV series could be as good as the *planet* Ceres and the *goddess* Ceres then finally we would be fulfilling our true human capacity, and how she and Jeff had been amazed that their children knew about outer space and mythology and had done all that reading by themselves.

Yeah, that was me, he hears his sister say.

It wasn't *her* who said the Ceres thing. It was him. *She* knows nothing about anything.

The visitor sounds like a member of the educated elite. She is here because she was doing something research-wise over in Worthing and stayed overnight last night here in a hotel. She says something he can't make out. Then she says,

and that makes you a terrorist. They're listed as a terrorist group now.

Everybody laughs.

His mother talks about the day someone broke all the windscreens on all the cars up the street.

His environ/mental sister starts blahing about how solar panels and not eating meat one day a week isn't going to make enough of a dent.

It's truly terrible. But this new generation of responsible young people will sort it out, his mother says. Thank God for the young people. I trust them.

Yeah, that's it. Give us the responsibility for everything you've all messed up but don't give us any power with which to change anything, his sister says.

His mother says something apologetic about her revolutionary daughter.

Yeah, because the planet is really dangerously near being fucked, his sister says.

Don't swear. And darling, his mother says. It's just not as simple as that.

Yes it is, his sister says. And you being patronizing to me doesn't make it any less simple.

The visitor says something about how important it is to have a voice.

Almost in unison his mother and his sister start telling the visitor about his father's girlfriend.

Visitor: Stopped speaking?

His mother: Just stopped. Can't make any sounds at all.

Visitor: She's lost her voice?

His sister: Yeah but it's somehow sort of more than just losing her voice.

His mother: Her ability to make any sound at all has literally gone. When we go next door all she'll do is shrug her shoulders. Even when Sacha stood on one of her feet when she wasn't expecting it –

His sister: – to see what would happen, not out of meanness or cause I wanted to hurt her –

His mother: – even then –

His sister: she just opened her mouth in an O and no sound came out, though you could see it was sore by her face. I said sorry, I told her I was doing it to try to be helpful, then we asked what if we tried burning her arm unexpectedly with a hot teaspoon, you know, something when she least expected it, would that help, and she wrote down on a piece of paper, *nothing works, don't think I haven't tried myself.*

Visitor: She'd tried to burn herself? With a teaspoon?

His mother: I think she just meant she'd tried, I don't know how, to get herself to make a noise.

Visitor: You can't trick your unconscious.

His mother: You think it's psychological? I think it's definitely psychological. I said it was. Didn't I say that, Sacha? I said psychosomatic.

His sister: Like Greta.

His mother: How?

His sister: *She* stopped speaking.

His mother: No, the whole thing about her was

that she *did* speak, Garbo Speaks. Garbo Laughs. My father used to say: *the ideal woman until she spoke.* [impersonates her father, Bradford accent] *Should never have opened her mouth. All downhill after that.* [back to her usual voice] He really did!

His sister: No, mum. Greta *Thunberg*. When she was a little kid she went into a state of shock when she realized what was happening to the earth, and she actually stopped being able to speak. And then she realized the whole point was that she *had* to speak. That she *had* to use her voice. I asked Ashley about that, actually.

His mother: Asked her what?

His sister: If it was about the world, if she was trying to save the world. And she wrote on the pad, *not any more.*

Robert Greenlaw, porous understander of his time and times, sits halfway up the stairs like in the A A Milne poem for children and remembers verbatim one of the first conversations he had with his father's girlfriend.

His father's girlfriend: In times of injustice you always have to be ready to speak up, to speak out loudly against it.

Robert Greenlaw: If you do, you'll be one of the first they'll kill.

His father's girlfriend: It won't come to that. Not if enough people speak out.

Robert Greenlaw: Yeah but what if it does?

His father's girlfriend: If it does, then I'm not worried, they can kill me if they like, because I trust and I know there'll be so many more who'll come after me to speak out just as loud.

Robert Greenlaw: They'll all get killed too.

His father's girlfriend: Justice will always win.

Robert Greenlaw: Yeah but that totally depends on what the people who make the laws decide to define justice as.

His father's girlfriend: You're impossible.

Robert Greenlaw: You're all too plausible.

Along with stopping speaking, his father's girlfriend seems to have stopped writing her 'book' about 'politics'. He rather hopes it's because he sneaked into her 'study' at the start of January and wrote with a Sharpie on the top page of the sheaf of printed-out pages next to her name MEMBER OF THE EDUCATED ELITE.

Because?

Robert Greenlaw knows there is no point in making lists of the lies a PM or POTUS tells.

It is an amazing time to be alive. World order is changing.

But he also admits to himself that some bits of his father's girlfriend's book made quite interesting reading:

(where blah marks Robert Greenlaw's loss of interest)

language distorted, used as tool of taking control of a populace by sloganeering and emotional manipulation, is in fact the opposite of giving back control to populace blah

use of classical references and display of knowledge as rhetorical power-tools are surreptitiously also used as a marker of class and of who owns culture, who owns knowledge blah

truth gives way to the <u>authentic lie</u>, in other words what the voter emotionally supports, or <u>emotional</u> truth, which is where <u>factual</u> truth stops mattering, which leads in turn to total collapse of integrity and to tribalism blah

It is more likely, though, that it's nothing to do with him. More likely she stopped writing it because a couple of nights before she stopped speaking altogether – as Robert Greenlaw, silent outlaw, knows because he has a key, often goes next door without anyone knowing, goes in quite often to see what's in the fridge, to pick things up in their rooms and put things down again, occasionally to pocket things, to listen to them having sex (when they still did) thinking nobody could possibly be watching or listening, to take a seat on the landing, they leave the door open – that night she was talking and talking, wouldn't shut up, telling his father in her mad girl way about a programme about WW2 home movies she'd just seen and how there was a sequence of old footage of a Nazi town having a summer festival, floats were going through the streets with women and children on them in national costume waving to people on the pavement, she talked about how the floats were hung with garlands of flowers and how at the very end, the very back of the procession, the very last image in the home movie was a caricature of a Jewish person looking out of a prison truck window through the bars, being driven away to jail and everybody laughing and waving goodbye.

It was supposed to be funny, she said. It was like a cartoon. The film was silent but everybody laughed and cheered all the same.

She was crying by then. His father said some sort of comforting-sounding things but Robert Greenlaw could tell he couldn't really be bothered, had already had enough of this. She didn't take the hint. She kept on being upset. She told his father about the other home movie of a country fair, the one showing people dressed as German citizens acting like they're sweeping the streets, with huge cartoon-sized brooms, and what they're sweeping off the streets is people dressed in costumes of Jewish caricatures.

What she was most upset about, she said, was the

way that then and now were meeting up and that it was such a *caricature time* then and *it's such a caricature time again.*

That's what she kept repeating through the noise of her crying. His father in the end fell asleep, or pretended to, and Robert Greenlaw didn't blame him.

What's her problem?

There is endless stuff always on TV and all over the net about the Nazis. All Robert's life there always has been.

Down in the lounge, meanwhile, the visitor has clearly just worked out that their father and his girlfriend are living next door.

She is saying something congratulatory about what a grown-up way it is to do things.

His mother says marry in May and you'll rue the day.

His parents are laughable.

They are having a meltdown about their own deaths getting closer and closer now they are so ancient.

His father: Call no man happy till he is dead.

His mother: Kill yourself. Then you'll be happy.

His father: Tell you what. It'll be you that's the death of me.

Remembering that particular fight Robert Greenlaw forgets where he is, forgets to take care, finds he's braced himself against the memory of the fight without knowing his body is even doing it, and in unbracing himself puts both feet on the creaker step by mistake.

CREAK

Shit.

Everyone stops speaking in the lounge.

Then his mother comes to the lounge door and looks up. She sees the top of his head.

Robert? she says.

Actress pause.

She comes round and up three of the steps.

Why on earth aren't you at school? she says.

She says it with parental indignation rather than the usual deadpan way because there's a visitor in.

Robert Greenlaw stands up so that he is even higher above her.

In one of my quantum lives I *am* actually in school right now, he says. Doing uh (he checks the time on his phone), maths.

His mother has no idea what quantum is or what he's talking about. As per. She looks at him in bewilderment.

So Robert Greenlaw, quantum son, who knows he can get away with quite a bit by simply acting like he has the right and believes in his right to do whatever it is he's doing, adjusts his stance to superior by squaring his shoulders and turning his head and comes down the stairs as if there's no question.

Oh, and Robert, his mother says. What've you done with the remote?

I *am* The Remote, he says as if The Remote is an anti-hero with the superpower of being, yes, remote.

Where is it? she says again.

It's somewhere miles away from here by now, he says going into the lounge.

And that'll be why they call it a remote, the beautiful visitor says.

Robert: sunstruck, first time ever.

First real time.

His surname melts away. He becomes just Robert, plain Robert, nothing but Robert, an unencumbered someone he hasn't been for so long now that he'd forgotten he could.

Everything is different.

Everything, changed.

The visitor is beautiful.

His mother says her name.

The visitor's name is Charlotte.

The name CHARLOTTE lights up like a word in a neon sign.

The visitor called Charlotte is lighting up this room.

Robert himself feels as if he too is neon, lightning zagging through him, he is shining, look at his arms, his hands, he is a source of light too because of her. No, he *is* light, actual light, light itself. Not just that – he is the kind of light that's in the word delight.

He is filled with a word from childhood. It's the word joy. It is not a word he has ever given a moment's thought before, never in his life, and now he is a self shot out of the dark into the light, arms out wide as if to take everything into them, the whole world, the universe round it with all its galaxies, and hold them up to the light, *his* light, because now nothing will ever end, everything is infinite. It is like smashed light imprisoned in him till now, in pieces, sharp fragments like smashed lightbulb in the pit of his gut, has been understood, known for what it was, is and could be all at once and is now assembling itself and turning him into a BALL OF LIGHT, also quite frankly yes his balls feel full of light, and the tip of his penis, no, his whole penis, and the tips of his toes and his fingers, tip of his nose, his whole body's become a pointed twig on a tree whose branches are a network of pure light.

!

Hi, the visitor called Charlotte says.

Hi, he says.

Visitor.

Visitation.

There seems to be a force which bodies, by their very presence, exert upon each other:

quote from Einstein, up on his bedroom wall up in the lofty heights of the house. This is something Einstein actually said about Newton, father of gravity. But look what it really means.

!

It is now clear to Robert for the first time that Einstein was a man in love, a man motivated by love, love for everything.

He sees his sister's hand.

It has a bandage round it.

His sister waves the bandaged hand at him.

Hi, she says.

Yeah, hi, he says. All right?

You might say, she says.

Oh – there's a man here too.

There was no sound of a man when Robert [Greenlaw] was on the stairs listening.

Who's he?

Is the man here with the visitor?

The man *is* here with the visitor.

But is he *with* the visitor?

His mother clearly thinks they're together. His sister clearly does. His mother is telling him that Arthur and Charlotte kindly took his sister to A&E after she had *some kind of accident* where she *cut her hand open*, then brought her home in their car.

Had to have a stitch, his sister says. Here. And here. The skin came right off.

She points at her bandaged hand with her other hand, up by the fingers then down at the bottom of the palm.

Right, yeah, he says. Wow.

Stitch in time, his sister says. You might say.

Will she tell?

Will she tell in front of the visitor?

Robert puts on his most unconcerned face, looks away, at the floor, makes himself look busy over at the cooker with the coffee maker while his mother talks some more about how kind the visitors have been. Then his mother takes up where she'd left off, trying to justify to the visitors why her ex husband lives next door with his much younger girlfriend.

What could I do? she says. He met her. He fell in love with somebody twenty years younger, now that's what I call middle-aged spread. But we're a family, we couldn't bear not to be together. Or at least close. So when next door came up for sale we bought it and he moved out. I mean, in.

Next door dad, his sister says. One big happy family.

Yeah, but mum. He didn't move out because he met Ashley, Robert says with his back to everybody.

His voice sounds weird out loud saying things.

He turns round. Nobody is looking at him like he just spoke in a weird voice.

He looks again at her. The visitor, Charlotte, is every bit as stunning to him as when he first saw her.

She really is that beautiful.

He is shocked.

He looks away.

He looks back.

It is like someone is shining a searchlight into him.

Come and sit down, Robert, his mother says.

He comes to the table, sits next to his mother where she patted the bench.

From here he can both look and look away.

His mother is attempting to change the subject and sound reasonable to the visitors by telling the story of the day a couple of months ago when she went into the Nationwide Building Society to pay in some money.

And the TV screen in there was playing, you know, electioneering coverage, news, his mother says. But with the sound down and the subtitles on. And the subtitles, you know the way they appear sort of jerkily on the screen because they're being typed up by a machine while the person is speaking, anyway the subtitles kept repeating a particular phrase, the phrase was GET BACK SIT DOWN, they kept saying GET BACK SIT DOWN. Which made me wonder what the news story was about. Till I realized that what the TV news reporter was actually saying was GET BREXIT DONE.

The visitor is beautiful even when she is pretending something with her face.

Like it's nothing to do with you that Brexit got done, his sister says.

Sacha, that's unnecessary, his mother says.

Anyway. All over now. Done and dusted. We're lucky. We're all in the dawn of a new era.

The thing *I* find most interesting, Robert says again in his strange-to-him voice.

He is fingering the ribbing on his sock while he says it because he daren't look up or he will forget what he's saying. Then he remembers what he uses his socks for. He flushes red and stops touching anything. He holds his hand well away from his shin. He levels his gaze at a cup on the table. The beautiful visitor Charlotte is a blur of light beyond the cup.

What do you find interesting? the beautiful visitor Charlotte says.

A particular feature of its lexicon, he says.

Then Robert flushes up because the word lexicon sounds partly like it's got the word sex in it.

They are all looking at him and waiting for him to say whatever it is he's going to say next.

Lexicon, his mother says.

What's that mean? his sister says.

It's a word about words, the beautiful visitor Charlotte says.

The visitor is not just beautiful, she is verbally brilliant.

Yes, in exactitude, Robert says. In that our father voted *remain* and our mother voted *leave*. But that it's our father who, in the end, was the one who literally had to. *Leave.*

Oh God, his mother says. Robert.

Which makes it, he says, like the people who voted leave were sort of also issuing a command. It's quite clever, really. Like, in my physics class there's a boy, I don't know his name, whose father is French and has a restaurant, a good one, with a, a, star –

Michelin star? the beautiful visitor says so beautifully that Robert is silenced and looks away, looks down, then a moment later dares a look back at her from under his fringe.

Yeah, and they're leaving, they have to leave, his sister says.

Robert opens his mouth but no sound comes out.

Something I've always wondered, his mother says too brightly (she is changing the subject). Maybe one of you young people can enlighten me. What *is* cancel culture?

Nobody answers.

The beautiful Charlotte leans forward.

(Her scent crosses Robert.

She smells amazing.)

The beautiful Charlotte winks at his mother.

You know, she says. All that Brexit stuff, it's nothing. It's like, pfft. Like a fly laying eggs on a corpse. Because everything's got to change. Everything.

And just to set the record straight, his mother says like the beautiful Charlotte hasn't said anything, our fight, my disagreement with my husband, was nothing to do with what I voted for and all to do with your father meeting Ashley.

Yeah, but mum, his sister says. He didn't meet Ashley till 2018. And he moved out in 2016.

His mother shrugs, breathes deeply in, breathes the air out towards the ceiling and does an actress laugh.

Done and dusted, his sister says. We've been done all right.

It's going to be better, his mother says. For everyone. In the long run.

Einstein says the future is an illusion, Robert says. *And* the past. *And* the present.

You can't stop change, the man who came here with the beautiful visitor Charlotte says.

It is the first thing Robert has heard him say.

Change just comes, the man says. It comes of necessity. You have to go with it and make something of what it makes of you.

Metamorphosis, Charlotte says. It's always the answer to the unanswerable. Even if it means turning into a beetle, like in the Kafka version.

Oh I love Kafka, his mother says. A book should be an axe to break the frozen sea inside you. I think it's one of the most beautiful things ever written.

Robert looks from the man to Charlotte and

back again from Charlotte to the man. No. They are not sleeping together. He can always tell. There is something between them. But it's not that.

And I was wondering, the man says. I wonder if your friend, I mean your neighbour, is it – Ashley?

It is Ashley, his mother says.

She says it like she owns Ashley.

I wonder if Ashley is finding language difficult, the man says, because there is so much to say.

You mean feeling getting in the way of language? Charlotte says.

She says it beautifully.

(Robert opens his mouth and the whisper comes out.)

Yes.

What's that, Rob? his sister says.

For the last little while she's been eyeing him, incredulous. She raises one eyebrow. Then she glances from him to Charlotte and back to him and she raises the other eyebrow too.

Because, because, Ashley's book is actually about that. I mean language, Robert says.

Book? his mother says.

She's writing a book, Robert says. Or she was.

Ashley's writing a book? his mother says.

How do you know? his sister says.

I've read it. Some of it, he says.

Ashley? his sister says. Let *you* read a *book*? That she's writing?

It's about lexicons, he says. In politics. The chapters have words or phrases as their titles.

Like what? his mother says.

Humbug, he says. Girly Swot. The People's Government. Big Ben's Bongs. It has a section at the back where it defines words. An Updated Lexicon. It looks at the meanings and histories of words like letterbox and, eh, bumboys.

The word comes out of his mouth before he can stop it. He blushes. His sister sniggers.

Bumboys? Charlotte says. What does she write about that?

Like how, he says. The first half of that word is a word that means uh

(oh no)

buttocks.

His sister sniggers at him again.

You've gone bright red, she says.

Keep going, Charlotte says.

How it also means like worthless, he says, or not working properly, or a person that's lazy or irresponsible or homeless. So that the word in the end doesn't just mean gay, because it carries all the other subcurrent meanings too.

Subcurrent. Fantastic, Charlotte says.

There's a chapter about the word fantastic as well, he says. About how in politics they keep saying everything's fantastic just now, how it's going to be fantastic, and about how that's a word that's always about triggering fantasy. And also a chapter about how people in politics talk about what's happening in World War 2 terms all the time to make people be loyal and take sides and get with the patriotic spirit.

What's this book called? his mother says.

The Immoral Imagination, he says.

His mother makes a scornful noise.

Well, there you go. There's no such thing as the immoral imagination, she says. Because there's no such thing as the moral imagination. The very idea that the imagination is anything to do with morality is spurious.

Well, the man says.

We *can* imagine anything, Charlotte says. But every human act, including the act of the imagination, bears a moral context.

Yes, Robert says. It does, mum.

That's not the same as saying the imagination is moral or immoral in itself, his mother says.

It's assuming we live at all by any code of ethics, Charlotte says.

Robert nods very vigorously.

His sister looks at him and laughs.

The imagination is as free as the wind, his mother says.

Yeah, but the wind isn't free, his sister says. It's driven by climate shift and now by climate damage.

Okay, not the wind, but as free as, as the free-est

thing you can imagine that isn't the wind, his mother says.

Well, that's the problem, isn't it, Charlotte says. It depends what you *can* imagine. And that does tend to depend on the Zeitgeist of the time, and who and what are influencing a mass imagination.

!

She is so clever it makes Robert feel weak. He sits straight like a choirboy in a church, one whose voice will never break and leave him with no singing voice. He is wearing those choirboy smocky clothes. They are bright white. He has never felt so humble. He has never felt so clean, from the top of his head right down to his toenails. He has been washed clean in light. He understands now why porn isn't at all the same thing as love. You could never do those things so unthinkingly, so humiliatingly, to someone so, so – truly adored.

Adored! Did he ever think in his life he would have a use for such a word?

His mother is still going on.

The imagination can and does do anything it likes and everything it likes, she says.

It can't, Robert thinks. It shouldn't.

Like Robert with the bike seats? his sister says.

Robert the choirboy is mortified inside his imaginary smock.

Bike seats, Charlotte says.

She looks at his sister then at Robert. His sister

waves her bandaged hand like a little caveman club at him, a mummy's stump. Robert looks down and away. His head feels very hot.

Mmphgm, he says.

Yeah, and anyway how come he knows anything about *anything* Ashley's doing? his sister says. Ashley won't even let him in the *house*. I bet he's making it up to get attention.

I'm not, he says. I'm not making anything up. I took some photos on my phone of some of the pages of her book. This is what she says about the word letterbox.

He scrolls his phone, finger-widens a photo and reads out the following in his best newsreader voice.

Letterbox is a word compiled of the two words letter and box.

A very banal opening, his mother says.

The word letter comes from Middle English via Old French, from Latin origin, littera, meaning an alphabet letter, and litterae, meaning an epistle. It means several things, from a symbol, and part of an alphabet, and something written to represent sound, to a written message, one that's often sent by post. It can also refer to literature and learning, particularly scholarly achievement, and to precision, especially in matters of law, as in the phrases to the letter and letter of the law. The word box is originally derived from both Greek and Latin, pyxis and buxis. It usually means a

four-sided receptacle for holding anything,
sometimes with a lid; or a small set-apart seating
area in a theatre; or an enclosure that's small; or
the seat for a driver on a coach; or a shield for the
genitals of someone playing cricket; or a –

he blushes

vagina;

his face is burning

or a coffin; or the name for a small evergreen
tree or hedge. Different derivation gives it as a
thump or blow on the head, or the act of hitting
with a fist, as in to box, and to box can also mean
to enclose or make enclosed, to shut in.

Oh for God sake, his mother says.

Is there more? Charlotte says.

He nods.

In British usage, letterbox means a hole in a door
or a box placed outside a house as a secure point
either for collection or delivery of mail, or a place,
compartment or slot whereby mail that's either
being delivered or waiting to be delivered can be
deposited and picked up safely by either deliverer
or recipient. Other words like it are pillarbox (so
called because of the shape of the collection box)
and mailbox. In more recent years it has also come
to describe an aspect ratio for films transferred to
video that recreates widescreen format on a small
screen.

Facile, his mother says.

Does anyone want me to keep going? he says.

Me, Charlotte says.

The iconic UK status of the letterbox is made clear in a publication like The Postman and the Postal Service, one of the Ladybird People at Work series from the 1965 UK Ladybird 'Easy Reading' imprint of books for children. (This book was reissued in 2016 to celebrate the 500th anniversary of the Royal Mail.) It featured on its cover a painted illustration of a postman emptying the contents of a bright red letterbox with the royal insignia on the front into a brown sack. He is standing near the kerb next to another British classic, a red Mini van (a typical post van of the time). Behind him, beyond a hedge and some fencing, is a typical British suburban house. Inside, the book featured illustrations of things from the first horsebacked postmen to the apparatus invented in the c20th to collect mailbags from moving trains; it detailed the purchasing of stamps, the mailing of a letter, the sorting, the delivery; it explained why letterboxes are painted the royal colour, red, and how Royal Mail got its name. In 1983 the Ladybird imprint published another book, The Postal Service, in its People Who Help Us series. This was a more modern look at a modern postal service, full of images showing the work of a dedicated community for the wider community. It explained and celebrated the astonishing and

*quotidian achievement of getting the written
message from place of sending to place of delivery
as speedily as possible via a national institution
working at its best to deliver on every level, and to
connect people for every imaginable reason. One
of its central symbols throughout was the bright
red Royal Mail letterbox.*

I mean, very informative, his mother says. But
hardly publishable.

You haven't heard the last bit, he says. About
what the iconic British letterbox means right now in
the updated lexicon.

Go on, Charlotte says.

*In summer 2018, after a disagreement with the
then UK prime minister, a backbench MP who'd
resigned from his post as Foreign Secretary – a man
who just under a year later would become UK
prime minister himself – wrote an article he
published in the Evening Standard where he stated
that though he personally declared himself not
intolerant enough to believe Muslim women who
wore full face veil burqas should be banned from
wearing what their religion often required of them,
all the same he thought it ridiculous of Muslim
women to choose to go around looking like
letterboxes. Their choice of clothing, he said, didn't
just make them resemble letterboxes but also bank
robbers.*

He was paid £275,000 for the article, which he

wrote in breach of ministerial code, and which was cited in the following days as the reason for a quadrupling of anti-Muslim attacks and incidents in the UK.

In the run-up to the UK general election of 2019 he repeatedly refused to grant that there'd been anything harmful, irresponsible, or troubling in the message sent by his rhetoric. This was at a time when attacks on people with Islamic beliefs across the world were rising, with first America then India closing borders to Muslims, India legislating against Muslims and orchestrating attacks, beatings, lynchings, arrests and killings of Muslims and the recent cordoning off of the whole of Kashmir, alongside a massive coordinated international right-wing militarization, and, in China, a simultaneous instigation of 're-education' detention centres for Muslims.

Wow, Charlotte says.

Kudos to Ashley, his sister says. Can I send that to Ayat?

No, Robert says.

Updated Lexicon? Charlotte says. Is that what she calls it?

Yes, Robert says.

Thank you for reading it out, Charlotte says.

S'okay, Robert says.

Why can't I? his sister says. She told me a horrific thing, about a man who stopped her mother in the street outside their dry cleaners and pretended he was trying to post a letter into her eyes then tried to get everyone passing in the street to laugh. Nobody did. He just looked like a lunatic. But it's what actually happened to them after that article. It made mad people go even madder.

Be really good material for Art in Nature, the man says.

It would, Charlotte says.

I've also got photos of the humbug, piccaninny and die in a ditch pages here if anyone'd like to see or hear them, Robert says. They're really interesting.

I would, his sister says.

I meant anyone other than you, Robert says.

Do you think Ashley'd mind if you forwarded some of these to us? Charlotte says. Have you got an email address for her?

She won't mind, Robert says. You don't have to ask her. I can forward them right now if you tell me your phone number.

Probably best we ask her first, Charlotte says.

His sister laughs under her breath.

So, Charlotte says. Ashley started writing a book about words. Then she stopped being able to *speak* words. Is that it?

In exactitude, Robert says.

Ashley, his mother says. Writing a book.

She shakes her head dramatically, ie like an

actress would. His mother is an educated elite. She thinks books are *her* thing, her personal possession that nobody else has the same right to as she does.

She must like you a lot, Robert, if she's let you read it and photograph it, Charlotte says. She must really trust you.

His sister laughs out loud.

Robert doesn't care because Charlotte has just said his name.

Ashley hates him, his sister says.

Writing isn't an easy thing to do, the man says.

Arthur and Charlotte speak from *real* experience. They're both *real* writers, his mother says.

Online, mainly, the man says.

They're here doing medical research, his mother says.

Well, no, Charlotte says. More like reportage.

About the mist that came in on Worthing beach and hurt everybody in the eyes and made people sick, his mother says.

In August, Charlotte says. And the sewage spills over the last few years. When they closed the front and the pier and they moved everyone off the beach.

His sister is scrolling her phone.

Tea cosy, his sister says. I'm going to text Ashley and ask her if she'll write about that. The prime minister said at the start of the week that CO_2 emissions were cladding the world like a tea cosy.

Which demonstrates exactly how un-urgent he thinks things are and wants other people to think, Charlotte says.

Ashley's phone is broken right now, Robert says. It can't get texts.

(But it's all right. His sister has already forgotten about talking to Ashley about tea cosies.)

And also, she says. Someone here tell me. What exactly *is* skunk?

You know what a skunk is, his mother says. God help us, probably someone somewhere is eating one right now and starting a new Asian virus.

Nobody laughs.

My mother the racist, his sister says. And I'm not talking about *a* skunk, just *skunk*. I don't mean the spliff kind. It says here some soldiers have just spent the morning spraying a street where Palestinian people live with it. With skunk. What exactly is skunk?

It must be something that smells foul, Charlotte says.

The limits of my language are the limits of my world, the man says. Wittgenstein. I think.

(The man is a member of the educated elite.)

Wittgenstein, wonderful, his mother says. Isn't he?

You very much remind me of my Aunt Iris, the man says to his sister.

Who? his sister says. Me?

She was at Greenham, he says. She was on the
first ever anti-nuclear peace march to Aldermaston.
She ran a commune near Porton Down, protested
against and did research and drew public attention
to biological warfare, nerve gas and tear gas
manufacture, hidden poisons people weren't being
told about. She's just back from Greece, again. She's
been working in the crisis in the Mediterranean.

She's quite a woman, Charlotte says.

What's Greenham? his sister says.

Famous activist university, Charlotte says.

Don't be sarky, the man says. Iris is the reason
the phrase salt of the earth has any salt in it. At all.

No, she's quite a force, Iris, Charlotte says.

We need a whole new education, his sister says.
The past's the past. What's coming's stuff we can't
even imagine.

She's even more like Iris than I thought, the
man says.

Are *you* writing a book? Robert says.

He is saying it to Charlotte, not the man. But
because he still finds it hard to look at Charlotte he
can't be sure she knows he was speaking to her
until she replies.

No, she says. We're not really that kind of
writer.

We're. Plural. Robert's chest twinges.

We're the online sort, the man says. We run a
website called Art in Nature which provides

thoughtful analysis of the shapes things take in art and nature and, yeah, things like language too, and the structure of the ways we live, and so on.

We're   We

Does that pay very well? his mother asks.

Charlotte and the man say it hardly pays at all but it's got thousands of hits and is on a steady upward trend so at some point maybe it will, and that at the moment they're living off an inheritance. Charlotte explains that she's also becoming really fed up of the net and the way it's taken over everybody's lives. The man she's with looks pained when she says this. Good. Things are uneasy between them.

I keep saying, the man says. A person who helps run an online analysis *can't* do it by boycotting going online.

Hits, his sister says.

She starts telling the story of the teacher at Robert's school getting hit in the head with a brick because she sent kids home saying foreign words from other countries to their parents.

(But his sister doesn't know the story. It's Robert who knows the story.

He was there. She wasn't. He was one of the kids watching when it happened.

Someone's father: You're using words on purpose that people don't know the meanings of. You're teaching our offspring foreign words.

The teacher: But rancour is just another word for anger. I suggest we stop the anger.

The father: If we want to be angry we'll be it in the Queen's English. You don't have the right to use words from other languages any more.

The teacher: The word Bildungsroman just means a story of a person's personal development. It's crossed over into English from German and now it's an English term. If you're going to write about this famous English novel in an exam, you have to know the word Bildungsroman.

The father: You're doing it again.

The teacher: Look. It's just a fact. A story about learning how to live and maturing into adulthood is called a Bildungsroman.

Which is when the brick got thrown and the police got called.)

It was about a word a class was being taught because of the book David Copyfield, Robert says.

David Copperfield! his mother says. That's it! Sacha, that's it! Whether I shall turn out to be the heroine of my own life! First lines of David Copperfield. Or whether that station will be held by anybody else.

It's hero, though, isn't it? Charlotte says. Whether I'll turn out to be the hero.

Yes, I know, but we did our own version, his mother says. Back in the 80s. Feminist. We took it round schools. Back in my acting days. We called it

The World As It Rolled, I don't know why we did, if I ever knew why it's gone. It was all about what happened to the female characters from the book. It opened with us all saying that line, those lines, in chorus, and we were all holding copies of the book and riffling through the pages. *Whether I shall turn out to be the heroine of my own life, or whether that station will be held by anybody else, these pages must show.*

His mother talks on and on about times she had when she was acting when she was young, because the visitors are shortly going to be driving somewhere she once had an idyllic summer acting in.

Funny, she says. I hadn't thought about it for years, until this morning. And then we were watching TV and I saw this woman on screen that I knew, back then, years ago, and then after you went to school, Sacha, I was sitting here and thinking and I remembered all sorts of people and things I'd forgotten. I remembered I had the loveliest time in Suffolk one summer. And you're off there right now.

Suffolk? Robert says. Is that near Norfolk?

It is, Charlotte says. Right next to it.

She smiles at him.

Because she does, he gets the words of his next sentence mixed up.

Is Cromer the place near? he says.

His sister laughs her speculative laugh again.

The man who came with Charlotte has tracked down someone who used to know his dead mother and they're going to visit the person there.

I'm so sorry. When did she die? his mother says.

They start talking about when the mother died etc which was ages ago, like over a year ago.

She was a person who never compromised, never much gave herself away, the man says. So it was surprising that she left a request like this, something so specific.

She left a note with her lawyer, Charlotte says, that she wanted Art to track down his family, remember her to them and pass on a memento.

Not someone she ever mentioned, the man says. Not that I recall. Anyway I looked him up, I found some info for him because he was a songwriter in the 1960s, and it so happens he's still alive. So we're off to meet him.

What's the sea on the coast you're going to? his sister asks.

The North Sea, Robert says.

Is the North Sea actually I mean water-wise in any real way different from the Channel? his sister says. Or is the sea round Britain all the same water and only different because of the names people give it?

His sister is an ignoramus.

It's a good question, Charlotte says.

Robert readjusts his face to look like he also thinks it's a good question.

Oh, lovely Suffolk, his mother says. Cornfields high. The cornheads swinging like their own golden wave of the sea. Blue sky above, sea beyond. The gold against the blue.

Bit early in the year for the corn, the man says.

I felt immortal that summer, his mother says.

Sounds like quite a summer, Mrs Greenlaw, Charlotte says.

Call me Grace, his mother said. Ah, now. Thereby hangs a tale. Back in those days we so much wanted to go brown that we'd spray ourselves with olive oil out of a plant-spray bottle then let the sun fry us deeper and deeper brown. How stupid we were. But what summers. They were wonderful. The smell of cut grass.

His mother is infantile.

Old Robert [Greenlaw] (silently): summer can fuck off, it's never as good as you think it'll be, usually shit weather and even if it is hot now hot just means a whole other kind of shit weather in which it's too hot to do anything, and the leaves hang off the trees going a duller filthier colour by the week and everywhere smells of shit and sick, all the litter bins smell of off milk, the whole season is like the smell round a rubbish truck as it moves through the city and like you're stuck on a bike behind it going way too slowly down a too-narrow street.

New Robert (out loud): Einstein. He went there.

Einstein? To Suffolk? Charlotte says.

Norfolk, Robert says. In person. In the year 1933.

Then someone else says something else. Charlotte turns to the something else.

The visitors are getting ready to go. They stand up in a valedictory way.

Robert's insides become a struggling bird.

But it's been really lovely to meet you all, the visitors say.

She is going. She is leaving.

Electro minus magnetism.

His chest starts to hurt.

He can feel his eyes grow round.

He now knows a pure and inarguable thing about the infrastructure of everything. When two particles are entangled then a change to one no matter where the other particle is in the universe will mean there's a change in the other.

But how do the particles know? How do they know whether entanglement has or hasn't taken place?

It is someone maybe 30 years old.

He is Robert, 13.

There is no way.

Not for several (at least 3) years.

Not that he is thinking of anything bodily anyway.

This is a pure love.

It is the first time Robert has ever thought of the world in terms of there being more than himself in it.

So how do you find the person you found if you lose the person after finding them and then there are a lot of long dark years between you?

If Einstein holds a mirror up to look at his own face and travels at the speed of light which is 186,000 miles per second, and the light leaves his face at the same speed, can Einstein ever catch up to the light leaving his own face?

It is the thought of the light leaving Einstein's face in the famous mirror experiment.

It is terrible.

It is one of the most terrible thoughts Robert has ever tortured himself with, the light leaving the face of Einstein. He has lain in bed at night and agonized at the idea.

But up to now, up to today, he had never truly understood, more truly he'd understood *nothing*, about what the words and the realities – light, speed, energy, mirror, face – really meant and mean.

The light is leaving.

It is leaving Robert's face.

Half an hour later and the light is still here.

Phew.

!

She's standing right here. He wouldn't even have to reach to touch her. (As if he'd ever.)

It's weird but they've all ended up standing crowded together into the place between the outer door and the inner door and everybody (except Robert, who is shifting his attention from one conversation to the other) is talking at once, even the man who doesn't say much.

The man is speaking about someone who has the word hero as his literal first name. He's in a prison close to here, near the airport. The man went and met him, Charlotte went too, the day before yesterday. He's telling his sister how hard it is to get in to see someone held in the prison at the airport and how ironic it is that someone called Hero is imprisoned, and at the same time that the person called Hero is truly heroic in the way he deals with being imprisoned though he's innocent.

He got beaten up by government thugs in the country he ran away from because he wrote a blog about something governmental he disagreed with, the man says. Then he had to get out of the country because he heard they were coming to kill him for writing a second blog about being beaten up by government thugs.

Meanwhile his mother is showing Charlotte the electricity meter cupboard, the door of which is still off its hinges leaning up against the coat-stand, and has started telling her about when she came home to find their front door ajar, was coming back from the shops and saw it wide open though she knew she'd double locked it when she went out. She thought one of the kids must've come home early. But no, there was a bailiff and a locksmith and two men from SA4A POWER in the doorway.

They forced your door? Charlotte says. And entered your house without permission?

They wouldn't let me into my own house, his mother says. I live here, I said. Who are you? They said was I Mrs Nureyev. Nobody of that name lives here, I said. How long have you lived here? they said. Since round about the time you were born, I said. They showed me letters they had copies of, saying a Mr R Nureyev lived here. They told me they were replacing our meters with prepay meters because Mr Nureyev hadn't paid his bills for over a year.

Charlotte glances at Robert.

It wasn't me, he says.

I showed them on my phone my own SA4A POWER account, his mother says, fully paid up as always, and they didn't believe me. Even when I phoned SA4A POWER and had one of their robot voices on the phone verifying me as a customer. Because somewhere in their computer files they had the imaginary Mr R Nureyev, who of course doesn't exist, never existed except at the Royal Ballet, listed as living here too. The bailiff and the

SA4A man literally blocked the door, I mean stood in the doorway and blocked it with their arms. Finally, but only when they'd finished what they were doing, they accompanied me into my own house again and waited on either side of me while I went through the bureau and got the house deeds out and showed them our name. And they said, you're clearly not a Mr Jeffrey Greenlaw, and threw me out of my own house.

So I called Jeff. But even when he came round and showed them his passport they refused to remove their new meters and put the old meters back. They got into their SA4A POWER truck and left.

Plus they really messed up the paintwork, see, here and here, and this was last September. I'm still arguing about it with SA4A automatons.

Art used to work for SA4A, Charlotte says laughing. Didn't you?

Charlotte is lovely when she laughs. Robert sees the man go red round the neck, up to his ears.

Then he worries about whether his own ears have been doing anything he himself can't see and others can.

They paid very well, the man says.

SA4A are the company that bus whole busloads of homeless people from other cities into this city, his sister says.

They do what? the man says.

A friend of mine told me, his sister says. They bus them down from places in the north because people tend to give more money here than they do in some other places, which means the government doesn't have so many dead people on the streets.

Sacha, his mother says. That can't be true.

Horse's mouth, his sister says.

The government would never allow that to happen, his mother says.

Robert follows his sister quite often and knows that she hangs out sometimes with an old homeless guy in town. He thinks she may well even be sleeping with him. He hasn't said anything to her. He is keeping it as a bartering tool in case he needs it. Any fragility his sister has is money in the bank to Robert [Greenlaw].

– never saw or spoke to a real human being the whole time I worked for them, the man is saying.

He has the canvas bag that Robert looked in earlier over his shoulder. He shifts its weight every few minutes.

What's in the bag? Robert says.

It looks heavy, his sister says.

It is, the man says.

That's Arthur's memento mori, Charlotte says. Show them, Art. The thing we're delivering today.

The man gets the stone out of the bag.

Wow. Very big marble, his sister says. For a very big game of marbles.

It *is* actually a marble, I mean, it's made of it, marble, Charlotte says.

It's the thing my mother was talking about in her will, the man says. Except, when we first read it, the will, we'd no idea what she meant. *A smooth round stone among my possessions.* We couldn't find anything like it. My aunt, Iris, she'd been living with my mother for a while, I asked her, but she was none the wiser. Then I took all my mother's things out of her wardrobe, I was taking them to the charity shop, and I found it under a lot of shoes. I've been carrying it around. I quite enjoy feeling the weight of it.

Bit of a masochist, Charlotte says.

Robert has seen the word masochist many times on the porn sites and ABUSEHEAP.

He blushes.

Not at all, the man says. But I'll be sorry to let it go. I've liked having it about my person. It reminds me. All the things I didn't realize. Things I never knew about her.

Robert exchanges a look with his sister. She obviously thinks it's weird too.

Memory. It can be heavy, Charlotte says.

Other times, so light, his mother says.

Anyway, we're off to pass it on, her memory. The stone. Like she asked, the man says.

They all go silent for a moment.

They stand at the open front door.

They still don't go.

It feels miraculous.

If Robert were younger he'd think there was some forcefield involved whereby nobody could leave the house until the curse was solved or the destiny was met or the whatever was fulfilled.

Whatever, they just stand, even though the front door's open, they've got their coats on, Charlotte is dangling a car key. They just stand, they stand and they stand, all of them, in the cold, between the inner and outer doors.

Which side's your ex's house on? Charlotte asks. And Ashley?

His mother nods her head towards his father's front steps.

The guy on the other side, there, she says pointing the other way. Last summer he called me to the back garden fence on his side and he said, can I talk to your husband? I said what about. He said, I want to ask him about your trees. I said, I'm in charge of my garden, not my husband, you can ask me. He said, no, I'll wait to speak to your husband. So I phoned Jeff, it was a Saturday, he was home, he came round. And the man shouted past me to him, though I was standing there too, and he said, I want to ask you to cut down your trees. We said why? It's not like the trees were doing anything, blocking or overhanging his property or anything, nowhere near the sewers, they're just

lovely old trees, an ash, a rowan, the apple tree.
And he said, the thing is, I don't get much time, I
work a lot, I only get a few hours a week in which I
can do stuff in the garden, and I want you to cut
down *your* trees so I can plant *my* trees. And we
said, we're not stopping you planting your trees, go
ahead, what's the problem? And he said, I don't
want to look out of my window and see trees that
aren't mine.

His mother and Charlotte and the man all talk
about how complex being a neighbour is.

Then Charlotte says she's had a thought, about
Ashley.

There's a filmmaker who made a film, years ago,
in the middle of the last century, a really good one,
she says. It's about trauma I suppose, and it's really
startling. The thing is, it's very much about not
talking. About two men who are friends and are
both deaf mutes, who can't talk like everyone else
does, so instead they find their own ways to. One's
thin and tall, one's small and squat, they couldn't
be more different, but they couldn't be more
connected.

She tells them it was made just postwar, the early
50s, a British film, the two men wandering and
living and working in a bomb-blasted landscape in
London near the docks.

And the film says all these complicated things,
and it does it without saying a word, she says. Wait.

Art. Lend me your phone. It's Free Cinema, British. She's Italian, she was the only woman to make one of the founding films of the movement, Mazzetti, uh huh, Lorenza Mazzetti, here it is – oh. Oh no.

She looks at the phone screen.

She just died, she says.

Oh, his mother says. Oh dear.

A month ago, at New Year, Charlotte says. In Rome. It says here she was ninety two. Oh.

Charlotte looks dismayed.

Oh dear, his mother says again. Is it someone you know?

No, Charlotte says, no, not personally. Not at all.

But a good long life, his mother says. Ninety two. I mean.

An amazing life, Charlotte says. Lorenza Mazzetti. Truly.

She gives the man back his phone.

The film's called Together, she says.

She looks at Robert.

You tell her, she says. I mean Ashley. You tell her about it, it's a powerful story, and it might just, you know. Make a difference. You tell her for me. Don't forget.

I will, Robert says, I'll tell her as soon as I see her. I won't forget. Lorenza. Mazzetti. Together.

It's true that the arts can often be a help, his mother is saying. Not always, though. I mean, some of the finest words in the world have passed

110

through me, and out again like so much excess vitamin c. But that's when I was young and foolish, and I thought it was just words, for effect, what you said out loud so you could watch the power you have over others when you make them feel. I played a dead person, a dead person who comes back to life. Every second night, for a fortnight. From town to town, that summer. In Suffolk.

That immortal summer you had, the man says.

Then Robert says out of nowhere:

Can I come? To Suffolk?

Don't be silly, Robert, his mother says.

Why not? the man says. If you'd like. There's plenty of room.

Nice idea, Charlotte says. Why don't you all come?

Excuse his rudeness, his mother says. He can't go to Suffolk with you. He's got school.

Yeah, I'd like to go somewhere, his sister says.

We can easily fit you all in, Charlotte says.

His mother starts to laugh.

I'm just laughing at hearing my daughter say she'll travel anywhere in a car, she says.

It's electric, his sister says.

Though when I say *all*, I don't think we could fit Ashley and your ex husband in too, Charlotte says.

Bonus, his mother says. Be nice, a bit of space. Lovely thought. Kind of you. But we can't. Look at Sacha's hand.

My hand's fine, his sister says. It wants to go.

No, no. I can't possibly do anything so spontaneous, his mother says.

Why not? the man says. You only live once. Or twice in your case. Every second night for a fortnight.

Everybody laughs. The man looks very surprised then pleased.

But we hardly know each other, his mother says.

I have an ethos, the man says. It's this. Time spent exchanging life and times with complete or comparative strangers can sometimes work out rather well. In some cases, it can even be life-changing.

Yes! his mother says. It's true!

She blushes.

Both Robert and his sister notice.

No, I've got to get them to school, she says. And where would we stay? And what about – what about everything?

I can't go back to school today with my hand like this, his sister says.

Then you can't go to Suffolk either, his mother says.

Saturday tomorrow, Charlotte says. You could stay over, somewhere near the sea, take the train back at your leisure.

But we live right next to the sea, his mother says.

It's a different sea, his sister says.

More or less, Charlotte says.

But you've things to do, family things, his mother says. We can't intrude.

I'm going to meet a complete stranger, the man says. For an hour or so. Anyway. You could do what you liked. You could peel off at any point on the journey, anywhere you fancy the look of.

Where exactly are you going? his mother asks.

The man says the name of a place Robert has never heard of.

No, I don't know it, his mother says.

Charlotte says the name of another place Robert has never heard of. His mother acts like she's having an orgasm.

That's it! It exactly! his mother says.

Is that where you were immortal, then? the man says.

It is, his mother says. What an amazing thing. And you're going there, of all places. Today.

His mother is flirting with the man.

Come too. You can tell us about your immortal summer. On the way. Summer on the way, even in February, the man says.

Is the man flirting with his mother?

Nicely put, his mother says.

He's a writer, Charlotte says. And you, she says (putting a hand for a moment on Robert's shoulder and sending something like an electric shock through Robert), can tell us all at last the story of the hourglass and the glue.

The story of the what? his mother says.

Charlotte knows.

She knows he is ruinous.

His heart falls inside him like a stone falling through deep water.

Then Charlotte winks at him.

In the blink of her eye the world is made possible all over again.

His mother forgets to ask about glue (thank God) and starts to wax lyrical about being young and spontaneous and having conversations about time and the nature of the imagination at half past ten in the morning and going on road trips.

She sends him and his sister inside to pack things for overnight.

I'm really sorry, he says to his sister on the way upstairs. I didn't know it'd hurt. Please don't tell.

You're dead, his sister says. My hand's going to be scarred for life.

Stitch in time was a really witty thing to say, he says. (Appeasement.) And at least now you will never forget me. Every time you look at it you'll think of me. The scar I mean.

You're a silly little wanker, she says. And what the fuck have you done with the remote?

I posted it, he says.

You what? she says.

I put it in an envelope, he says, and put some of dad's stamp collection on it –

The presentation stamps? she says. Which set?

The war folder. Four of the Star Wars 2015, three of the Dad's Army, he says.

He'll kill you, she says. He will. Where the fuck did you send it?

Deception Island, he says.

You posted it to an imaginary place? she says.

Deception Island's real, he says. I looked it up, I looked up *what is the most remote place on earth*, and it's one of the places that came up, it's a hollow island in Antarctica, like an island with a hole in the middle of it like the top of a volcano. That's because it *is* the top of a volcano, and nobody lives there because the volcano might go off, there are these old whaling stations from like a century ago, they're all collapsed in on themselves. The beach is covered in whale bones. Nothing there, birds, gulls and petrels. Penguins. Seals and their babies.

You posted a lump of plastic to some place where it'll sit and never rot and be a piece of rubbish for ever because there'll be no use for it there? she says. And some plane'll have to cross the world to deliver it just because of some stupid whim of yours?

He shrugs.

You've lost your mind, his sister says. Who did you send it to?

Mr WH Alebone, he says.

His sister stops in the middle of the stairs and has to hold on to the banister with her unbandaged hand because she is suddenly laughing so much.

One of the best things ever, to be able to make your sister laugh like that.

1 May 2020

Dear Hero,

You don't know me, we are strangers. A while back some friends told me a little about you being in detention. It made me want to write just saying hi and sending you a friendly word or two.

First and most, I hope you are well in this terrible time.

I am sending this letter via my friends. They told me you got here by being sealed inside a box in transit for more than six weeks, that you are qualified as a microbiologist, and that when you arrived here you ended up wrapping fridges in plastic in a warehouse.

They also told me that you aren't one of the detainees let out because of health reasons in

March and that you have been in the detention centre now for nearly three years.

They told me not just how you taught yourself English from a dictionary so small that it fits into the palm of your hand, but that the last time you wrote to them you talked about insomnia, cumulo nimbus clouds, the atmosphere, and the problem of trying to look through a window that is opaque, that you really like birds and wildlife but that the window in the cell you live in is opaque plastic, not glass, and doesn't open.

I'm 16 and live in Brighton, roughly thirty miles from where you are if you're still in detention.

I go to a great school – when it's not closed because of the virus. I love it. I'm really missing it. Now I know how much I <u>love</u> learning. Now that I'm not getting to learn in the way we were.

I've got a little brother. He drives me crazy, particularly right now because he hates lockdown so much. Our mother keeps telling him he has to stop being so animalistic and apply logic. Talking of animals, I'm planning to study to be a vet when I leave school, so if I get qualified in veterinary studies I'll be able to look after my brother. Joke! No but in reality I care a lot about wildlife, the environment means everything to me, and the way it is being harmed is what gives <u>me</u> insomnia.

Though considering the iniquity of your own situation, I really don't have a right to not sleep well.

I was thinking, what will I write to Hero about that could be of use to him?

So I'm going to write about the swifts.

You probably know already they're the birds that live some of the year in Africa and some of the year here and in other places in Europe and Scandinavia. They are about to arrive here again any day, at least I hope they are. Last year they arrived May 13th. In Brighton we're among the earliest to see swifts returning to the UK. My mother has this saying, about the swifts being what make a summer happen: 'it's when the swifts arrive and when the swifts leave that marks the start and the end of a summer.' Apparently her mother said it, and her mother's mother said it. I think that makes swifts a bit like a flying message in a bottle. There's a poem by the poet Emily Dickinson that I like. It says (though it says it more poetically than I am here) what would happen if you split a lark open? I have a vision that if you were to open a swift, metaphorically of course, the rolled-up message they carry inside them is the unfurled word

SUMMER.

In case you don't know, they're the birds that look like black arrows high in the sky. They are in fact a kind of grey colour, with a bit of white under their chin, and beautiful tiny heads shaped like crash helmets, wise eyes like black beads.

Their latin name is apus apus, which is something to do with how they look like they don't have feet. Actually they have very small feet evolved for clinging to buildings or rocks, they are built to be aerodynamic which means in the end they need big feet less than other birds, they are quite small in frame but their wings are the biggest in ratio to the size of their body of all of the birds in the air because they spend a massive amount of their lives on the wing.

They feed while they're flying, they eat flies and insects and have adapted to sorting the ones that sting from the ones that don't – for example they can actually tell drones from other bees. I mean the bee kind of drone, not the camera and bombing machine. They drink rain on the wing or descend to skim the surface of a river without landing, and they even sleep on the wing – their brains can shut down on one side so they get some rest while the other side stays awake.

But what is also pretty amazing is that they can fly 3,000 miles in five days, if they don't get put off course by bad weather, and they know where they are going pretty much as soon as they're born, by means of earth's natural magnetism, and that the average journey they make is between 12,000 and 13,000 miles and look at the size of them, they're such little birds.

I am watching the sky for them to arrive every

day. As if this year hadn't been bad enough, there's been reports from Greece that a high wind killed off thousands of them on their way north at the start of April.

Why would we ever imagine that anything in the world takes a shape more important than the eye or the brain or the shape in the sky of a bird like that.

Well Hero, I think that is way more than enough for one letter. I hope I haven't bored you. I wanted to send you an open horizon and this is one of the things that has kept me sane in this time when we are all in lockdown.

But lockdown is nothing compared to the unfairness of life for people who are already being treated unfairly.

I will write again soon.

I know we have not met or anything but with respect I very much hope you are okay.

I also know your window isn't that good, but I think sometimes you get to go outside into a yard?

If you see a swift in the sky, it's carrying a message from a stranger who wishes you well and is thinking of you.

Friendly greetings.

From

Sacha Greenlaw

2

So here's another fragment of moving image from across time.

Two men, both young, one short and stocky, the other taller, slighter, are walking across an expanse of rubble. There's a grey sky above them and a cityline that's all walls and chimney stacks beyond them. They're deep in conversation. But the men are both deaf mutes. So they're crossing this rubble talking intently to each other with their hands and by watching the shapes each other's mouths or faces make.

A boy about ten years old and up at the top of a lamppost on lookout shouts something we can't hear to some other children climbing a heap of oilcans and barrels. It's as if they've been waiting. The boy shins down the lamppost. Children jump off broken walls, down off the barrelheap. Across the bombed-out space with its bricks scattered here and there children run to gather behind the two men, who are walking along a piece of pavement on a neat clean road cut through the rubble of what's still standing of this bit of the city, oblivious to the children, who've formed a little gang now, girls as well as boys.

First the children yell into the eye of the camera some laughing insults we can't hear. Then they make faces, stick their tongues out. One puts his hands to his head like horns and waves his fingers. They run away laughing. Other children run at the camera. They pull their eyesockets down, flatten their noses, push their lower lips out with their tongues. A girl puts her thumbs in her ears and waves her hands like oversized ears.

The children march behind the men like a mock parade. They make fun of how the men walk. They laugh and strut and kick their way past a terrace of houses sliced open at one end by bomb damage. Even more children join in. One boy punches the air.

The men walking along the road talking so intently to each other have no idea that anything or anyone's behind them.

Two women, one young but already haggard, the other more middle-aged and stony, are watching it happen. They are standing with their arms folded at the shabby closed door of a house in a terrace.

They have a speculative air, especially when one of the men tips his hat to them. The two women exchange with each other words we can't hear, then watch, impassive, as the men go in through the next door house's open door. They say some more things we can't hear, then nod to each other as if something's been decided.

**On a fine summer's morning Daniel Gluck is
standing behind the wooden huts in a ruined field,**
a place until quite recently a firing range going by
the bit of the shape of a man, shoulder? bit of a
shoulder and neck? on the shred of litter he's just
picked up and unfurled from under his boot.

Ascot.

A word – and a place – that's changed its
meaning. It means something quite other now.
Everything means something quite other now.
Clearly this field was also something quite other till
recently, was a small wood, before, going by the
craters in the ground, still raw, not yet weathered.
Trees all gone but one. The others hauled out, roots
and all.

His father, he hopes, is somewhere under that
one surviving tree towards the middle of the field.

So many men are under it pushing to get out of the sun that there's no room for anyone else.

There's no other shade.

There's some wooden buildings they can't get into, out of bounds. There's nowhere else to go.

There's nothing else to do.

First thing in the morning there's waiting for the milk cart to come to the main gate.

Then nothing, for the rest of the day.

Every morning so far the milkman has brought news, but the news he brought yesterday and today was the same news as the day before and the day before that.

Germans in Paris.

(Hannah may still be in Paris.

There's no way of knowing.)

So.

There's the bunk buildings and the toilet smell.

Or there's full sunlight, in which there's a choice of walking the length of the new barbed wire fence in the sun then walking the length of it back again, or standing about in the sun near the bunk buildings, or standing about in the sun in the ruined field, which is where he is now.

Too hot to do the fence walk.

Far too hot for boots.

Wear your boots, put your boots on, you'll need them, his father said. *Pack something warm. You hear me?*

A fine summer's morning with no cloud in the sky again, blue for ever above them all lined up for roll-call. Half an hour later the fine summer's morning with its blue sky means skin burnt on the top of your head.

His hat went walkabout, day before yesterday.

With one eye he's watching all the heads to see if he can spot it.

With the other he's getting ready to be cheerful about it, not cause trouble to himself or anyone, when he sees it on whoever else's head.

He leans on the broken fencepost, the wood warm under his hand.

Glorious day, a man says, walks past.

Again, Daniel says.

He looks at the furl of paper in his other hand with the bit of combat shoulder on it. He shakes it open. Quite thick paper, serviceable.

He holds it up above his head. Might work.

He leans against the fencepost, folds the paper along its edge, folds it again. How you used to make a boat, remember. With any luck there's enough.

He unfolds it, starts again at the beginning.

He came downstairs to breakfast, Monday morning, and William Bell – not in uniform, in his suit jacket and tie like Sunday church – was at the table drinking tea with his father. Paying a formal social visit at quarter to eight in the morning.

Outside the open front door in the hum of bees, kicking his heels near his father's pinks and the rose border, another West Sussex Constabulary man, this one wearing a long raincoat. On such a sunny morning.

It's you, Dan, William Bell said. Thought you'd've been off by now. Navy, isn't it?

They don't want him, his father said. His piss test came back diabetes.

I don't have diabetes, Daniel said. Mystery to me.

Anyway they won't have him, his father said.

Yet, Daniel said.

His father swirled the pot, poured Daniel tea.

Get some breakfast, Daniel, he said.

Get it now, he said under his breath shooting Daniel a look.

Take your time, gents, William Bell said with his arms up and his hands behind his head.

What William Bell meant in his ostentatious leisure was: hurry it up.

Just a bit of questioning, William Bell said. Won't take any time.

I'll nip upstairs and pack a bag, his father said. Two minutes.

Oh, you won't need a bag packed, Walter, William Bell said. He won't need a bag, Dan. Just down to Charlton Street. Back by lunchtime.

He's category C, Daniel said.

It's all the category Cs, we're told, William Bell

said. It's not just Statutory Rules in Respect of the Aliens in Protected Areas any more, we're told. It's blanket category C. Don't concern yourselves. Just a few questions, we're told. Finish your tea, Walter, plenty time.

I'll come along, can I? Daniel said.

You can do, boy, William Bell said. Nice of you. Keep the old man company.

You've no need, Daniel, his father said.

Daniel followed him upstairs.

What else use am I? he said too quiet for William Bell to hear. I'll be more help in than out.

His father stood there shaking his head in his bedroom doorway, a shaving brush in his hand, an unlaced boot, one of the winter boots, in the other.

Oh God, he said.

It wasn't that he was shaking his head. It was that his head was shaking. His whole body was shaking. The shaving brush in his shaking hand shook.

No. I'm coming, Daniel said.

Wear your boots, then, his father said. Pack something warm. Be sure to take all the money you've got in the house.

Thought you'd like to stroll down to the station yourselves, William Bell said. Make your own way there. We'll follow you down in a couple of minutes. When you get there tell the duty sergeant who you are and wait for me at the front desk. All right?

Take what's left of that loaf, Daniel, his father said.

All right sir? the younger policeman said as they came out through the front door. Manage your bag?

He had the raincoat on over his uniform, presumably so no neighbours would see uniforms outside his father's house.

They'll carry their bags themselves, Brownlee, William Bell said. Brownlee and I'll just do a quick check round, just for the books, as it were, keep things right, if that's okay by you, Walter. Anything untoward or dangerous we've to report. There won't be, I know. But all the same. Just for the books.

Feel free, please, Bill, his father said. Lock the door after you, will you?

Will do, William Bell said.

They didn't see William Bell again. At Charlton Street station they waited at the front desk till past eleven, when a Black Maria (*just these two then? that all?*) took them to Brighton.

At the station in Brighton their matches, razor blades and a little fruitknife that Daniel carried in his jacket pocket got confiscated. A constable went through their cases. He opened Daniel's manicure case and removed the nail scissors.

What did you bring that nonsense with you for? his father said.

134

To look after my nails, Daniel said.

A quandary you are, his father said shaking his head.

They'd taken his father's killing fluid bottle too. The bottle was sitting right there on the sergeant's desk.

Think they thought you were likely to drink it yourself, Daniel said. I'm happy for all the butterflies who'll live.

I've used laurel before, his father said. I can find it again, I'm sure, if I see a rarity.

They sat on their suitcases on the floor because the three chairs and the bench were taken. Daniel's father put his back against the wall below the notices and had a sleep. Daniel spoke with a man in his forties, a journalist from London who'd been picked up in Brighton, here for the long weekend.

It's wholesale internment, the man said. It's for our own good.

He said the last phrase with a wry eye. The place filled up, men and boys. Some had no luggage. Some had come in their shirtsleeves, didn't even have a coat.

Nothing happened.

More people, wandering about.

At four in the afternoon his father woke up from the doze and shared out chunks of the morning loaf with the nearest men.

The army trucks arrived. Nobody asked anybody anything. The police gave the officer a sheet of paper, the officer signed it, gave it back. They loaded them all on.

His father sat on his case, Daniel let an aged-looking chap sit on his and sat crosslegged on the floor of the truck near the back where he could see through the stringholes in the canvas, keep a lookout for where they were. Hard to tell, after Brighton, though the going was slow. Men threw up; the truck was foul, fogged with a burnt fuel smell from its own exhaust pipe, and though they were going along pretty slowly the men in the back were occasionally shunted very suddenly from one side to the other by the swing of the thing.

One man kept saying he'd not said a proper goodbye to his wife.

One said he'd left his front door wide open.

A panic went round the truck.

I hope Bill locked that door, his father said quietly to Daniel.

Five minutes later he said it again.

Then –

do you think Bill remembered to lock the door? he said an hour later.

Evening light.

The truck stopped somewhere leafy.

It sat and didn't move for another two hours.

Dusk.

Finally someone opened a gate and shepherded them all to a stone building. Animal stalls.

Bertram Mills Circus, a corporal with a bayonet on the rifle told Daniel. They winter the livestock here.

(The last time Hannah and their mother came to London, Christmas 1933, they all went to the circus. Grand Hall, Olympia. There was a sea lion that whispered into a woman's ear. Bombayo the Hindu, a miniature man, stood on a pony as it galloped fast round the ring followed by four girls in tutus balanced one on top of the other on the back of a massive carthorse. Beauties and the Beast. A woman appeared as if by magic out of a cloud of white doves. A troupe of acrobats was painted gold all over. Mademoiselle Violette D'Argens and her Lions: First Appearance in London, she wore a skimpy satin top that barely hid her chest, commanded a beast with fierce claws and a body all muscle to sit neatly on a little stool and behave. Daniel, nearly twenty, was enchanted. Hannah, was she thirteen? fourteen? scoffed at him all the way home in the cab.)

There were a couple of long tables, not many chairs. On either side of the long room there were structures with wooden boards on them, three, then three, then three. Bunks. The three by threes stretched further down the room than Daniel could make out in the dark.

Plenty straw outside! Each alien is advised to fill his mattress bag and make it as thick or as thin as he likes, an NCO shouted.

Daniel filled one.

He filled another.

He's got two, a man younger than Daniel shouted. *I* want two.

Old and young everywhere, all the ages under the sun. Men were running to bag the bunks closest to the door and furthest from the toilet now. Daniel ran with both straw bags. He got them a middle and a lower together halfway down the building. He waved to his father, told him not to let anybody else have them. Then he went and got the blankets. They'd only give him two. They thought he was being cheeky wanting four.

The blankets were old, rough wool, didn't smell great. His father sat meekly on the lower wooden board fingering a piece of straw.

Up at the end of the room was a queue of men. That was the toilet behind a low brick divide next to the beds. Then the room was full of smoke and coughing; someone was trying to light a stove. It was 3am, the light outside coming up. Someone got the thing lit, boiled water, made tea.

There weren't enough cups for the number of people.

People shared what cups there were.

Things slowed. Something akin to silence

happened. Snoring, sleep-moaning, the occasional panicked shout.

I am seventy eight years old, Daniel heard the man in the lower bunk next to his father say. I cannot be expected to live like this.

It'll be better, brighter, tomorrow when we're able to see where we are, Daniel's father, below Daniel, said.

Don't you know? We are at Ascot, the man said.

He said the word Ascot as if he were saying something made of glass and didn't want his mouth cut.

Racecourse, his father said.

I have been here many times, the man said. Many times in the Royal Enclosure. Many friends here, many memories. What is your business, sir?

Beer, Daniel's father said. Imports, and sausage, pickles. General foodstuffs, general goods. These days, soap.

He knocked the base of the bunk above with his fist.

Up there is my son, he said. He looks after my accounts and works as a salesman for me.

Pause.

I mean he did. Was, his father said.

All past, the man said.

Then he said,

my dear wife. She has died.

I'm sorry to hear it, his father said.

Ten years ago, the old man said.

Mine three years ago, his father said. Time is nothing.

You are a German, the man said.

I grew up in England from infancy, never got the papers, his father said. A serious mistake, I should have known after the last war. But that war ended and I thought I didn't need them. Then when I went to get them this time round it was too late, the war was up and running, they wouldn't give them to me.

I surmise from your reply that you are not a supporter of the Reich, the man said.

You surmise correctly, Daniel's father said.

I am expected these days to sleep next to a Jew, the man said.

Hard not to, in here. And I can't speak for the fellow on the other side of you, or the one above. But it's with regret I inform you. I do not have the honour of being a member of that race, his father said.

But I do, Daniel said.

Me too, the man on the other side of the gent said.

And me, someone else said.

And me, and him, and him, someone else said.

A guard at the door called to them to be quiet, told them men were trying to sleep.

A well-off blackshirt. All the blackshirts and sympathizers were supposed to be picked up by

140

now. Category A went last autumn. B went in the spring. Daniel turned on to his front, saw in the half light the metal ring fixed in the wall.

We're all at the circus now, he thought. We're all at the races.

He closed his eyes.

He opened them.

Terrible noise.

His father below him felt him shift, he spoke, told him what the noise was.

Reveille.

First thing Daniel saw in the bright summer light was how filthy everything, blanket he'd slept under, board he'd slept on, bag with the straw in it he'd slept on, floor, wall, ceiling, even the base of his own suitcase when he picked it up, was.

His father sat on the edge of his own filthy straw bag and watched Daniel see how things were.

Morning, Daniel said.

He gave his father a rueful smile.

Son, do you think Bill Bell locked the door? his father said.

I do, Daniel said. Bill's a good fellow.

And what about the cat? And the roses? Who'll do the tomatoes? The tomatoes'll need doing today. They'll need doing every day, if they're not to rot. What about the soap? What if someone pilfers the stock?

His father was a salesman for Sunlight soap and

soapflakes now, *do they lather? rather!* He said
these worried things, and variations on these
things, all through the wait for the porridge, all
through the eating of it, all through the standing in
the sun that first morning, the milling around, the
nothing else to do.

So they went that first afternoon and got the
requisite writing paper and wrote the requisite
twenty four lines only, to William Bell c/o Steyning
Police Station.

But Daniel saw, though his father didn't, what
the corporal behind the post desk did with the letter
his father wrote, thrown over his shoulder on to a
pile of other letters in the metal bin overflowing
with letters, letters, letters all over the floor.

Now?

Daniel stands in the ruined field and puts the
paper hat on his head.

Instantaneous relief!

Thank you, old target practice.

He goes towards the tree.

But he can't see his father among the seething
people under there.

He'll go and see if he can find him at the gate,
where the crowd waits every day after the milkman
in the hope mail will arrive.

Warmth on his hands, on his arm. Warm
going cool.

He opens his eyes.

He looks at his hands.

Someone is rubbing at him, old skin loose on the inner arm, light but firm with a warm damp flannel.

Oh, hello, he says.

Morning Mr Gluck, the nurse, what's her name, Paulina, says. How you today?

I'm very well, Paulina, he says. How are you?

Fine, Mr Gluck. Are you ready to get up? Bit of breakfast?

Thank you, Paulina.

He is in his neighbour's house, which has lately become his home. It is a very nice house. It is a lovely room. The room used to belong to his neighbour's daughter.

Paulina pulls the covers back and helps him swing his legs over the side of the bed.

Toilet. Then back to bed. Breakfast.

He's been talking about camping today, he hears Paulina tell his neighbour's daughter.

His neighbour's daughter, what's her name, Elisabeth, is home again. That makes today Friday.

And Paulina will be leaving the country soon.

End of an era, he said to Paulina when they talked about it.

Eras end, Paulina said. I'm Romanian. I know. They have to. So that new eras can begin.

He closes his eyes.

Today he has been chatting in his sleep, he hears

Paulina say. About his friend Douglas who went camping. And then about going to the races, and how he camped there.

Douglas, his neighbour's daughter says. It's not a person. It's a place on the Isle of Man, they interned him and his father in the Second World War. At least we think so. It's difficult to know.

Yes, Paulina says. But that makes some sense of what he is saying.

I think he's thinking about it, his neighbour's daughter says, because my mother or Zoe will have reminded him, there's a man who tracked him down on the internet, he's driving over to visit him today. I have a theory that he hears the word *internet* and thinks the word *internment*.

He has a very curly mind for a gentleman who has lived so many years, Paulina says. A hundred and four years. He is the oldest person I have met in my time living in this country, and I've been here for fourteen years working with many people of many years. He told me today a story about apples. That one day at the gate of a prison someone brought crates of apples for the men in the prison and that it took only a few seconds for all those free apples to get taken and the crates lying empty on the ground. But nobody saw the apples, nobody ate the apples, nobody saw anybody else eat the apples – and then for weeks afterwards someone would say, like they were offering you a forbidden drug, would you like to buy this apple? And soon one apple cost fifteen times more than the first price. The world's way.

Certainly is, his neighbour's daughter says.

Your mother and her friend left this morning, she told me to remind you there are lentils in the fridge already in a sauce and they'll see you on Sunday before you go back to London. I'll see you tonight to tuck Mr Gluck in. I hope your day is a good one. And his day too.

Cheery goodbyes.

The front door closes.

Memory comes to Daniel now by unforming itself the way a flake of snow will melt on something warm, your face, your hand, like it does on your collar when you come in from the cold. Sometimes he hears the hooves of the horses on the roads of the cities he grew up in on the road outside this window.

That's not horses, they tell him here in his neighbour's house. That's people from the AirBnB studio along the road. It's the wheels of their suitcases going over the cracks in the pavement.

How long d'you think we'll be here? an Irish-sounding man wrapped in a blanket (no other clothes with him, says he was brought in off a building site) asked Daniel's father a fortnight into their time at Ascot.

(Word had got round that Daniel's father knew about internment.)

No idea, friend, Daniel's father said.

(They moved them nearly three weeks later.)

How long d'you think they'll keep us here, Mr Gluck? the retired professor of medieval French asked Daniel's father when they unloaded them into Kempton Park and told them to make beds for themselves in the Tote building under the betting pigeonholes.

Your guess is as good as mine, sir, Daniel's father said.

(One night only. They took them in trucks to Liverpool next day and loaded them on a ship, gave each fifty-man group a lump of cheese the size of a forearm, told them to divide it among themselves for the journey. One of the soldiers cut it into pieces with a bayonet. Daniel got a piece an inch and a half square, size of half a finger.

Don't eat it all at once, his father said. Keep some for later.)

How long d'you think we'll be here? Daniel asked his father when they saw the barbed wire palisade and double fence at the Hutchinson gate.

His father took his glasses off, wiped off the rain, put them back on. He looked at the rows of houses behind the wire. He looked at the fenceposts newly sunk into the pavements. He looked at the small crowd of men inside the camp standing soaked at the fences waiting to see if anyone arriving was someone they knew.

Looks permanent to me, he said.

On the march up the road from the port in the rain a man in his forties told Daniel how the CID had picked him up from Hampstead Public Library by arriving in the morning and shouting in the Reading Room *all enemy aliens to the front desk now*. Then they went round looking in everybody else's faces deciding who looked Jewish but hadn't reported to the front desk. Even on the way to the police station they kept halting the group and making them wait while they stopped people in the street they thought looked likely and asked for their papers.

The local island people lining the road as they marched up the hill were watching them with their mouths hanging open.

I think they think we're Nazis, Daniel said. They think we're Nazi prisoners of war.

See, I never would've imagined, the NCO marching alongside them said then, that there'd be so many of you Jews who was Nazis. I can't comprehend it. Why would you like the Nazis so much when the Nazis don't like *you* so much?

We're not Nazis, Daniel said. You couldn't get more opposite from Nazis. Didn't they brief you?

Briefed us nothing, the soldier said.

We're the ones who thought we'd got away from

the Nazis, the man next to Daniel said. We're doctors, teachers, chemists, shopkeepers, labourers, factory workers, you name it. What we're not is Nazis.

Told us nothing, the soldier said. Enemy aliens is what they said. Are you not the Germans, then?

The Germans are not all Nazis, the man said.

The parade slowed, quickened, slowed. This was because the enemy aliens up ahead were stopping, taking their hats off, as they passed something. As soon as the people who got to it saw it was a war memorial to the dead of the island in the first war, they stopped too and took off their hats, if they had hats.

That sure enough don't seem very Nazi, the NCO said.

A sergeant shouted from the back at the rows of men up front to get a move on. A smartly dressed man ahead of Daniel turned and told the sergeant to stop shouting, they couldn't go any faster, that the man in front of him was more than seven decades old and was going as fast as he could.

That sergeant laid off the shouting right away.

Now *there's* a turn up for the books, Daniel's father said. *There's* a different fishkettle. Might be all right here, you know.

They got sorted into groups of thirty, told to take a house on the square, told which houses were free. The houses were holiday houses, guest houses, the landladies long gone taking the carpets and most of the furnishings with them. The windows were painted blue, blackout. The houses were lit with red bulbs. They were bare, a few chairs, makeshift tables. But the bedrooms had beds. There was water, cold. The kitchens had gas for cooking. There wasn't much to eat anything with in the way of plates, spoons. People made do with bits of wood and as soon as they got a chance carved themselves something in the way of a spoon. Each place chose a cook from among its house members, someone sorted a rota, duties, cleaning, so on.

Poor man's riviera! That's what they call this place when there's not a war on.

But there's a green grass square in front of the houses and it's got flowers, annuals, in the borders fresh-cut into it, and beyond it through the wire down the hill a view of the sea.

The Daily Mail says you're getting a sea air holiday here, a boy of ten says to Daniel a week later through the wire, where Daniel, bare-chested, is hanging his just-washed shirt on the fence to dry. The Daily Mail says you've luxury sunbathing beds and miniature golf and more money than we've got and hot water and coal. You get sugar and milk and eggs for your breakfast. Fried by landladies.

Miniature golf. Eggs.

Daniel looks over his shoulder at the slow-moving men wandering the street, aimless, hunched, as if the mild summer air isn't air but anaesthetic. Any minute, the invasion. Everybody expects it now. France and Belgium and Holland gone. Any minute, and an island of men, mostly Jews and people the fascists want dead, ready parcelled up to be handed over, lock and stock.

What's your name? Daniel asks the boy.

Speak some Nazi, the boy says. Go on.

I'm not a Nazi, Daniel says. Want to swap places?

The boy goggles his eyes at Daniel.

Tell you what. I'll come out, Daniel says. You come in here instead and have the holiday.

We can't holiday here, the boy says. We're already home.

Lucky you, Daniel says.

You're luckier, the boy says. You got miniature golf.

There's no golf here, Daniel says.

Daily Mail says there is, the boy says.

They put the Nazis down at Peveril mostly, a different boy kicking about in some fence rubble behind the first boy says. Them're the enemy aliens.

Speak some enemy alien, the boy says.

I'm Daniel, Daniel says. Tell me your name.

That's not alien words, the boy says. That's just English.

I am English, Daniel says.

What you doing in there then? the boy says. Come on out.

I belong in here, Daniel says. My family's here.

Your family's enemy aliens? the boy says.

In a manner of speaking, Daniel says. But also not at all.

That don't make no sense, the boy says.

His name's Keith, the other boy says.

Brothers? Daniel says.

What's it to you? the other boy says.

Move it! Away from the wire!

A guard is shouting at the boys, waving his rifle.

Tell the Daily Mail from me, Keith, Daniel calls after them, from me as a representative of us all here, that we're internees in a prison camp, we're not enemies, and that a prison is always a prison, even in August when the sky is blue.

The boys' backs disappear down the hill.

A prison. Daniel goes back to the House of the Fairy Tales, where they have a room to themselves, his father and him. It was called this already when they moved in because someone had cut the shapes of fairy-tale creatures with a razor into the blackout paint on the front window of the house.

A man with rabbit ears.

A legendary-looking tree.

A scarecrow.

A fish with the wings of a bird.

Three suitcases with mouths and eyes.

A mouse towering over a cat.

These figures all mean that daylight gets in.

There's a House of the Bathing Belles, with its windows all voluptuous, and a House of the Zoo Animals – the famous lion tamer lives there and an elephant keeper from a zoo. The zoo is trying to get a release for him as fast as possible because his elephants have stopped eating since he left.

The orthodox Jews complained to the street father about the Bathing Belles. Then someone cut biblical figures into their bay window and they stopped complaining and were really pleased about how the light filters in through the biblical.

One sunny morning Daniel comes out of the store and sees a commotion happening near the fence. One of the most elderly of the internees, a man with a long grey beard, has caught the beard in the barbs on the fence. Three internees on the internee side of the fence are tugging gently at the beard. Two guards on the other side of the fence are doing the same. Everyone is puzzling, on both sides, over how to free the beard.

One of the guards watching at a distance takes the bayonet off his gun and comes towards the commotion.

Two thin young Germans from one of the houses across the square are watching too. One of them's the tuneful whistler, Daniel's heard him round the place. The other, they'll be family the way the whistler always has an eye on the other, is a shadow version of him, a ghost, and when that soldier raises the bayonet the ghost brother hollows himself into his own shoulders and somehow goes near invisible, very like vanishing himself by magic.

The soldier raises the blade, a blade as long as his arm. With precision he uses its tip to cut through the part of the beard caught on the fence. The old man steps back, rights himself, flourishes his arms. He smooths his beard, checks it for gaps. Everybody on both sides of the wire laughs and congratulates everybody else. Close shave!

The soldier tells the old man to *watch the hair on your chinny chin chin.*

The ghost brother is visibly shaking. Daniel can see even from here. The tuneful brother sees Daniel notice. He nods to Daniel. He takes the other by the arm and comes over.

Cyril, he says. Klein. This is Zelig, my littler brother. We are recently of Croydon, and before Croydon and before this Hutchinson Camp of Douglas, Isle of Man, we are lately of the city of Augsburg.

Zel lost his voice in Germany, in the camp called Dachau, Cyril tells Daniel later.

My brother has a fine tenor voice, he says, but he no longer sings. He can speak, but now he does not speak a lot. His voice is in hiding. He got taken away when they found books in his satchel they didn't like. Story books. Der Krieg der Welten. Das kunstseidene Mädchen. But they are burned books and he is a Jew. Three crimes. The Nazis hate Jews, they hate the stories of the women who are independent, and they hate the stories of the bacterias that will kill invaders. He is political prisoner. He has fifteen years old. He is there for five seasons, fourteen months. What he has seen he cannot peel from the fronts of his eyes.

But miracle, we get him out.

Then we get us both out and get us here. I am chauffeur in Surrey, Cyril says. I am also partly doctor but of course ejected from university before completing my education.

Daniel already knows that they stand at the gate every day to watch the new arrivals. Cyril tells him they're watching for their father. They don't know where he is, or their mother, or anyone else in their family.

One evening in Daniel and his father's room up in the eaves, Cyril tells Daniel cheerily the story of how he and Zelig were picked up by London Constabulary and taken to a vast London cave.

Olympia.

Where exhibitions are happening when it is no war, Cyril says. And many Nazi sailors came in the night off a boat. There was very much heil hitlering, very much singing about our blood spurting from knives. Then some days later they move us in trucks together with these same men to Butlin's Holiday Camp. In Butlin's Holiday Camp a pastor stood up on Sunday and asked God for Nazi victory.

Cyril laughs.

He laughs often. He puts an arm round his brother's shoulders. The boy, Zel, hardly a man, smiles an absent smile whenever his brother laughs.

Your English, my friend Daniel, is hole at the top, Cyril says.

Top hole, Daniel says. That's because I was born an Englishman, whelped as a German, and after the age of six became an Englishman again.

Helped as a German? Cyril says

Whelped, Daniel says.

He spells it and explains it.

Like a puppy, a young dog, he says.

He is embarrassed at his own showing off with language. But Cyril looks delighted.

Whelpéd, Cyril says. Whelpt.

I'm only a summer German, Daniel says. I grew up here. My father's a German Englishman. He met my mother here, she was German, didn't think of herself as Jew till they stamped it on her papers, she died three summers ago, the triumph of so many wills sapped her own will to live. She had me here, in Watford, in 1915. War was already on, father interned, mother and son sent home to Germany. I didn't meet him till I was six years old. After the war I was schooled here. Except for the summers. We spent them in Germany.

It is summer now, Cyril says. So, you are a German right now, my friend.

Daniel smiles a broad smile.

I ask will you help me, Cyril says. My German English, to make it a German Englishman. Yes?

Daniel says he'll do this thing with pleasure.

Cyril pulls his hand out of his pocket and puts something, small, made of flattened metal, in Daniel's hand. It's a little enamel lapel badge, the pin on the back is gone, but the front still has most of its enamel, peach colour and blue, in the shape of a girl's head and shoulders. The girl has a swimming cap on and is holding something gold-coloured to her head. It says in black and white at the bottom of it:

BUTLIN'S CLACTON 1939.

I found it near the. What is the word, for the letters in the box?

Letterbox, Daniel says.

Ah!

Cyril laughs. Zelig smiles wanly.

Der Briefkasten, Cyril says. Letter. Box. *Letterbox*. I was looking to the *letterbox* because the mouth of the *letterbox* had been closed by a metal bar that has been fixed over the *letterbox*. Now I know this word.

Ha, Daniel says. You are an excellent pupil. But you were looking *at* the letterbox.

Genau! Cyril says. And I look *at* the ground, because I felt beneath my foot this swimming girl.

The girl on the badge has a cresting wave done in blue enamel over the place her breasts would be, white enamel foam on its top.

I give to you, my friend Daniel, because here we are all of us in one boat, Cyril says.

In the same boat, Daniel says.

The same boat, Cyril says. The same boat.

Thank you. But I couldn't possibly accept, Daniel says.

Why is she holding this thing here, to her ear? Cyril says. Is she, what is the word for not to hear?

Deaf, Daniel says. No, no. I don't think it's a hearing trumpet. I think that's meant to be a glass of champagne, I think she is toasting us. Like she's saying: Cheers! Look. Bubbles in champagne. The little dots here in the enamel.

Glasur. Schmelz, Cyril says.

Zelig, who has been sitting staring at the table, a suitcase on a chair, says something so quiet that Daniel can't catch it.

Zel remembers to me that der Schmelz is also a word to say a voice or a music sounds very pleasant, Cyril says.

Zel reminds you, Daniel says. Thank you Zel.

Zel nods.

It is yours. Please do not be too Englishman. It is after all summer. Please accept, Cyril says.

Thank you, Daniel says. I do accept your gift. It is kind of you.

Look at Zel, he is thinking I give to you my girl, Cyril says. There is no gift better. We are now life's long friend. I give you a way to escape this island on the back of this swimming girl.

Daniel smiles. He puts the badge down on the lid of the suitcase.

Next moment, gone.

Where's it gone?

He looks for it but there's nothing on the suitcase. There's no suitcase here. Someone has put a tray on his lap.

Sandwich. How kind.

Elevenses, his neighbour's daughter says.

Ah, he says. Here again.

I am, she says. It's Friday.

She misunderstands him, thinks he's talking about her. No matter.

How are you, Mr Gluck? she says. How was your week?

She means, *ask me how my week was, Mr Gluck*.

He smiles. She is a kind and lovely and clever girl, though no longer quite the firebrand she was when she was a child. Sometimes Daniel is sad about this, for her. She is in a kind of work that is eating her soul. She is lonely. That's for certain. It is like watching her being eroded.

Much of a muchness and the muchness is good, he says.

I got back from Siena on Wednesday, she says.

Ah, he says.

I took twenty students there for the day to see the Lorenzetti pictures in the town hall. The Good and the Bad Governance.

I have never seen them, he says.

The Tyrant, she says, has lower jaw teeth sticking out of his mouth like a wild boar's teeth. And Peace, Fortitude, Prudence. Generosity, Temperance, Justice, all the figures at the centre of Good Governance, are women. Fortitude in her suit of armour is surrounded by armoured knights.

What else? he says.

The Good Governance wall, she says, has this perfect balance and harmony to it, which is also somehow deeply present in the fact that it's in amazing condition. Whereas the bad governance wall has deteriorated quite badly.

Tell me one of the pictures, he says.

A good or a bad? she says.

Let's always choose good governance, he says.

She thumbs her phone.

From memory, he says.

She smiles.

She puts the phone down. She closes her eyes.

Bright architecture under a night sky, she says. Houses, sweet communal living. People selling things, people working, writing, making things. People getting married. People on horseback, people holding each other by the hand. A human train or chain, maybe a dance by the children of Venus, maybe just happy people holding on to each other. A peaceful city. Summer has come. They're sprightly, the figures. A bit of damage, but not much. Well restored. Holding its own, still bright down the centuries.

They both open their eyes.

What's in the paper today, then? she says.

Thugs and showmen in power, he says. Nothing new. A clever virus. That's news. The stocks and shares will shake. There'll be people who do very well out of that. One more time we'll find out what's worth more, people or money.

He thinks of his mother's face. All her family money went in the hyper. She died old, in her fifties.

I for one don't want to die young, he says.

His neighbour's daughter laughs.

What my mother'd say if she were here is, it's a bit late for that, Mr a Hundred and Four, she says.

Whatever age you are, he says. You still die young.

His neighbour's daughter beams a smile at him.

His neighbour's daughter loves him.

My father lived through the Spanish flu, he says. I only once heard him talk about it. He said you had to remember not to take it personally. Then you stopped being scared. Never mind that. What you reading?

Mostly right now I'm reading the news on my phone, she says. But also this.

She holds up a paperback book.

Novel, she says. It's okay. Sub Woolfian, well. Thinks it is, anyway. It's about Rilke and Katherine Mansfield. Did you know they lived near each other in Switzerland but never met? Have you read Rilke ever?

Ah, he says. Rilke.

He has things he wants to think about Rilke. But he can't think of him right now because Cyril is here again kneeling by his side next to this nice chair in his neighbour's conservatory.

He nods to the ghost of pale Zelig, always there with Cyril. Zelig nods back.

Of course neither of them's here in the conservatory at all. Zel died in 1947, didn't stay long, how could he, he'd already been made so old so fast. Cyril, gone in 1970, was it?

Yet here he is now, bright and alive and next to Daniel as they look out ahead, eyes on the silver sheet of the sea beyond the wire.

His brother had the worse time of it, is all Cyril will say. His brother's memory, Cyril says, is what gets left after a fire has gutted you and everything in you has melted and changed its shape.

Cyril they just tormented, hardly at all, a bit of goading. He was lucky. They brought him in to headquarters, punched him in the head and the stomach, told him he was a homosexual and would be hanged, told him he'd seduced too many Aryan

161

girls to be allowed to live, death sentence for undesirables like him so he'd be hanged that afternoon in the yard, told him to sit down then pulled the chair away from under him just as he went to, so he fell to the floor, room of laughing brownshirts. Did it again. Again. Again.

In the end something else happened somewhere else in the building to distract them and they forgot about him. He took the chance and slipped out. He saw as he went how they were lined up on either side of the corridor with their rifle butts ready for whoever was next to walk their line.

Even just that, being punched, insulted, was terrifying. Even just sitting down on a chair that was never there beneath you, and knowing you'd better make to sit down on it though you *knew* there'd be no chair, because if you didn't they'd kill you then and there, was so terrifying, Cyril said, that he nearly lost his mind. *But I keep getting up. Every time I hit the floor I get up again. I say inside my head, you can do it, you can be like Chaplin. Up. On the feet. That's it. Now. Brush your jacket down.*

He is finding it hard to hear what his neighbour's daughter is saying, or to listen.

BUTLIN'S CLACTON 1939.

He looks down at his slippered feet on the carpet in case it's fallen.

But of course it's not going to be here.

It's somewhere else in time, isn't it?

Where?

Where and when did he let it slip?

It was such a fine thing for anyone to give anyone.

He is deeply annoyed with himself.

He is a very careless man sometimes.

He can't articulate enough how much he dislikes himself for forgetting things he can't remember.

For instance. A girl he loved. One night he woke in the dark in a panic. It wasn't Rive Gauche she wore! He's been telling himself it was Rive Gauche for years. But he's been telling himself wrongly, the wrong name. It was something else!

He lay in the dark ashamed.

He didn't, he doesn't, know how to atone. He has to put it right.

But how do you put a memory right?

I'm so, so sorry.

It was another French one she wore. Jolie. Jolie something.

Jolie, it says on one side of the bottle on her sideboard in her room. The other word is on the other side of the bottle. He tries to see round its corner in his head.

No.

Can't.

She worked at the Soup Kitchen for cash. Then

she sold some paintings. Then she acted, Royal Court, BBC. Then she died.

Soup Kitchen. It wasn't a soup kitchen, it was a restaurant that served soup. It got more and more fashionable the further away from poverty London got. Artists worked there. The girl artists all got jobs there.

His neighbour's daughter is saying something more forcefully now.

I'm so sorry, he says. Tell me again.

She's asking him about the Isle of Man.

Oh.

How do you know about that? he says.

She tells him he was talking about it earlier and Paulina heard.

Oh.

Yes, he says. Well. I was hardly in, in for comparatively no time. And it was awful.

It was exceptional. And it was still awful. But we weren't in for long. My father, he'd been interned for near six years, the whole first war. Wakefield. Lofthouse. Lofthouse was a good camp, high class, fee-paying, my mother paid for it. But still he came out mad, very weak, bleak. Ruined his health. Sick man the rest of his life.

Daniel closes his eyes.

He opens them in the dark of the House of the Fairy Tales. His father has the mattress and the bed. For this he's given one of his blankets to

Daniel. Daniel is on the floor, one blanket over him, two between him and the floor. His father's voice, in the dark:

Wakefield was a holiday place too. For the workers on the local trams. They like to intern people in the holiday places. Anyway a girl, one day, she was maybe sixteen, a pretty girl, she must've been out walking beyond the gorse, and she saw me reaching for meadowsweet. I thought if I could get my hands on it I could put it in water and a drop of sugar, if I could find some, the butterflies love meadowsweet. But I couldn't reach it, and she saw that, she saw me try, so she came over through the bushes and picked it and very simply gave me it through the wire. I heard she got three months in the Wakefield Prison for that. They very particularly told me. Loitering in government grounds. Consorting with the enemy. My fault. I think of that girl often. I hope it didn't do harm to her. It was such a gift to me.

How long d'you think we'll be in here? Daniel asks him.

(It's been weeks. The weeks have been like years.)

I have real hope, his father says in a quiet voice.

Daniel in the dark, astonished.

He has never known his father carelessly hopeful about anything.

It's different this time. It's a different place, now, England, his father says. Its better self has come to the fore. I know, I know, there's been a bit of whipping-up. Inevitable all that fifth columnist living off the fat of the land stuff, the collar the lot intern the lot stuff, every German's an enemy agent and so on.

But Mrs Rathbone speaking in the parliament. The Bishop of Chichester speaking in the parliament. Mr Wedgwood, young Mr Foot, so many, even though it looks like invasion, even though everything's up in the air for *them*, still taking time in the parliament to talk about *us*. And Mr Foot, he said they were missing a trick, because we hate the Nazis so much and we know so much, we've got special skills, could form an underground army, fight for England, be bloody useful. Nobody said such stuff back then. It couldn't be more different. They know about fairness now, and why to go to war, and what happens when you do. They know about newspapers that lie for money. They know you don't put innocent people in prison. The British are just. They're practical. They're forbearing. They're not childish. They're calm, they're civilized, now. They'll put it right. We'll be out of here in no time. See if I'm wrong.

His father was right.

Daniel got home by the end of January 1941. His father got release papers at the same time.

They went back to Steyning, cut back the roses in time for spring. Daniel had another medical, clear this time, joined up, British subject so no problem, Royal Navy.

His father died that summer. Daniel was already at sea.

Wakefield? his neighbour's daughter is saying. Where Barbara Hepworth grew up? The artist who made your stone.

Daniel opens his eyes in another century, in the conservatory.

She means what's left of the mother and child maquette.

A woman he slept with once stole the child piece of stone. She just took it, pocketed it, years ago.

But he still had the mother stone so he didn't mind. Made it unsaleable though. Which was a good thing. Means when he sold everything else, this he kept. Good. He very much likes it.

He stretches to remember where it is. It's in his bedroom in

(he stretches to remember where he is right now)

this house, his neighbour's house, on top of the bookcase.

Never mind that, Daniel says. Have you seen, by any chance, anywhere around, a little colourful metal thing?

A little metal what? his neighbour's daughter says.

Shaped like a swimmer, he says. With a glass held to her head like so.

He puts his arm up above the side of his head and cocks his empty teacup to his ear. Jaunty. She laughs.

No, she says. I'm pretty sure I haven't. What is it?

In any of the years that we've known one another, he says, did you ever see, anywhere about my person, or my house, a little flat metal thing, lapel badge shaped like a girl, a girl swimming?

If I did I don't remember it, his neighbour's daughter says.

Little thing, Daniel says. Never mind. My loss.

He waits until she's reading her book again.

Then he surreptitiously checks the floor round his feet, feels with his slippers for anything that might be under them.

One fine summer's morning a man comes to see Daniel at the canteen. It's the man Daniel saw on their arrival at Douglas port, the man ahead of him in the march, the man who yelled at the sergeant about how the man in front of him was too old to go faster.

He introduces himself as Mr Uhlman. Fred.

Something about him is very formal, ceremonious. So much so that Daniel can't think of calling him Fred.

Mr Uhlman says he has heard that the young Mr Gluck is a native English speaker as well as a man who understands German.

Born here, Daniel says, then whisked away, I spoke nothing but German till I was six. After that, nothing but English. My German self is six years old.

I am interested in translations, the man says, and the different things they will find themselves saying, while all trying to say the same thing. With your skill between the languages I like to think you will make an interesting case. I am gathering versions of this little verse.

He gives him a four line poem in German, it's been handwritten on a very nice thick piece of paper, like paper used to be.

My grandmother liked to repeat it, he says. I would like to hear it in your English.

Daniel reads it.

He takes the little stub of pencil kept for the accounts and he sharpens it with the knife. He writes on a sheet of toilet paper. He crosses things out.

He writes the whole thing again and he crosses out the workings.

I've had to change the rhyme scheme, and I've taken an unforgivable liberty with grammar, he says. A first attempt.

Mr Uhlman reads it.

Don't say Kaddish, not for me.
Don't sing Masses, not for I.
Nothing sung or spoken be
On the day that I will die.

It's a good start! Mr Uhlman says.

He looks pleased.

I don't know that Heine would agree with you, Daniel says.

And you recognize Heine, Mr Uhlman says. For all your English schooling.

I have a German sister, Daniel says. What do you think? Is it of use to you?

I like it, Mr Uhlman says. I like it very much. Good. Thank you.

Perhaps in exchange, Mr Uhlman, Daniel says, you might lend me three sheets of paper like the paper your Heine is written on. I say lend, because I promise, I'll give you back three sheets as good or better, as soon as I have them. After the war. I won't forget.

Mr Uhlman opens his eyes wide.

Daniel puts a tube of toothpaste down on the counter. (Toothpaste, like chocolate, costs.)

And this, a gift to you, he says. Yes?

Mr Uhlman is old, forty at least. He is one of the artists who signed the letter they're going to send to the press. A copy has been circulating in the camp. *SIR, The undersigned artists, painters and sculptors, at present interned in Hutchinson Camp, Douglas, I.O.M., would like to appeal urgently to all our British colleagues and friends. It is only too well known that we have left our homes and our countries as our persons as well as our work were*

*greatly endangered there. We came to England
because we believed that here*

It continues

*last hope of Democracy in Europe   indefinite
period of time   create something   greatest use
to this country   mission of Art. Art cannot live
behind barbed   by some newspapers   tension
under which we live   close community with
thousands of persons   no news for weeks
'White Paper' makes provision for all sorts of
been forgotten*

and it ends

*and restore to us – all refugees from Nazi
oppression – the one thing no artist can live and
work without: FREEDOM.*

Mr Uhlman's wife, Mr Uhlman tells Daniel, gave
birth to their first child a few days after he got
arrested, a daughter he hasn't yet met.

Daniel thinks of that artists' letter.

You will, he says.

Mr Uhlman smiles a sad smile as a thank you.
He says he was a lawyer. He tells Daniel how when
he was first qualified and went into work one
morning he sat down in his office but there was so
much hammering and sawing going on somewhere
in the Law Courts that he couldn't concentrate. He
went down and out into the yard to see what was
happening.

Some workmen were erecting a scaffold.

No. It was a guillotine.

He got out in time, went to France, became a painter, went to Spain, met a young English woman who was travelling, daughter of Sir Henry Croft, kind of girl who taught Marx – blasphemy! – to her baby siblings. Then she did the unthinkable, married a penniless Jewish refugee. She'd put some ink and a packet of charcoal in his jacket pocket at the police station. She'd packed a block of this good paper into his suitcase. He draws every day on the block of paper, he says, at least one drawing, sometimes more. It depends on whether he is feeling less depressed or more depressed. Either way, it helps, to.

That evening he comes over to the House of the Fairy Tales before lights out and waits for Daniel at the front door. He hands him three blank sheets of the very good paper.

There is almost nobody to whom I'd give this paper, Mr Gluck, he says. It is three drawings' worth.

He smiles.

And see how clean my teeth are, he says.

One day he lets Daniel watch him do his day's drawing. He sits in his room and leans the paper on the lid of the little suitcase balanced on his knees.

I'm not so keen to paint just now, he says. Drawing is the true thing.

He puts his pen down and gets up off the bed. He

opens the case and takes some papers out. He shows Daniel an ink drawing, dark.

It is the bunk room at Ascot! It is so like the bunk room in atmosphere and darkness that Daniel can smell it again. He breaks out in a cold sweat.

Mr Uhlman tells him how he nearly went insane waiting for mail in Ascot.

A month, he says. A whole month. London so close, nothing from anyone. My child, born any minute.

He shows Daniel some more of the pictures he's working on. They are dedicated to his new born child. In many of them a small girl holding a balloon bobbing on a string is walking through hell. All the way through hell the balloon stays in the air above her and the girl walks about, curious, detached, untouched, and just as powerful as – increasingly more powerful, as the drawings multiply, than – any of the hellish things happening round her. There are ruined buildings, scaffolds and gibbets, people hanging off trees in bits,

homage to Goya, look, Mr Uhlman says pointing,

and the child walks through the gutted landscape past heaped-up hills of skulls. She passes a hanged woman. The horror doesn't touch her. She does a dance with a jolly skeleton.

The day he lets Daniel watch him draw, Mr Uhlman is adding birds to a picture of a hayfield with a scarecrow in it. A path cuts through the picture. The girl with the balloon has walked down it, met some other children, and they're all smiling beneath the scarecrow, a bloated dead soldier, because he has a small bird singing on his hat.

Are you a lover of art, Mr Gluck? Mr Uhlman says.

I know nothing about it, Mr Uhlman, Daniel says. My sister is sometimes a painter. But I know nothing.

Do you like to see things as they are *and* as they aren't? Mr Uhlman says.

I can't not see both, Daniel says. Sometimes I wish it were otherwise. But I can't not.

Then congratulations. You are one step away from artist, Mr Uhlman says.

I fear you're mistaking me for someone I'll never be, Daniel says.

Mr Uhlman laughs.

He talks about a carnival he went to in the 1920s hyper.

And suddenly everyone in town was dance mad, it was a contagion of dance, Mr Uhlman says. The whole town danced and danced, because of madness and poverty. Driven to joy.

He draws more birds. The pen hardly moves on the paper and the birds congregate above the field.

Another day, Mr Uhlman is so depressed he can hardly draw.

I fought against Hitler while the Cliveden people fraternized and flirted with him, he says.

He says it gently enough but he is full of rancour.

Then he changes his demeanour. He says,

would it give you some pleasure, Mr Gluck, to meet Kurt?

Kurt is notorious. He's the artist who barks like a dog in the evenings and his barks can be heard all across the camp's streets. He sleeps in a basket, they say, like a dog, not in a bed. Daniel was there in the artist's cafe when he did the thing with the cup and the saucer. Pretty rare to find a cup that matches a saucer anyway, but Kurt had, and was sitting at the table in the cafe surrounded by people talking to each other and slowly the room went more and more quiet because of the hum of Kurt's voice and what he was doing, he was circling the cup and the saucer slowly round and round in front of him, and he was saying the word *lies*, *lies*, *lies*, over and over again. No, it was German, the German word *leise*, a word that means quiet, as in *be quiet please*, and he was saying it very very quietly *leise leise leise* over and over, until people *leise* round him were quiet and listening, and the *leise* quietness spread like a ring in water *leise* widening through the room as he said it *leise* with a little more force *leise* slightly more loudly each time *leise leise leise* until the whole room *leise* was listening to him saying it *leise* more and more loudly *LEISE* now he was

175

shouting it *L E I S E* then he was shouting it at the top of his voice as loud as he could *L   E   I   S   E* with his whole body thrown into the shouts and on his feet now still circling the cup and the saucer in the air – and then he smashed both saucer and cup down hard and they hit the ground hard and they shattered.

Silence.

Everybody in the room, shocked.

Then everybody shouting, laughing, angry, happy. All of these at once.

What Daniel felt was himself breathing fully for the first time in, he didn't know. Since before they got arrested? Since, years, nearly ten years? The time before days got terrible?

Everybody in the camp knows Kurt's had work ridiculed by Hitler himself.

If we ever get out of this here, and we get out of it alive and not dead, Cyril said listening one evening to the dusk barking, I will buy a dog and I will call it Kurt. It has real usefulness, the barkings of Kurt. When that old fellow in the next room to ours wakes up shouting for help and how they're coming to kill him, go back to sleep I tell myself or I tell Zel, because it is just someone barking back in reply to Kurt the dachshund.

Kurt takes Daniel's hand in both of his with great firmness.

I feel lucky and happy to make your

acquaintance, he says. You are a man with luck and happiness always with you.

He shakes Daniel's hand.

Now I have shaken the youthful hand of happy luck, he says. Now I'll make it out of this war. *And* you work in the canteen. Which is why I asked to meet you. I have a request.

He takes Daniel up to show him the studio.

He is making a collage. It looks like it is made of iridescent lace.

Daniel sees that what it's made of is fish skin.

The room smells strange, high, sweet. Then Daniel remembers the story that went round the camp about Kurt kicking over his chamberpot and panicking that the several days' worth of what was in it would seep through the floorboards and down into the room below and because of this his studio would be taken away from him.

(The story goes that Kurt tore off his clothes to mop up the spill.

And then he put them all back on him again, Cyril says.)

All round the room, balanced on broken lumps of wood, some on the broken-off legs of an old piano, are the greeny-blue-coloured sculptures of heads, beasts, indefinable shapes. They are lumpy, gritty-looking. Something about them is strangely familiar.

Kurt asks Daniel if he will have the kindness to

put aside and pass on to him anything in the canteen or the store that nobody wants to use or to eat, the things often thrown away. Empty cigarette and toothpaste packets, chocolate wrappers. The gone-off leaves of cabbages. Also he most urgently wants any porridge that goes uneaten, if there's any that he comes across left in a dustbin after a breakfast.

That's when Daniel sees that the sculptures are made of solidified porridge and that the porridge they're made of has gone so mouldy that each of the sculptures is sprouting green hair.

These sculptures are alive, he says.

Kurt frowns.

There is no higher accolade, he says.

His frown is a kind of smile.

Daniel opens his eyes.

You've been in the wars, his neighbour's daughter says.

Her hand is on his shoulder.

Tossing and turning and calling out, she says.

She's brought him some soup on the tray.

I was, he says. I really was.

Where were you? she says. What did you dream?

I was walking along in Douglas town, Daniel says, we all were, we were off down to the Picture House, and the guard who was with us, he gave me his gun to carry because he was tired.

You could've escaped, then, in your dream, she

says. You had a gun. You could've held up that guard with his own gun and all made a run for it.

He laughs.

Oh, it wasn't a dream, he says. It happened. Escape to what? Only fascists tried to escape.

He puts the spoon down on the tray.

Afterwards I met Mr Uhlman on Charing Cross Road. We said hello, we shook hands, how are you? Then after that, what do you say? Nothing to say. So I pointed to the bookshop. I said, I heard your book of the drawings you did in Hutchinson came out, I haven't seen it yet myself, though, and I'm looking forward to it.

He laughed.

Looking forward, he said. Such a phrase. Everyone was looking so forward that nobody bought that book. Nobody wanted anything about the war any more. Nobody wanted it as soon as it was published.

I owe you three pieces of good paper, I said.

I cancel your debt, he said.

We wished each other a cheery goodbye.

I never saw him again.

But I saw a copy of his book years later, after he died, I saw all the pictures, some I'd seen before, and I remembered, I remembered as if someone had etched them into my head, and that little girl with the balloon in the pictures, the daughter, the child just born, she keeps going

179

through hell, right to the end of the book, and in the last pages she –

he starts to laugh

– what she does is, she takes hold of the bottom of, you know, what churchmen wear,

A, a – cassock? his neighbour's daughter says.

Yes, exactly that, the cassock, and she tips, there's a giant churchman, his cross is a swastika, she takes hold of him by the hem of his cassock and just, easy as that, she tips him over. Then she stands, with one foot off the ground, like a circus dancer or an acrobat, hand on her hip, and she balances on his vast stomach, and her balloon is high in the sky.

I wish I'd been able to tell Mr Uhlman I saw that, and to thank him.

And did you say you went to the cinema in your dream? his neighbour's daughter says.

Oh, it wasn't a dream. We went in real life, he says. They took us. Two guards. Four hundred of us. A day in November. The Picture House. It had a mock tudor front. Very pretty. The Great Dictator. Chaplin the barber loved a fine-looking girl. Same name as my sister, the girl. It was really something, taking on Hitler like that. And back to the camp to a concert that evening. Schubert, I believe.

It sounds very unlike a prison, she says.

A prison is a prison, he says. Whatever you fill the time with.

He finishes the soup.

Thank you, he says. You are so kind.

You are so welcome, she says.

She helps him through to the bed for the lie down he has in the afternoons.

And Mr Gluck, she says. Can I just ask. Did you say you have. You had. A sister?

I did, he says.

He doesn't say anything else.

I'll wake you a little before the people are due to arrive, she says.

People, he says.

The people who are coming to visit you today, she says. The man. You knew his mother. Remember?

Daniel shakes his head.

Oh yes, he says.

She goes to pull the curtains shut over the French windows.

Let's leave them open, he says. It's good light out there today.

She opens them again.

Thank you, he says.

He closes his eyes.

He is seventeen. His sister is twelve, a mere child. It's in the front room in the Berlin flat, he is there for his summer, they are leaning next to each other out of the big open window with their elbows on the sill, both watching the afternoon traffic below.

They are arguing. They always do.

He says Max Linder is the better comedian.

She is all for Chaplin.

Yes, but Linder's the one that'll last, he is saying. No question. Sophisticated, inventive. A social comedian, a man with social intelligence. Chaplin's a mere clown, a shadow-boxer to Linder. Thinks he can steal someone else's tricks and be as good as the original. And he can't, because he isn't. Linder's the source. Linder's the real thing.

Hannah shakes her head like she's sorry for Daniel.

Social comedian, she says.

She laughs like he's said something naive.

Chaplin is evergreen, she says in English. Max Linder is one of those pretty things that last only a year. Wait and see, summer brother.

She has lately taken to calling him this, like he isn't really her brother. Like he's only a brother one season a year.

He put on his most superior air.

We'll wait and see, he says.

Whether we do or we don't, she says. The tramp will outlive the dandy, I reckon, and do it by thousands of years.

On a morning in late summer, still fine and warm in the daytime, cold at night, well, late September, Daniel sits in the sun behind the House of the Fairy Tales and unfolds the sheets of paper.

There are three.

He takes two of them and holds them on his knee against the breeze while he rolls the third up again and tucks it back into his inside pocket.

The young guard with the bright red hair (Daniel calls him the Irishman, he calls Daniel the Englishman) has lent him a good sized piece of a pencil.

He has the kitchen fruitknife, for sharpening.

My dear little Hanns

he writes, very small, small as he can and still make it out, at the top of the first page. Hanns is what he calls Hannah when she is most determined to do what she likes regardless of whether the world will let her

how is it where you are my wander-vogue?

she will like that, wander-vogue for wandervogel or will she just think him immature?

his handwriting is execrable

My handwriting is execrable, my apologies, I am out of practice, I don't do much with my hands now that involves many words

cross out everything from I don't to words

I am working to improve this though as I will tell you and you will see in the course of this letter. Which comes with a smile and a laugh to say a hello to you, how are you? are you getting some fight practice in? I am thinking of you. Father is

in reasonable spirits

weak

a terrible roommate and it is a very small room

in reasonable spirits, sometimes he is even hopeful

yes

If he knew I were writing to you he would send his love. One good outcome of coming here is that they took his killing fluid away from him in Brighton so the butterflies of the Isle of Man are free to come and go on both sides of the wire like 'the souls of summer hours' that the Poet Laureate says they are. There, I have remembered that piece of poetry to tell you, are you impressed?

he can see her handwriting in his head, clever, flowing, sharp, leaning like she does when she's on a bicycle right over the handlebars as if leaning will make it go faster

here I am, sick for home, not just standing amid the bewildered alien corn, no I am the bewildered alien corn, and very corny too, yes, thank-you

she will like the poetry what-have-you, she will appreciate it

forlorn! as John Keats would say and tolling away to myself like a poetic bell I'm on the lookout for a more melodious plot but where we are and what I've got will have to

no. Cross out the forlorn and the tolling. Cross it all out from here I am to will have to

Here in this Island of Men on the Isle of Man

*your brother is pleased to be able to report to you
he has friends, I have in fact made a real pal, a jolly
chap, we pal around together and it is a comfort to
have a friend in this strange Zwangsgemeinschaft
of a mineshaft*

she will like that, good,

though he won't tell her

(or anyone)

about how Cyril knows exactly how to take him
and hold him till he comes, which he now does for
Daniel and Daniel for him most days of the week.
He can see her now in his head. If she saw, she'd
know. She would not disapprove. He knows that
she would laugh and laugh, empty herself laughing,
at the rumour that the camp authorities are now
lacing the porridge with bromide to help them all
control their urges, the main result of which is that
most people don't eat the porridge any more, the
secondary result of which is all the more material
for Kurt

*here Hanns it feels far away, but we are all in
anticipation all the time*

cross that all out

*here Hanns though it feels far away I find myself
among such artists and clever folk that I am sure
you would approve, and say, you're a lucky boy,
Dani, in fact I'd go so far as to say if you were here
yourself you'd be in your element. If the element
wasn't a prison*

put a line through that last sentence

remember when she wrote to him after their mother died and said that the people left behind after someone has died are liable to become inhabitants of Grief Island and must be sure to carry an inflatable life jacket with them to help them swim away if the weather roughens and they haven't got access to a boat.

She is so clever. She has always said, always been able to say the unsayables. He is a poor substitute, especially for a letter writer.

But he will pass on no fear, he crosses out

we are now much less fearful of an invasion than we were

as soon as he writes it

he will not mention the lurch in the stomach, the fairground swing of hope / despair, he won't say anything about the boredom, she'd just scorn him for being it, he will not even write the beautiful line he was so proud of thinking up

we have been here behind the wire all through the bright open door of the summer

even though it seems to him a beautiful sequence of words. He will not mention how easy it would have been for him or their father to find themselves on a ship to Canada or Australia just by the accident of being in one room or another when the selections were made, and he will not write about the boat that was torpedoed, or how red the sky went over Liverpool burning, even all that distance away. He will not say how time is not recognizable as time any more, how he can't bring himself to eat sometimes, how sometimes he finds he is walking about like Uncle Ernst did when Ernst was drunk.

Ernst. Dead now or alive?

We tell nobody your name or where we imagine you might be. There are ears everywhere and they are not always listening for a Keatsian melodious plot

is a paragraph he will not write in her letter instead

I have been reading for you in case you are right now too busy or otherwise preoccupied or not getting the chance to read for yourself, most unlikely I know, but there we are, and it is like we are companionable when I do, and because our camp Commandant is such a fine fellow he has said there can be some books in the camp, so there are some old volumes doing the rounds, they fall more apart the more more and more people read them

he'll have to sort that, there are too many mores

but I have read in a pretty good copy David Copperfield by Charles Dickens. I would tell you my favourite quotations from it but now some other fellow has it and is no doubt enjoying it. I must say when the mother holds the baby brother up high in the air to show him to David when

David is being driven away to school, at that point in the story I thought of you. I am grown sentimental in my older age but there you have it. I have also read Kafka. The story of the brother and sister who go past the gate of the manor house and maybe knock on the gate or maybe don't. It is more true, that tiny story, than many a thing I have read and it has gone deep

leave Dickens but cross out everything Kafka, replace with

and a little Christmas story by Dickens too where a man asks a ghost to take his memory away so he will stop feeling sad about painful things he remembers. So the ghost does, it removes all the memories that cause the man pain. But the pain itself doesn't go away, though the knowledge of why there IS pain has vanished. Then the man becomes bitter and angry and bewildered as to why he feels pain. And then, like a contagion, this bitterness and anger and the loss of memory of difficult things infect everyone the man comes in contact with, and soon everybody in the town is angry and bitter with no idea why.

Right now I am also reading most of a volume (I am waiting for someone to finish the broken-off part of it and pass it on to me) of Tess of the D'Urbervilles by Thomas Hardy. 'On a thyme-scented, bird-hatching morning in May.'

We are fortunate in how many really talented

and scholarly people speak here and give lectures,
just the other day there was a talk on Goethe, there
is a professor of Plato here, and an expert on Rilke
and of course I thought of you when he was talking
of the Rose Bowl,

>but now you know how to forget about those things
>because the rose bowl is here before you
>and it cannot be forgotten, it is full
>of being, the roses leaning forward,
>holding out, never giving way, holding their own
>so we too can go as far as we can, like the roses do

How do you like my translation? It is from
memory, so might be very wrong. All the speakers
here speak from memory. It is quite a feat. The
other day I was really thinking of you when the
debate we had was: Should The Artist Portray His
Own Age. I tell you Hanns there was nearly a
fistfight. And you would be so proud of me,
because I spoke up and said, but what about the
artist portraying _her_ own age, and when I did I was
nearly laughed out of the room, but at least it
stopped the fistfight and let them all agree with
each other and have something in common again.
But I am thinking of your pictures a lot too. There
are artists here. They are good but it is yours I have
in my head. The one with the flowers that I thought
had faces discernible, if you looked, in the shapes
of their petals, means that now I can't not see a
face in _all_ real flowers

189

am I saying it wrong? She was annoyed when I said the flowers she painted had faces. She is no longer sixteen, she is twenty now, maybe she thinks such things childish and behind her

and one of the other things I have been remembering to tell you is that I am carving you a wooden bird out of a piece of chair leg. I regret to pass on the information too that nowadays I have none of that nice lotion with me that you told me about and had been keeping my skin soft as you said it would, and even worse I no longer have the ointment the doc gave me for the place behind my ear where the wart came off, and so I am using any oil or grease that comes my way, but sparingly, because not often very nicely scented.

I know you will be interested that I went to see Dr Streliska, he is a handwriting expert and graphologist in the camp. Our father had been to see him and Dr S looked at a piece of his handwriting and said, 'you are a man who loves to grow things.' So our father felt most pleased.

'He said nothing about you being a person who likes to suffocate butterflies, open their wings when they're dead and stick a pin through their torsos, then?' I said.

I wish above all I had had something written of yours to show Dr S. He would have said, 'why this is a king of queens! A queen of kings!' I don't doubt.

I showed him a piece in my own hand and he said, 'you are a man for many seasons.' I am pleased though I have no idea what it means or how he can say such things by looking at scrawl. I was most disappointed that he didn't say, you are a great singer and will be famous for your singing. Of course you remember exactly how good a singer I am. But I am persevering. I am writing a summer song with my friend Mr Klein, he is musically talented, we are planning to record our musical notations on the wire here by hanging our socks on the fence like the fence is our stave and the island's view our page, and when I have finished it I will dedicate it to you. Its first line is: 'on a thyme-scented, bird-hatching morning in May.'

Talking of music, I mean the real thing. Mr Rawicz is here. Mr Landauer is at another of the island's camps. Our camp Commandant asked Mr R to give a concert. Well. Mr R tried out all the old pianos left in the camp and they were all terrible, one fell to pieces literally as he was playing it! (There are paintings now on the wood of its back and sides, the wires are conducting electricity in the technical school, who knows what's become of the wheels, the ivory keys went to the dentist to be made into teeth.)

Our Commandant is Major Captain Hubert Daniel. He has given the artists studios, given the writers books and paper. He made sure all our mail arrived and arrives. That's the good chap he is. He had two grand pianos shipped in from Liverpool and a special arrangement sorted between the camps so that Landauer could play at our camp though he is not an internee here.

Rawicz and Landauer! who perform for the King and Queen! They were arrested on their journey home from playing for the King and Queen and brought here to be interned. Now they have played for me too! We sat on the grass and listened to the Viennese Strausses.

The fine people of Douglas crowded in their hundreds up against the wire to listen together with us.

It was a marvellous evening.

Well my Hannsel, this letter is nearly done for today and the Irishman wants what's left of his pencil back before he goes off duty.

So till we meet again.

Keep your Innerlichtkeit lit and shining in the window for me,

> *as mine is for you*
> *my autumn sister*
> *from*
> *your ever*
> *summer brother*

Daniel reads it through.

He unfolds the last sheet of good paper.

Leaning on his knee, pinning the draft pages of

the letter beneath him with his heel where he can see them, he makes a final fair copy in even tinier writing and with (almost) no crossings-out.

Then he sits back against the wall, looks towards the sea beyond the wire.

High above the island, high above the gulls, a bird that's not a gull. A summer bird? this late in the season? If it is, it's a very late traveller, possibly lost, quite alone.

Take this letter to my sister, whatever you are, bird up there.

Now he shuffles the three pages, the crossed-out and the fair copy, all together neatly.

He tears them in half.

He tears them in half again then in half again.

He takes the pieces to the kitchen in the House of the Fairy Tales, where he borrows the cook's matches. He comes back through the bare hall and out the front door.

He makes a little heap of paper on the stone of the house's front step. He sets light to the edge of one of the pieces of paper.

The others catch.

The heat the fire sends through them strengthens, then wanes.

When the fire's over and the remains are cool enough, he cleans the burnt stuff up. He rubs the ash of them into his hands, then opens his empty hands and looks at them.

The lines on his hands stand out clear through the blackening.

He puts his hand behind his ear to feel the place where the wart was, three years ago,

no,

eighty years ago.

His ears have wakened.

That wart's long gone.

But he can still feel the place the doctor took it off and left a line of stitches. He can still feel the line where something was that's gone, where the gone thing healed.

But wait. Now his eyes have wakened too.

He is in his neighbour's house, in his neighbour's daughter's room.

What time of day is it?

He has had breakfast. He has had a sandwich. He has had soup. It is afternoon. It is still light.

What month is it?

Low sun.

Winter-spring.

There are people outside the house. He can hear them. He can see a car in the driveway through the French windows. People getting out of it are talking and laughing outside the house.

Well, it's a fine sunny afternoon for the wintertime, and a fine thing to hear people happy out in the air.

They shut the doors of the car and stand talking

for a bit longer, young people and older people, a family.

They sound like happy birds.

He thinks of the birds above the scarecrow in the picture. They were moments in ink, and he saw them come to life, and there they still were all the years later in the book he saw, when he saw that book.

One of the young people from the family of visitors comes and looks in through the French windows, stands right up against one of the doors looking in through the reflection.

What Daniel sees then is his sister.

Is it?

Hannah?

It's Hannah herself standing there looking in.

It is.

It's her.

It's her young self.

It's the copy of her young self.

She opens the window's door and it's Hannah, God help him, there in the room, aged twelve, in the shape of a boy.

Oh hello, Daniel says.

Hi, Hannah says.

Where've you been all this time? he says.

The traffic was busier than they thought it'd be, Hannah says.

But so very long, Daniel says. I thought time had quite undone us.

On the contrary, time and space are what lace us all up together, Hannah says. What makes us part of the larger picture. Universally speaking. The problem is, we tend to think we're separate. But it's a delusion.

Ah, Daniel says.

Of course I'm quoting Einstein, Hannah says. Well, paraphrasing. He said the only real religion humans can have is the matter of freeing ourselves from the delusion first that we're separate from each other and second that we're separate from the universe, and the only peace of mind we'll ever get, he says, is when we try and overcome this delusion. He said this in a letter to a man whose son, who was eleven, had just died of polio. In exactitude you know if today was February the 12th it would be the seventieth anniversary to the day of Einstein sending this letter to the man. But the actual anniversary will happen on Wednesday this week. In exactitude.

Ah, Daniel says.

Yes, Hannah says. He was actually a man, the man Einstein wrote back to, who had done a lot to help save a lot of children's lives at the end of the Second World War. But he felt bad because he couldn't do anything to save his own child from dying from a disease. So he wrote to Einstein and asked him to explain, what was the point, or if there *was* a point, in being innocent, and gifted, and dying and becoming nothing but dust.

There is no doubt, Daniel says. You really are you.

Yes, Hannah says. I really am me. And you really are you. But if we follow Einstein's thinking and add together you plus me plus time plus space. What does that all make?

Then she waits, like she always did, for Daniel finally to catch her up.

What? What does it all make? Daniel says.

It makes you and I more than just you or I, Hannah says. It makes us us.

Here's a tale to drive away the time trimly. Once upon etc there was a king or a lord or a duke that had a fair daughter, the fairest that ever was, with hair and skin as white and as red and as gold and as black as etc and once upon etc his daughter was stolen away etc.

Today Hannah Gluck has been trawling the graveyards of the smaller places out of town, cycling between them with flowers in the bicycle's basket, wheeling the bike past the graves, checking the dates, memorizing the names of the ones who died young.

This is a good source. It's not completely safe but birth and death certification are usually held in different lists, often in different drawers or cabinets, sometimes even in different buildings if you're lucky. If you're lucky, if you're moving fast, nobody thinks to check both sources, that's if they check at all.

This'll change. Change is the nature of luck.

But it's still working well at the moment.

She has started going out of whichever town or city she's in, out to the surrounding villages especially. People can be more suspicious though. Or they tend to be, in the smaller places.

No, it's more that when people see her in the graveyards going from stone to stone they can be either foul or kind. It's always interesting. You can never tell which way they'll go.

Who the hell are you?

Can I help?

Hannah Gluck is ready for both.

In this readiness, Hannah Gluck is more than Hannah Gluck. At the moment she is Adrienne Albert, seamstress. Adrienne Albert died at eighteen months old, in Nancy, in 1920, of Spanish influenza. She's buried there in the same grave as a grandmother who died of the same thing at much the same time. But here she is, regardless, living and breathing and as warm as any living flesh and blood, though just a touch younger than it says on her papers, and today she's trawling a graveyard and looking to resurrect other lives like her own.

You see the name and the dates on a stone.

You ask a silent permission of the person gone.

You bow your head to their memory.

Then you pass on the gifts, the names and the dates, to the person who needs the new self.

It's not subterfuge. It's much more complex. Something real happens, something as metamorphic as caterpillar and butterfly. The gone person is as here and as real and as much a part of the act of balancing against the odds as a girl at a circus Hannah saw years ago, on one toe on one foot on one leg on the back of another girl on the back of two other girls, all on the back of a huge horse going at a lumbering canter you'd have thought it impossible to balance on top of even if there were only *one* of you on its back, thundering round the ring to a circus band playing Did You Ever See A Dream Walking.

How did they do it?

They did it against the odds.

And, like it or not, we all get ground down to a name and a date and what looks like nothing much in the end.

But when the words that once meant a person meet a living breathing shape, it's like when a lone bird sings in a tree like that one above her just did, and then a bird many gardens away sings the same song back to it. Particle sings to particle, crumb of grime to crumb of grime, fragment-hank to fragment. Something connects. A smatter of dust meets the thought of water, and then the thought of oxygen, carbon, nitrogen, hydrogen, calcium, phosphorus, mercury, potassium, magnesium, ion, so on, molecular alphabet.

Something heats up round the words that once, even so briefly, meant a person.

You don't know anything, the first thing, about that person. Still, something family happens.

It starts to happen the moment she memorizes the name and the date.

Then she telephones a number, a different one every time, and passes on to someone she doesn't know and will never meet the things she's memorized. That person, a kind of cousin, passes these on to the artists, and the artists make the papers that give that name the new life. Something shifts seismically. The dead name takes the new person on, and a live person takes the dead name on. Life happens for someone whose life will otherwise end. Life happens to a life that didn't happen. Life enters, graciously, with respect, the unlived life. With luck, with one eye on surviving the cold and the other on thanking the heat, *thank you, summer fires, bless our crops and sheep and cattle, may the gods give us a good year*, the reborn person will withstand a few more seasons.

So the thing to do, then, she says to herself as she walks the paths watching for the too-soon dead, the pebbled paths of the bigger cemeteries, the cat-paths and no-paths and grassy plots where the little towns and villages bury their families – the thing to do, when life asks for acrobatics, is behave like that circus girl on the top of the pyramid of girls on the back of that giant farm horse, remember, how she leapt down off the top of the others, somersaulted, landed in the sawdust on her toes, skipped to the place where the ringmaster'd sprayed the paper hoops on the stands with something flammable and set a match to them all, and threw herself through the burning hoops.

Then even the clown, remember. He looked like he'd be useless, clumsy, falling over himself, stupid wig sticking out and wrong size clothes flapping like petrol rags near a furnace. But what an athlete he turned out to be, he dived like a seabird, a champion, Olympian, through the rings of fire not once but twice, then again, and again.

One late summer's morning in 1940 in Lyon a man who looks very like her brother walks past Hannah in the street.

Of course it's not her brother. That's obvious almost immediately.

But there's been a fragment of a second when her brother was there in front of her even though he wasn't, isn't, and the man has such a look of him that it makes her turn her head then turn right round on her heel on the street.

It is so nice to see him!

Even though it's not him.

Even the shape of his back. Even though it's not his back.

So she follows an inclination, let's see where it takes us. She follows the man. He goes to the station. She follows him through the station. She joins the ticket queue, stands behind him. She doesn't hear where he's buying his ticket for but when she gets to the ticket desk she casts a glance at the man's back like he's her husband and they're having a quarrel and says, Same as him, please.

The ticket woman looks at the going man who's paid this lady no attention, turns back and gives Hannah the eyebrow. Hannah shrugs her own eyebrows, gives a little shake of the head, keeps her face long-suffering.

The woman charges her half of what it says on the ticket is the price.

Hannah gives the woman her warmest smile.

She sets off after the man who's not her brother, stays five or six paces behind him.

She sits in the same carriage.

Actually he is nothing at all like her brother. A very slight physical resemblance. Still. Even slight is lovely. She can imagine it's him and that they're just sitting in a railway carriage ignoring each other, which is something they quite often did.

The carriage fills with people and luggage. People sit between Hannah and the man who's not her brother.

From here she can still see the side of his head.

The city flashes past, grey on blue. A woman in a torn poster paddles along a coast on a boat made of the word MENTON, some torn-open mountains in the background, the ripped words Sai d' té above her head. BUGAT. Avec Energol démarrage foudroyant en hiv. The hoardings are bright rags placed over the dark. The surface of things is a lie, and everybody who sees the hoardings for what they are knows it.

(Why are you travelling?

My mother is very sick, they think she will die.

Where is your mother?

With her sister, near St Julien.)

Countryside flashes past, sunlight, green on blue, quite migrainous. The summer when she was thirteen, remember, was a summer of migraines. The migraines were partly enjoyable, like a private light-show on the inside of her eyes, the triangles pulsing like cartoon characters, their colours piercing, splendid. Black lines held colour-shape after colour-shape like the shapes were walking a road together, geometry of a travelling band.

The headaches and the vomiting? Much less enjoyable. Worst of all she couldn't read. Whenever she looked at a page she saw the insides of her own eyes on it, same as on the insides of her eyelids when she shut her eyes. A blank circle formed, round which the geometries pulsed, in the middle of any words she'd try to read, a blur surrounded by words her eye could make out but couldn't focus on, because trying to focus on them eclipsed them in turn.

So she was spending a fair amount of time in a darkened bedroom.

She lay on the bed. On one side of her head beyond the shut door there was the summer noise of family (her brother and father were back). On the other there was the summer noise of the city through the window shutters, traffic. Happy-sounding people in the daytime. Thug-songs through the night.

What do you make of it all? Daniel said.

He'd come in and was sitting on the side of her bed.

Make of what? she said.

Everything, he said.

He meant what was happening.

Then he pretended he didn't mean that at all.

What's it like? he said. In there.

He knocked with his fist, but gently, on her forehead.

She always tried to speak to him in English; she was proud of her English. She read a lot of books in English, all the ones she could find, precisely so that when the summer came round she'd surprise her English brother by speaking exceptionally well to him in the language he spoke every day. Was it rivalry? Yes. Was it love? Yes.

In here? It's like. Hm. Imagine hand-painted animation at the cinema. Imagine a team of assiduous (she was pleased to have found a use for the word assiduous, her first time, she hoped she'd said it correctly, so she said it again just for the pleasure) assiduous girl painters sitting at a tinting table in a film factory. And they spend their day colouring by hand, dipping their brushes into pots of paints filled with the colours of blooming English roses, pinks and yellows shining like after a rainshower, then colouring each of the little triangles that's about to do a dance across my eyes. And each time the frame changes, these colours, and the line of blackness that holds them together, like a road they're all walking along, vibrate as if electricity is going through not just them but the road they're on.

Well, he said. Sounds like quite a show.

Truly I rather like it, she said. I'm quite well entertained.

Is it doing it now? he said.

No, she said. Kino Hanno is closed for now.

How does it feel now, then? he said.

Now then, she said. An interesting verbal construct.

A what what? he said.

The past and the present together, she said. Now. Then.

A bewildered silence came off him.

He went to sit on the window seat across the darkened room.

She'd gone too fast for him again. She forgot. He is not flippant like she is. He is not quicksilver. His energy is steady, something like a tree root.

Now? I'm all right, she said. Then? It's like something wild, which is eating me whole, decides it doesn't want me after all and so it regurgitates me. That's my now and my then. Most of all I regret that I'm missing some good summer days.

He looked through the little gap in the shutter where the slice of light came in.

You aren't missing so much, he said.

He thinks I've shut myself in here because things are changed out there, she thought. He thinks I'm frightened. He didn't see it coming, hasn't seen it happen, not like we have. He doesn't know the everyday nature of it. *He* must be frightened.

I'm not frightened, she said.

I didn't say you were, he said. I'd never assume such a thing, not of you.

Good, she said.

Though it may be the case that your head is acting scared without telling you, he said.

I do not give it permission to do that, she said. Neither should you. So. If I may, I'll ask of you the same question you asked of me.

What question? he said.

What you're making of it all, she said.

Ah, he said. I'm not much of a maker of anything, me. You know that.

He jumped up. He went to the door.

(He was agitated.

She was right.)

I'll leave you to get the rest you need, he said.

I'll alter the question a little, she said. What will you make of it all?

He shut the door.

He heard her. He can't not have.

(Also, she was particularly proud of her use, there, of the future tense.)

The next afternoon her brother opened the door of the bedroom and carried in something dark and heavy, bulky, something under a blanket.

You have the shape of a pregnant woman, she said from the bed.

But she'd embarrassed him by the word pregnant. She could hear it in his awkwardness.

Anyway he put the bulky thing on the chair and unwrapped it from its cover. He stood holding the cover as if unsure whether to fold it or not. He did, very neatly. He unwound from the machine a wire and a plug.

The whole room began to whirr. A circle of light, like a square moon, a square of sun, appeared on the bedroom wall.

She put her hand over her eyes.

Too bright for you? he said.

No, she said. What is it?

Kino Danno, he said. You don't need a ticket. Today you're our guest.

She peeked through her fingers and watched as he adjusted the focus.

Chaplin. Der Einwanderer.

A ship, a lot of people lying seasick on the deck and on each other, groaning in silence.

A shot of someone bent over the side of the ship, convulsing, being what looks like sick over the side. But no – it's Chaplin, and he isn't being sick, he's catching and landing a live fish, which he turns to show them both with a brilliant smile.

Hannah laughed.

She took her hands away from her eyes.

She laughed and laughed when the people all over the ship who are acting so seasick hear the dinner bell get rung and rush to get to the dining room before anyone else.

She laughed as they arrive in America and Chaplin kicks the behind of an officious customs man who cordons them all off with a rope.

A title came up in English. *Later – hungry and broke.*

(It was exciting to see the other language.)

Is broke the same as broken? Hannah said.

No, her brother said. It means you've no money left.

Hannah memorized it. Broke. Broke.

As she did, Chaplin with his sweet white face on Hannah's bedroom wall (the little moustache Hitler has been canny enough to copy as if to suggest he's benign and endear himself to the world's millions, and to the kind of millions that Chaplin makes, too) finds a dollar on the American street. Then he finds Edna, the girl he fell in love with and was kind to on the ship. They eat a meal in a restaurant. But a funny plot happens round whether the money he found is real or not, which of course it isn't, and they have no money and can't afford to pay for the meal. The waiter, a monster of a man, has a habit of beating people to within an inch of their lives when they can't pay.

But an artist in the restaurant thinks their faces are remarkable and very meaningful, faces symbolic of the time he's living in.

He wants them to model for him.

He pays them in advance.

Happy ending in the pouring rain.

Her brother knew she loved Chaplin.

Where did you get your cinema from? she said.

Camera shop. I had to carry it here, and I've to carry it back tomorrow. Chaplin's not all that's on today's bill, he said. I've one more little thing of wonder here.

He ran the Chaplin film back through the projector – it was funny backwards too, in a whole other way. When the end of the film flicked out and round and round itself even that was a bit thrilling.

He switched off the projector, replaced the film with another, switched the square of inner sunlight / moonlight back on (this time it didn't hurt her eyes at all) and threaded the film through the reel wheel.

This time the film was covered in even more scratches and looked like it was from some other century. It was.

A man in a room full of roman-looking statues, like a gallery or an artist's studio, is chiselling at a statue that's not even a statue, it's just a drawing, of a fine lady or a goddess holding a jug and a cup.

Then the drawing turns into a real person. It offers the artist a drink from its jug and its cup but he's too shocked to accept, so it steps down off its pedestal and walks across the room to a pedestal on the other side, where it takes up a pose with a harp which it starts to play. The artist goes to throw his arms round it, but it vanishes to nothing and he falls over himself. The goddess appears behind him. He goes to grab it again and it turns into – a turban !

The turban is the size of a small child. It walks about the room by itself.

The artist catches the turban and picks it up, puts it on one of the pedestals. But the living statue appears again. The artist runs to hug it. It vanishes, jaunts across the room, mounts the first pedestal (the little walking turban has vanished too) and returns to being nothing but a drawing. The artist puts his hands to his head and collapses on the floor of his gallery.

Hannah laughed. She clapped her hands.

The artist's envy of the muse, she said.

The what? Daniel said.

It's a version of the story of Pygmalion, she says.

Oh, Daniel said.

In this case both the muse *and* the artwork out-artist the artist, Hannah said.

But did you like it? Daniel said.

Very much, she said.

He ran the film backwards, unplugged the projector.

Now he was lying at the foot of her bed in the dark telling her what Mr Wirtz at the camera shop had told him about the early filmmaker who made the vanishing statue film.

He was filming one day in a street in Paris, Daniel said. And something in the camera stuck, the film stuck, the apparatus wasn't working, so he opened the box and he sorted it and started filming again. And when he got home and watched the film he'd made, in front of his eyes a bus full of passengers suddenly turned into a hearse, and people on the street vanished, horses just vanished, and new people appeared there who hadn't been there before, men turned into women, women turned into men, people turned into horses, horses into people. And the filmmaker thought, I have found a way not just to witness and record time but also to conjure with time.

Something wakes Hannah.

The woman sitting next to her on the train has jogged her elbow.

(ALBERT Adrienne, seamstress)

The train has arrived. Everybody off.

Because it's near the border the checks here are chaotic. Good.

She says a silent goodbye to the back of the man who looked for a moment a little like her brother.

She chooses a poorly dressed old woman carrying a pile of sacking and an empty wicker box, the kind that holds hens. She places herself directly behind the old woman.

My mother's ill. I don't know. That woman you've just let through, she is taking me, she was sent by my aunt to fetch me from the station, I've come from Lyon and I don't know this place and she may not wait for me, she's deaf, look, she's going without me and I won't know where to go.

She holds her arms out from herself. She gives the uniform the man's wearing her most beautiful angry look. The man blushes red, hands her back her papers without looking at her and nods her through.

She breathes fully in, then out.

She quickens her pace as if to catch up with the old woman. She follows her at a distance through the busy streets to the less busy streets, past houses until there are no houses, nothing but gouged-up grass and dried mud where trucks have turned in the road, to the edge of the town then out beyond the town where the fields begin.

She can see the military grey and the signage, the roadblocks skirting the border.

They walk a lower road through a scatter of farmland.

When the woman turns away from the hills rather than towards them, Hannah stops and stands under a tree, takes off her shoe and looks inside it as if to find a stone. She lets the woman disappear towards a cluster of houses.

She sets off herself in the opposite direction along the side of a meadow.

It is a completely beautiful evening. Heavy summer light. She walks until she comes to the place a signpost has been removed from a village. She walks past its houses like she knows where she's going. The people working see her and leave her alone. She walks between fields for over an hour on a dirt road in the birdsong, the evening's grassy air.

Then there's a house by itself with a yard full of geese settling themselves for the night, the mountains rising behind it.

She opens its gate.

A dog barks.

A woman comes to the door and opens it, holds the dog by the scruff of its neck.

What do you want? the woman says.

A man is standing behind the woman and the dog in a doorway that leads through to the rest of the house.

I was wondering if I might trouble you for a glass of water, Hannah says.

A glass of water, the woman says.

I have a little money, if you'd take recompense for the kindness, Hannah says.

She smiles her smile.

The woman turns to look at the man.

Yes, a warm evening, and you've been walking, the man says.

I've quite a way to go, Hannah says. But there's still light in the sky.

We'll gladly give you something to eat, too, if you can pay us something small towards it as you suggest, the man says.

It's kind of you, Hannah says.

She sits at the table. The man says something to the dog. It stops agitating. The woman puts a spoon on the table in front of Hannah.

Thank you, Hannah says.

They put bread down, and a glass of water filled from a jug, then a bowl of some kind of stew. It tastes good. She tells them. The woman straightens herself with pride.

Hannah tells them her name is Adrienne and says the name of the place she bought the train ticket to.

That's more than an hour on foot from here, the woman says. And the curfew. We can give you blankets, you're welcome to sleep in the barn if you'd like to wait till the morning.

It is a real kindness, she says. It's my very good luck that I knocked on your door.

She puts two banknotes on the table.

I'll set off as soon as it's light, she says. I won't trouble you more.

You're no trouble to us, the woman says.

Hannah goes out to the barn with the man, who carries a roll of blankets. The dog walks peaceably beside them both.

The mountains, she says. It doesn't matter what time of the day or evening it is. Such beauty.

Yes, the man says. We've always thought of them as our own.

He smiles at her.

Where does France end and Switzerland begin? she asks.

The man takes her beyond the barn and points to a small muddy yard full of goats at the back of the house in the dusk. He takes her to the edge of the yard. He slides one foot through the wire in the fence.

I am now in two countries, he says. My goats, when they put their heads through this fence, benefit from the good grass of more than one country. They always have. We get excellent milk.

He pulls his leg back through. He stands in his yard and looks at her with utter candour.

How lucky you are, she says.

He crinkles his well-sunned face.

If I were to bring family, just every so often, especially the little ones, there are many children in my family, just now and then, to visit you to enjoy your beautiful view, she says. Or perhaps send a cousin with some family of mine. Perhaps you would be as kind to them as you've been to me. Of course, for a little recompense for such kindness.

We'll always be happy to receive visits from your family, the man says. And there,

(he points beyond the fence across a grassy expanse which ends in a forest)

that's where a path through the woods begins. Just one high fence, and my goats get under it easily if they try. Beautiful wildlife, those woods. It's a very nice hike. I also know a man in town. He's the mayor. He is himself a great lover of family life. I will leave you a note addressed to him telling him you and I are old friends, I'll leave it on the doorstep for the morning, you can take it with you.

When the man has gone back into the house and the sun is down, she folds the blankets on top of

each other in the corner of the barn where there's a
tall bank of hay. She sits back against the haywall
on the blankets, flicks a tiny fly away from her nose.
She checks for her cash. She checks for her papers.
She settles her hands in her pockets and closes
her eyes.

Good people.

Lucky break.

Claude will make it work.

Claude got her the papers, good ones, real
artistry. When the park was overrun with flowers
and the city first overrun with thugs, she'd sat in the
park with a book in her hand, Rimbaud,
Illuminations. He came and sat beside her. He was
good-looking, he was serious but smiling, he spoke
with a lightness. O saisons, he said, o chateaux.
What soul has no faults? I've done an enchanted
study of it, happiness, it won't pass us by, long may
it live, with de Gaulle to wake us.

When she'd turned to him and smiled, he'd said
the word: yes?

Yes, she said.

They watched people strolling about the park,
women on the arms of the Luftwaffe like
everything wasn't happening. They sat among the
flowers, flowers falling over themselves, and he told
her with the same light demeanour three things
he'd seen.

He'd seen a casino in Nice that was no longer a

casino, had become a mattress store, you couldn't move for the high piles of them that local people had donated to give to refugees to sleep on.

He'd seen people shot by the planes dead on the sides of the road out of the city.

He'd seen a mother and child who'd been executed, shot into the same grave. The mother'd been made to take her clothes off, the child the thugs had buried clothed, tossed it in on top of the mother.

Now you don't need to tell me anything else, she said.

But he told her his name, the name he's now inhabiting. Hannah told him her French name. She told him she didn't have papers.

He told her how he'd picked up an actual Bentley on the road. What? She didn't know what a Bentley was? He laughed. A Bentley was an English car, a very fine one, and it had been abandoned, door hanging open, engine still running, by English people rushing to get the last ship that'd take them back to England. He'd also picked up on the same road a bicycle left the same way, he'd tied the lid of the boot down on it and driven as far as he could get. When the car ran out of petrol he got on the bike and cycled the rest of the way to Toulon. He'd met the gardeners there. They pass as gardeners. They're pretty good gardeners, too. They garden all across the Midi.

Ever been? he said. You'll like it.

He sorted it. He got her papers. He got her across the zone line. It won't be non-occupied for long. The Italians want it. The Germans will let them have it till they decide to take it for themselves.

He never asked her about anything.

She told him about her mother, said that what she was telling him had happened to someone else's mother. This other person's mother'd been ill and medicines were forbidden and dying and nurses were forbidden. Meanwhile the thugs took the flat and everything in it.

Now there's no need to tell *me* anything else, he said.

He gave her the bicycle.

He told her laughter was the best way to conceive, so whatever she did, best not to laugh. Then he made her really laugh. It was impossible not to; he was an excellent mimic. He mimicked the concierge. He mimicked the Nazis. He mimicked the Maréchal watering his red white and blue flowers in his Azur garden. He mimicked any film star she could name, could do Colbert *and* Gable. He mimicked the grim woman at the baker's. He made her laugh at all of it and then he held her body in a way that completely understood her, he was good at doing *her* too, then, a whole other kind of mimicry.

She'd woken, she'd thought he'd be gone. He was

still there next to her, smoking a cigarette. The light was coming up outside.

New day, he said.

There was a caterpillar in my dream, she said. It was walking the length of a rifle. It's a sign, what do you think?

In which direction was the caterpillar heading? he asked.

Away from the handle towards the shooting end, she said.

Away from the trigger, he said.

Yes, she said.

Good, he said. If you're going to get shot, don't get shot by a caterpillar. Tell it you'll wait to be shot by the butterfly.

That's when she told him the first real thing about herself, by mistake.

(It was dangerous. You had to blank your brain. You had to think way beyond yourself. Life depended on it, and not just your own. Her father, her brother. Her mother was safe in heaven dead, thank God.

You had to *not* know, to know as little as you could. You had to find new ways of thinking and saying and not saying everything and anything.)

She'd spoken thoughtlessly openly about her father and how he liked to catch butterflies, and to kill them, pin them behind glass. She regretted it as soon as she did. Her stomach dropped inside her.

She felt sick. She thought she might well be sick any moment.

But Claude shrugged, flicked the done cigarette into last night's dirty water in the washing bowl.

You can't put a pin through a summer, he said.

They'd kissed, got up, got ready for the day.

What she knew about Claude was that he was a man who could make damp newspaper catch light and burn.

Because of him she'd be warm enough through a cold winter.

Mad dogs and Englishmen. We're out in the Midi sun.

Hannah puts her face against the shawl that's round the child when she says it, so close that the shawl is partly in her mouth making her words not actual words, so nobody can possibly have heard her say anything, or anything meaningful.

The city of flowers – the bright coast under the bright blue sky next to the bright blue sea, with its flower fields on the hills above it in a riot of bloom for the perfume industry – is ragged with refugees.

Some of the big hotels are making a fortune because some of the refugees still have money. Most of the smaller hotels are going under.

After Claude goes, she has to move. She chooses this city. She chooses the hotel she'll stay in by the delight on the face of the woman who comes to the door when she sees the baby.

When the woman tells her a name Hannah replaces it instantly. The name the woman said is gone. Her name in Hannah's head is now Madame Etienne.

It's Madame Etienne, young and sweet, so keen that she runs up the stairs ahead of Hannah and the baby and waits on each landing for them to catch her up, who opens a door in the slope of the roof and shows her a room.

It's worn, I know, Madame Etienne says now toeing a rip in the carpet. But if Madame Albert will look. It has the sea.

Madame Etienne is quite lovely to the baby. She also promises with all her heart that some days there'll be more than just turnip for supper. She does this with a wink in case she can't fulfil her promise. She tells Hannah, whom she refers to respectfully and repeatedly as Madame Albert, as if Hannah is twenty years older than she is, which she isn't, they're clearly about the same age, that last night at one of the cinemas in the town the authorities had come in and made the staff turn the houselights up! So they could pick out whoever was shouting or throwing things at the screen whenever the Maréchal or Hitler or Mussolini came on!

She tells her this with an air of blithe disconnect, same as you'd say, but it's raining! or, what a lovely day! or, look at that funny-faced dog, it does make me laugh! or, you're wearing such a pretty blouse today!

Her husband, she tells Hannah in the same jolly manner while she punches a pillow into better shape, told her last night when they were listening to the radio that people caught listening to Les Français parlent aux Français can be fined up to 10,000 francs and also put in prison! For two years! Does this room please Madame Albert?

Very much, Hannah says.

Madame Etienne pulls open the bottom drawer of a chest of drawers. She pulls it out as far as it'll come. She takes a blanket off the bed, goes down on her knees and folds the blanket into the drawer like a thick lining then tucks the pillow in at one end. She stands up leaving the drawer open and gestures to it like a ballerina might, but with no idea of the delicacy of her own gesture.

For the child to sleep in, she says. Does Madame Albert think it's good? Does she think it is too small?

I think it will work very well, Hannah says.

Madame Etienne kisses the baby one more time then flurries out and down the stairs.

Hannah sits on the bed in the room.

The baby kicks her legs.

Claude, gone.

Three others from the group, also vanished.

They're dead.

He's dead.

She hopes for his sake he's dead.

She's here to do his job, to meet a *cousin* at one of the big hotels tomorrow.

She dandles the baby, sings the song about horses going to market and coming home again. The baby laughs.

The baby is beginning to form words already and wants to test the strength of her legs, every chance she gets bracing herself against her mother.

It is a happy baby, which is a lucky thing.

Hannah spends the days between the child and despair. There's a happiness in these days that's unquantifiable up against the foulness.

In the first days here she goes out with the baby in her arms along the Promenade des Anglais with its vegetable gardens in the lovely sun.

Almost every day she does this she reminds herself that a child makes you too visible, that too many people will start to recognize you.

She walks the baby back to their hotel room again.

Even so, the days since the baby came pass so fast it's as if they're jealous of happinesses.

She meets the go-between every fifth day of the week, always in a different place. The go-between, for now, is a fourteen year old schoolgirl who gives her name as Sylvie.

Sylvie is as simple as a wooden door; she is plain and elegant, closed and solid, locked. Hannah gives her the bicycle, indicates without saying that it's a gift. Sylvie understands, nods impassive thanks with all the articulacy of such a door.

Don't underestimate the articulacy of a wooden door. Everything has a voice. What Sylvie is made of has its own good seasoned voice, even in a girl still so young.

Sylvie settles in to being the usual contact. It works well. They pass each other in the appointed street or square at the appointed times. As they do, Hannah slips the packet of papers into the basket of the bicycle under Sylvie's folded raincoat or under the (very) occasional slab of meat wrapped in the brown paper, or the turnips or beets or chard she's delivering to the big hotels.

One day Sylvie takes Hannah's wrist in her small hand as she manoeuvres the packet under the food.

For you, Madame, she says.

She hands Hannah a folded cone of paper. She puts a foot on one pedal, swings herself up on to the seat and she's gone.

Hannah opens the paper cone. It's full of wild strawberries.

That's a locked wooden door for you.

Then there are the hours of the day when Hannah does nothing but sit and watch the baby asleep in the drawer, like the baby's afloat in a tiny boat.

Hannah herself is a broken-oared boat on a sea so wild she already knows any minute she'll be flotsam.

So.

What will I make of my broke broken self?

She watches the child breathe and shift in her sleep. Rilke says that by having a child at all you've already served that child its own death, placed it in the mouth of the child like a little ball of greyed bread, the core of the loveliest apple.

Her own parents, did they know this feeling? And theirs before them? And theirs before them, too? And yet, no anger.

Instead, the last word of that poem is the word unbeschreiblich. The knowledge defies words.

The baby breathes in.

The baby breathes out.

Her mouth is so small and so here.

Wer den Dichter will versteh'n, muss in Dichters Lande geh'n. Translate it, for your brother.

If you want to understand the poet, visit poet-land.

I'm in poet-land now for sure. This is time on another plane.

Weeks pass.

(The baby gets too big for the drawer.)

Hannah passes on the papers.

(The child breathes in, out, in.)

She sorts the tickets to Lyon, a little food, the instructions.

(The child is beginning to form words into phrases.)

There's a silk map to pass on to a contact in Switzerland who'll pass it on to London.

More people to disappear.

Hannah has to travel north.

(Madame E minds the child on the days when Hannah's away. The child throws her arms open when Hannah comes back.)

This week there are two groups. One of seven kids. They're to look like they're on a hike. Sort the right clothes.

(Soon Hannah is leaving the child at the hotel for days on end.)

This week five adults. Check the health, the stamina, sort the papers. More can go wrong with adults. Locals are more uneasy when they see adults crossing land. Kids they tend to care about much less. The guides have to look like the kind of young people who'll lead other young people on a hike.

(Madame Etienne and her husband, a man who looks thoughtful, says nothing and can mend anything that's broken, welcome the cash.)

The laws change. Now you have to be ten kilometres inside the Swiss border before the Swiss will let you stay. Check the stamina.

North.

Then back south.

North.

Then south.

There are so many nights now when Hannah's not with the child.

On those nights, before she goes to sleep, wherever she is, she sits and imagines the child on her knee and herself singing the horse going to market song to the child.

Whether she's with the child or not she tells the child a story before sleep.

Like the one about the summer day that argued with the gods about never wanting to be over.

I will last for ever! the summer day said. Night will never fall! Winter will never come!

Well, the gods all laughed like they'd heard the best joke, the funniest thing ever. Because as soon as someone or something says to the gods, this is the way things are, this is the way they'll be, the gods and goddesses gather at the balcony and they look down over it at our nothing-much world, us running about on its surface like ants, and it's worth noting, they're sometimes cruel, the gods. They like a laugh, they laugh at us sometimes so much that they have to hold their sides so their sides won't split with the laughing and all their godliness leak out of them. Best never to split a god. And here was a summer day, asking to be longer. As if a summer's day wasn't long enough.

One of the gods stopped laughing and threw out a sudden lightning strike made of ice and the lovely blue sky of the summer day was gone. In its place was a great mass of clouds, black and grey. And from those clouds it isn't rain that fell, but snow. Big fluffy flakes of snow fell on the hottest day in July. They were so big that as they fell they stuck to each other and became a lot of little snowballs. And a summer's day feels long, though it isn't any longer than a winter's day really, but that day, in the light that went on till late in the evening, so much snow fell that if you'd been standing on the doorstep the snow that fell would have reached as high as your nose.

The child put her hand on her nose.

It covered all the summer flowers. Their petals shivered and shrank.

No! the child said.

She covered her mouth with her hands.

But the next day, Hannah said. What happened then?

Sum, the child said.

Yes. Summer sun. The sun melted all the snow away. Some poor flowers had been scorched by the cold, though, because cold can burn you just like heat can.

Poor fowr, the child said.

But most of them raised their heads to the sun, Hannah said, and what did they do?

Hirsy, the child said.

That's right. They were thirsty. They drank all the melted snow. And after a while there were soon more flowers. And there were butterflies, and bees, who visited the flowers to make honey and to make the fruit grow on the trees, and make more flowers open.

And the new summer day bowed its head and it said to the gods, I'm sorry I asked to live for longer than the length of the day I am. And the gods on the balcony bowed politely back to the summer day, and the townspeople of the city of flowers saw the flowers slowly lifting their heads after the sudden frost, and they were glad to have the flowers back, even for the short time a flower lasts. The townspeople knew that the flowers only last a summer, that a summer is soon over. So, they said – what did they say?

What we ache, the child said.

That's right, she said. What will we make of this. So what did they make?

Very big fume, the child said.

A very big bottle of perfume. And when the summer was gone and the autumn and the winter came?

Nos, the child said.

That's right, they opened the bottle and they put their nose to its opening and they sniffed, and enjoyed the lovely perfume. And what did they remember?

Fowr, the child said.

The flowers, Hannah said.

Other nights she tells the child about the children who sleep all night under the stars under a canvas in the marketplace in town, so they'll be first in the queue for the next morning's vegetables.

What are they? she says to the child.

Cever, the child says.

That's right. They're clever, she says.

She tells the child the story of the mother who has to go away and leave her baby, and that it doesn't mean the mother doesn't love her baby, it means she loves her baby how much?

Venor, the child says.

That's right, Hannah says. Even more.

When the fields go dark, your eyes go bright, Hannah says one night. Soon a star starts to shine, and the insects sing the night. Every sound becomes a picture, everything you thought you knew, turns strange and dark in the pale sky, but the tops of the trees get brighter too. And you don't notice as you pass, how the dark makes the light grow, till light frees itself from the darkness, and it holds you as you go.

Old poem written by the son of a woodsman. When the light touches the tops of the poem's trees the child flickers, closes her eyes.

Hannah puts her own hands over her own eyes.

The Italians are gone.

The Nazis are all over town.

She tucks the child into the bed, slips downstairs and asks Madame Etienne if she can have a word.

Madame Etienne pours three glasses of something that looks and smells like actual brandy. She sets them on the table.

It's the real thing, Madame Albert, she says.

She gestures in her graceful way for Hannah to sit down.

Hannah, still standing, tells her that work has become very pressing.

Yes, Madame Etienne says.

Hannah asks her if she and her husband will let the child live with them permanently if she should happen to be away for a length of time.

I mean as a paying guest, of course, she says. Because your good care for us both means I know she'll be safe here. But the likelihood is that I'll be away for a long time.

Frown lines appear in Madame Etienne's pretty forehead.

We won't take any money, Madame Albert, she says. We don't ever need money for this.

I insist, Hannah says.

She puts a roll of notes in the pocket of Madame Etienne's apron.

You'll teach her to read, she says.

Madame Etienne nods.

Thank you, Hannah says.

Madame Etienne calls her husband. He comes through from the kitchen drying his hands and stands with them both round the table.

His wife tells him, shows him the money.

I'll come as often as I can, Hannah says. If it looks like something's likely to change, I'll come back straight away and collect her.

Paul, my love, Madame Etienne says.

Hannah hasn't even known his name till now.

She can't know his name.

She can't have his name in her head.

She blanks it.

She can't have her own child's name in her head. Of course she knows it, it's written all through her. But she is disciplined. She is ready. She vanishes it all the time.

To do this she imagines a gravestone, a headstone, but with nothing written on it.

That's her child.

What shall we drink to? the wife asks the husband.

Brotherhood, he says.

They clink the glasses.

My dear old (decrepit) (ha ha) summer brother (I will always be younger than you and there's nothing you can do about it)

235

Here's something of a self portrait. It's of me walking towards you.

Recognize me?

Shows how long it's been since I did any drawing. I'm very out of practice. But it's me. Dear Dani. It's been a long time. I'm cancelling out that long time by writing something of the time down, on paper which, you will be interested to know, I've very neatly torn, without hurting the book, out of the back of a copy of Gide's Prometheus.

Dani, when I think of you it's of us sitting saying our something and our nothing in the sunlight, and I've always got one of my arms slung round your shoulders, at least in my imagination if not in actuality because I know how hard you'd punch my arm if I did it in real life.

I often think of the care you always take with me. Your kindness in putting up with my bluntness and my snobberies, your taking such real pains, and it was, I'm sure, very much a pain! to have to listen and try to understand me, but you always did, you always do try, with such good grace putting up with even my most impenetrable and argumentative and obtuse demands on you.

We said we'd write and we'd burn what we wrote. You remember?

The heat that will come off this note when I burn it will alter the balance of heat and cold in the world in its own way.

That energy I send <u>your</u> way.

Look at me. Hopeless. It's like I can't help but be grandiose in English.

So I will say it plainly.

I think of you.

I think of father.

I hope he's not too ill and his spirit not too low, and not making your own spirit go low.

I will see you after this is all over.

I'm looking forward to that.

Here's my news.

I have a child now.

!

She looks like her father, who was a good friend to me.

She also looks, in certain light, quite like you.

For me this is a good sign! The days when I see my brother in her make me wildly happy.

I don't know that I believe in gods enough to ask of them. But if they exist and I might be so bold as to say, excuse me, if you're there can you please make that sunlit summer day longer and these dark days shorter — remember the story mother used to tell us? well she definitely told me at least, about the summer day and the gods, and she used to list the gods? I realize now that what she was doing was <u>teaching me gods</u>, since nothing was ever not a bit prussian and instructive one way or another with our fine mother. Well.

*The good gods, I ask them all in all their guises,
the whole panoply of Pans, and Zeuses, and
Dianas, and Floras and Poseidons and
Persephones, and Brighids and Maeves, and
Apollos and Athenas and Minervas and Marses
and Odins and Thors, and Mercurys and Hermeses
and Baldurs and Plutos and Demeters and
Neptunes and Venuses, and Bacchuses and Bentens
and Kores and Kalis, and Gamas, and Artemises,
the Gods and the Allahs and Buddhas, all the other
ancients, the ones whose names I don't have in my
head right now, hope they'll forgive me, there are
so many – most of all the Jupiters,*

 *above all I ask the Jupiters
that my girl will grow up
and that time will be kind to her.*

 *Those bloody gods are laughing already. I can
hear them.*

 *God-laughter sounds like, well, right now,
bullets hitting stone.*

 But they'd better not cross me on this.

 You know she reminds me of us both.

 *She is so small and new but already she is quick,
sensitive, argumentative (me), slow to anger (you),
she sleeps like she's a bearcub in hibernation (you),
she doesn't like the taste of turnip (us both, if I
remember rightly, and a small daily disappointment
given that there's not much else to eat most days),
she loves to be told a story (me), she is keen, from*

238

some inner stillness I have never had, to do right by people (you) and be good mannered and polite (definitely you), she is loyal (us both), she is soulful (you), also a laugher at everything, she finds unfunny things very funny (me, I think).

The other day she slid her foot under a pillow on the bed and then called me over to her as if to tell me something of great import to all the world's nations. She flourished her arm in the air over her leg (with its foot under the pillow) and said like a little circus magician, Foot gone! Then she pulled her foot out from under the pillow and said, with the same flourish, Look! Foot!

But most of all, I have never met anyone like her. She is herself.

A child hardly formed, hardly speaking, and yet she is so much an assured and completed self already in some ways that she is often a puzzle to me and clearly regards me as a puzzle too, sometimes looks at me very questioningly.

I said to her one day when she was looking at me, <u>who do you think you're looking at?</u> She replied, with real seriousness, <u>you</u>.

One other thing. She can sing, already, tunefully, and she knows without being told how to make up harmonies, and does them naturally. She sits and sings to herself and I have heard her sing too with the lady who keeps the room we live in. Now this talent is definitely not one of ours.

It must come from her father.

In fact I owe to her harmony, dear Dani, what I thought tonight lying next to her as she fell asleep.

It's that the foulness happening every day round us is a growth without roots. Goodness is more like turnip!

The foulness just wants one thing, more of its self. It wants self self self self nothing but self over and over again. I begin to realize that this makes it very like the blowaway moss that spreads fast across everything but can easily be kicked away because its grip is only about surface.

Just the act of thinking this kicks it loose and blows it away.

Big thoughts. You know me. I won't spare you from them.

When I was a callow schoolgirl full of my own cleverness (yes all right dearest Dani I still <u>am</u> – at least the latter, if well past the former) I thought such a load of rot about things.

I really believed I could hold all the knowledge in me, all the narratives, all the poems, all the art, all the learning – and that this gathering and holding of all of these things meant I now owned these things and that to do this was the reason for living.

These days what do I know?

Close to nothing.

But one thing I do know now is that I don't hold <u>any</u> of those things I thought I owned.

Instead, all those things hold me. They hold us
all under the sky.
   I'm about to burn this. Like we said we would.
   I wonder if you've remembered?
   Not that I doubt you. I never will.
   Its warmth will reach you one way or another
   so rest assured
   your autumn sister
   sends it with love
   to her summer brother.

15 June 2020

Dear Hero,

We haven't yet met, and if you didn't get my last letter you will wonder why someone you don't know is writing to you. Suffice to say I am a friend and I am writing to send friendly wishes.

How are you?

I really hope you are well.

I'm sending this letter via our friends' email this time so they will forward it to you wherever you are.

I've been doing some online studies into your name. It is an every day kind of thing to you, but believe me to the rest of us it is a pretty amazing thing to be called. First I looked up the Greek inventor and maths genius Hero, who pretty much invented the wind farm, was one of the first people to realize human beings can harness the wind for power, plus he invented the first engine powered by hot water and a very early form of self powering fountain. Apparently he was an atomist. I just shouted through to my little brother Robert who thinks he is teaching himself to play a violin in the next room, in other words he is making an appalling noise, and asked him about the atomists, and he tells me atomists believed that individuals are complete indivisible atoms, separate from each other, and if you take an atomist view then you are looking at separate parts of an idea or a subject rather than all the things that go to make up the whole thing. The good thing is, me asking him stopped him making that noise with the violin. But he has started again now.

I also found in folklore a female character called Hero – and the fact that it can also be a girl's name really pleased me. Hero, the girl, was a Mythical Figure who was in love with Leander, a boy who would swim every night to Hero's tower, lit up like a lighthouse. In the end though of course this turns into a tragic story. One night at the end of their summer of love a sea storm blew Hero's tower's light out and Leander got lost in the waves and drowned.

Well some old stories are like that!

I suppose this is so that we can deal with the sad things that happen to us.

Anyway the poet John Keats wrote a version of this story saying that Leander pretty much gets drowned by the light of Hero's beauty. Like <u>she</u> was the lighthouse. It seemed a bit sexist to me, so I made up my own poem:

> In the waves Leander
> Went for a meander
> Hit a spot of bother
> And now he is quite other
> Dear oh dear oh
> Don't worry Hero
> Hero don't cry
> Love will never die

Hope you don't think it too cheeky. But I wanted to change an old hopeless story to something a bit funnier. I have really had enough of sadness. There is so much this year. And we are <u>lucky</u>. None of us have been ill. But an old lady from across the road who went into a home last year, I don't want to key in the word died, but she did, she died. So did twelve other people in the home she was in, over one weekend, and a careworker, and the healthworker who saw the careworker, who had symptoms. And one of the teachers from the primary school down the road from here. And an NHS nurse my mother knew.

It is so sad.

Our postman is brilliant. His name is Sam and he works so hard it's like encountering a small dynamo. He thinks he probably had it in March but he never had a test and still hasn't been able to get one. It means he can't go and see his family. His parents are elderly and miles away from here, in Blackpool. We also know more than fifty people in all who have had what sounds like it symptom-wise, but couldn't get tested by anyone. So they don't know, and they were really ill at home, like Sam, and scared, and no one helped them, and no official body has listed them in any statistics. A lot of my friends know a lot of people this happened to. <u>Now</u> the government wants them for antibodies and plasma but <u>then</u> nobody wanted to know, they were just left on their own thinking they were dying. And some of them did die.

My father's business is garrotted. Right now we'd have no money for anything if it wasn't for his partner Ashley, who is generously paying the bills and buying food not just for him but for us too, till my father can get any money out of the government, who keep saying he's not valid for any.

Personally I had so many plans that now have had to be chucked out of the window that I am determined to make something better out of this time. These teenage years are supposed to be amazing. I'm 16 and the highlight of my last three months has been watching crap movies on Netflix party with my friends.

But I believe one good thing that will come out of

this is that my already trampled on generation will be evermore resilient. We will be aware of how lucky we are to spend time with our friends because we will know what it's like to live without them. And by God we will treasure our freedoms and we will fight for them in the name of all that is good.

I also feel like we are shortchanging the thousands and thousands of people who have died – just by still being alive.

My brother Robert is holding out for medical geniuses to invent a vaccine. I am holding out for the geniuses who invent the vaccine to also be climate change geniuses.

Then we might have a future.

It is why, Hero, you along with all the key workers in the NHS and the people working so hard keeping things going, like Sam, are my heroes, along with the people fighting to protect climate, and every single person protesting what happened to George Floyd.

I have a vision that the modern sense of being a hero is like shining a bright light on things that need to be seen. I guess that if someone does this it brings its own consequences. For instance if you are a bright light on social media, then people get quite angry and will attack you equally as much as they are drawn like moths to your flame.

But now maybe we will realize that we have to stop being poisonous to each other and the world. I know how naive that is, because poisonous stuff has never stopped happening. Our history class on zoom was zoombombed with a porn image which we all saw, for example. But I guess there will always be porn and poison, and human beings will always have to decide whether to be poisonous to others or not, whether we are in a pandemic or not.

I suppose what has happened here and all over the world in these few months with the lockdown has given us all a very mild dose of what it is like every day for you. I know it is not at all the same, nothing like being kept in prison conditions – and this when you are not a criminal.

It is also amazing to me that you might now <u>not</u> be in detention any more and might be homeless with nobody knowing where you are. Our friend wrote and told us that people in detention have just quietly been getting released but with nowhere to go or to stay and no money to survive on.

Dear Hero, I hope you are okay. I have to say it is amazing to me that the thing that gets people let out of <u>illegal</u> indefinite detention when they are innocent in the first place is a virus – not a more kindly human nature, or understanding, or a good law. I'm also quite worried for someone else I know, who is homeless. The news says homeless people have been give rooms in hotels. I've no idea if he got one or not. Why would we do these things for people only when there is a virus and not all the time?

But these are not the only reason I am writing.

I am writing again because the swifts came back! I was shouting with happiness in the street when I saw them in the sky. There aren't as many as last year apparently, but all the same they are here.

I've just realized, if you didn't get my last letter you won't know what I'm talking about. In it I wrote at length about my favourite birds – the swifts. They always come back to the same nesting place they left last year if they can, so long as it hasn't been renovated and made into an AirBnB – which no one except swifts can stay at now anyway because of the virus! I can't help but find that funny though I know a lot of people will be angry about it.

The swifts have come across the world singly not with their mate. They meet up when they get back to the nesting place. They stay together for life when it comes to having their babies here. Then when they've had them they split up till they meet again next year for more mating. It seems to me it might save a few marriages if human beings did this too for 3/4 of the year.

The nests they have are like small flat rings made of feathers and paper or stuff they collect in the air. They glue it all together with their saliva in a little ring shape or shallow bowl or cup shape that will hold the eggs in place. Then they take turns incubating or keeping the eggs warm. Their babies hatch out with a day between each one so that it's not too full on for the parent swifts. Nature is so intelligent.

In pictures of what their babies look like right now they're nothing like swifts yet, more like grotesque pink skin bags with no feathers, huge heads that look heavy to lift, eyes that can't yet see.

But nature's so clever that the babies can go into a kind of comatose state if the parents for some reason don't come back with food, and can last quite a long time in case of misfortune to a parent or bad weather.

Even without misfortune the parents have to work pretty hard collecting something like 1,000 flies and insects each and every time they go out, which they keep in pouches in their throats rolled together into a food ball and deliver on their return to their baby swifts.

So if you see or hear them now above you, you can be pretty sure what they are doing is collecting food. Soon their babies will be doing push ups in the nesting place with their wings, strengthening themselves for the long flight back to Africa. What is really astounding is that when they fledge and leave the nest it's the first time that they actually fly anywhere, and as soon as they hit the air they won't touch down again for at least a year, more usually a couple of years.

Six weeks or so from now, that's when they'll leave.

'That's the summer over' my mother will say
when we look up at a swiftless sky.
But not yet!
There are still some weeks left.
Whenever you hear them above you, remember
they also bring friendly greetings from me.
Best wishes and good health to you.
I hope you get this letter,
with warm wishes
from your friend
Sacha
(Greenlaw)

3

So, when she's in her early twenties, at the start of the 1950s, Lorenza Mazzetti arrives in England as part of a group of students invited here from the University of Florence on an initiative to bring people from mainland Europe to help with work on British farms.

She's the filmmaker whose images I described earlier, the image of the men who can't speak or hear crossing the rubble conversing with each other and the image of the man with the two suitcases on the edge of the high building.

The Italian students land in Dover and the first thing that happens is a thorough police search of each person bodily, then of each person's luggage. The police take Mazzetti's passport from her. When they give it back she is astonished to see that it's been stamped with the words *Undesirable* and *Alien*.

As it happens Mazzetti will be useless at farm work, too weak and too nervy. With hindsight it's clear that this is because she's had quite a war: in 1944, when she was in her teens, a group of Nazi officers arrived at the house in Tuscany where she and her twin sister Paola were being brought up as part of the family of their father's sister, Nina: the Mazzetti twins' mother had died not long after giving birth, and so far in their lives they'd been passed from person to person, family to family. But now they were finally home, living with Nina and her husband, Robert Einstein, who was a cousin of Albert Einstein, and their slightly older cousins, Luce and Anna Maria.

That summer the Germans in Italy were being driven back by the oncoming Allied forces. One beautiful sunny day the Wehrmacht officers came to the house and when they couldn't find Robert, who'd decamped to the woods because he knew they were after him, they did two things.

They wrecked the house.

They killed all the Einsteins they *could* find – Nina and her daughters.

They decided not to kill Lorenza Mazzetti or her sister because their surname wasn't Einstein.

The twins, who'd been locked away with other villagers while the killing happened, came back into the house to the dead bodies of their cousins and their aunt.

Their uncle came back to the bodies too. Not long afterwards he committed suicide.

In England, now, Mazzetti is as close to nervous breakdown as you might imagine given such a history. She infuriates the farmer to whose farm she's been assigned by not being strong enough to carry heavy sacks, by not being good enough at picking the bad potatoes off a conveyor belt, by burning the dinner she's meant to be cooking for the other students and by not being fast enough at mucking out a manure heap.

He throws her off the farm.

So she gets herself to London to find a job and somewhere to live.

But something deeply fractured in her means that each job she takes results in a kind of surreality.

A woman employs her as a live-in maid in the suburbs but ends up throwing all her stuff out into the road, calling the police and accusing her of stealing. (Later Mazzetti discovers it's she who's been being stolen from by the woman.)

A lovely happy family in a lovely happy house in the city give her a maid's position and welcome her warmly into their lovely life. But in the lovely happy family she is suddenly even more surrounded by the ghosts, standing and sitting and walking all round her, silent, smiling, bleeding from the places the teenage Mazzetti saw the holes the bullets had made in them.

With my suitcase I run away in search of some unhappiness.

She wanders the streets by herself.

Men follow her about, harassing her for sex.

But London policemen, it turns out, are exceptionally kind to her. They take her out of the rain and give her cups of tea and repeatedly allow her to spend the winter night in the warmth of a police station. And one day when she's wandering the streets lost, a family sees her lostness and invites her in off the street for a meal in their house. It's the first time she ever tastes curry.

She eventually gets a job serving and washing dishes at a restaurant near Charing Cross that sells nothing but omelettes and soup.

She manages to keep this job.

But it's not her real job. What she has always been, since she was a child, is an artist. Very late in what will turn out to be a long life (she'll die in Rome at the beginning of 2020, at the age of ninety two), her friend Ruggero will recall the way his own family would wake after a siesta when he was a child to find paintings by both the twins filling their garden, paintings leaning up against all the trees.

So while she's been surviving the foggy London years by the skin of her teeth she's been painting and drawing all along.

One day she takes herself and her work to the Slade School of Art.

She stands in the entrance hall and asks for a place at the school.

They say a polite no. They explain that you can't just walk in off the street and ask for a place in the school.

She stands in the front hall and won't move. She says it again. She wants a place at the art school.

They tell her firmly that it's not how things are done here and they ask her firmly to leave.

She starts to shout about how she wants to see the director of the school.

A man comes out of a room because of the commotion. He asks her what she wants to see the director for. She tells him she wants a place at the school. She tells him she's a genius.

He looks at her drawings.

He says, *okay, starting tomorrow you'll be our student.*

(He's the director.)

Soon after she starts at the art school she walks past a cupboard with a notice on it. FILM CLUB. She opens its doors. It's full of film equipment.

She has never made a film. But she gathers some friends together and they take as much of the equipment as they can carry and move it to her lodgings.

With these friends, and with the help of some very kind strangers, she makes a short film based on one of her favourite stories, Franz Kafka's

Metamorphosis. *Metamorphosis*, she says much later in her life, *seems like a powerful act of accusation against the daily grind that makes us indifferent to past, present and future injustice.* She calls the film K. She charges the cost of the *rather complicated* technical stuff on it, developing, dubbing and so on, to the University.

Some days later she's called in to see the school director again.

He asks her about a large sum of money she's signed for in the name of the University without asking anyone's permission.

He warns her she's liable to go to jail if she's falsified a financial signature.

She starts to shake. But she tells him about the film.

Okay, he says. This is what we'll do. We'll show this film to the rest of the students and I'll decide when I see whether they like it or not what I'm going to do with you.

At the film's first showing he introduces her to someone he's invited to see the film too, a man who's the director of the British Film Institute.

The British Film Institute director, the art school director and the art school students clap and cheer at the end of the film she's made.

The BFI awards her an experimental film grant.

She starts working on a new film with this money.

It's a story about two deaf mutes who live and

work in the rubble and the looming old architecture of London's east end, where they walk the streets talking to each other in sign language, about love, about how to keep properly clean and decent in the dusty postwar aftermath and about things they find strange or beautiful. They're often followed around by a crowd of funny and merciless children.

This film is called Together.

Like K, it is small, slight, immensely powerful, it is both everyday and near-apocalyptic and it is like nothing any other filmmaker is making at the time.

She meets the filmmaker Lindsay Anderson.

He helps her with the edit of Together.

With him, Karel Reisz and Tony Richardson, she becomes one of the founders of the Free Cinema movement. Their film work and programming revolutionize the possibilities in British filmmaking. Meanwhile, at the 1956 Cannes Film Festival, Together is applauded and loved by both critics and audiences.

Around this time Lorenza Mazzetti returns to Italy to live with her twin sister for a while. Don't imagine those ghosts have left her in peace throughout all the above; the bleeding ghosts still accompany her, wherever she is, whatever she's doing. *They'd been in my unconscious for too long.*

So she writes a novel called Il Cielo Cade. The Sky Falls. It's about the murder of her family, about the religious and political divisions that divide and rule people, and is told from the point of view of a very young child.

After it, she writes another, Con Rabbia, the literal translation of which is With Rage, or Angrily. It's a sequel to The Sky Falls and it's told from the perspective of an adolescent revolutionary soul infuriated by the indifference she sees everywhere after the war regardless of what has happened to so many people. *I couldn't live in calmness and boredom any more. My hand has touched blood and tragedy and I know that while boredom was dozing reality was preparing the apocalypse.*

Over the course of her life Mazzetti will paint, exhibit, write and publish in many forms and make more short film interludes; like all her work these short film pieces are about the rupture that happens when innocence and knowledge meet, and about how to retain that innocence even at the core of a smashed-up adult psyche. She will build a puppet theatre in the Campo di Fiori in the centre of Rome and perform over the years to countless audiences her version of Punch and Judy.

Her last great project, Album di Famiglia, or Family Album – a set of paintings featuring portraits of her family up to the time of the murders, and visions of the Tuscan countryside in a sunny, gorgeous summer with Nazis under the trees and fascists teaching the schoolchildren – will bring to mind artists like Henri Matisse and Charlotte

Salomon, by their style, by a shared understanding of the way light falls regardless of what it falls on, and by their sheer colourfulness.

Does a life end at the death?

How do we define a life?

How do we come to understand what time is, what we'll do with it, what it'll do with us?

Everybody's lifeline is broken somewhere.

Much of what I've told you here can be found in Lorenza Mazzetti's novels, and in her memoir, Diario Londinese, published in English as London Diaries.

The English word for summer comes from the Old English *sumor*, from the proto-indo-european root *sam*, meaning both *one* and *together*.

I can't remember where this next quote you're about to read is from. It's nothing to do with Mazzetti, though it's everything to do with her, and us all. But I copied it into a notebook some years ago and now I can't find its source.

Creativity is cultural not because it is derivative of it, but because it aims to heal culture. Art saturated with the unconscious acts like a compensatory dream in the individual: it tries to rebalance and address deep-rooted problems.

As Mazzetti tells it, not long after the summer killing of her family, a vanguard of Allied soldiers arrives at the house in Italy where they've been murdered. English and Scottish soldiers find a couple of shellshocked children sitting beside some newly filled graves.

The first thing they do is teach those children to sing some songs, in English.

The first song they teach them?

You Are My Sunshine.

Meet me here in two hours exactly, Grace said. I'm going for a walk.

It was Saturday morning. They were still in Suffolk. They were standing on the pavement outside a cafe in the sunny cold.

A walk? her daughter said.

Yes, Grace said.

By yourself? her daughter said.

By myself, Grace said.

You don't go for walks, her daughter said. I don't remember you going for a walk ever.

You are not the expert on me, Grace said.

Can't we come? her daughter said.

No, Grace said.

Why? her daughter said.

You'll be bored, Grace said.

I won't, her daughter said. *He* might.

You need to give me some cash, her son said.

What for? Grace said.

The people will get angry if we wait here for two hours and don't buy anything to eat or drink, her son said.

You just ate a huge breakfast, Grace said.

Yeah but we can't wait around for all that time in a cafe and not pay for something, her son said.

You don't have to stay here the whole time, Grace said. You could go and do something, anything. Go and explore. It's a lovely day.

It's freezing, her daughter said.

Go down to the beach, Grace said. There's a putting green. Go to the putting green.

It won't be open, her son said. It's February.

Why don't you want us to come with you? her daughter said.

Her daughter didn't really want to come with her. Really she was just being meddlesome because she sensed Grace wanted some time to herself for some reason.

Because believe it or not I want some time to myself. For my own reasons, Grace said.

Where are you going to go? her daughter said.

To look at an old church, Grace said.

You *are not*, her daughter said.

How about you two go the amusement arcade, Grace said. That'll be open. Go to the pier.

I'm not going to an arcade, her daughter said.

I'll need some money if we've got to spend time in an arcade, her son said.

Grace got her purse out and gave him a £20 note.

That's not nearly enough, he said. That's only ten shots on a Terminator.

It is more than enough, and in any case you've to give half of that to Sacha, Grace said.

I already factored Sacha in on the ten shots, her son said.

We can get them to change it here at the till, her daughter said. I'll do it.

No, I'll do it, her son said. I'll do it at the arcade.

I'm not going to an arcade, her daughter said. Give it to me now and I'll get the man at the till to change it.

No, her son said.

Right, Grace said, whatever. Go and do anything you like, I don't care what it is you do, so long as you both meet me right here outside this cafe, nowhere else, at twelve, I've ordered a taxi, there's a London train from Ipswich at two thirty.

She wants private time to herself for a secret reason, her daughter said.

That's correct, Grace said. Bye.

She set off in the direction she thought was right. It might be completely wrong. It'd been thirty years. She didn't remember the name of the church, or maybe never actually knew it. She didn't remember anything more than that she'd found it by chance, it was out of town, about a mile maybe? Then down a single track road skirted by bramble bushes.

At the edge of the town there was a housing estate that wasn't there before.

It was perfectly possible the church wouldn't be there any more, or that someone'd have turned it into a bijou second home, or even that it'd have fallen into the sea. It wasn't that far from the edge of things if she remembered rightly.

Behind her, her children were still squabbling in the street. She didn't even turn her head. She walked on as if they didn't exist, as if she'd never had them, they were someone else's responsibility and nothing to do with her. She crossed the bridge between the town and the marsh and went towards the housing estate on the hill.

Then turn right at the marsh.

Then look for the little road.

If she turned left here, she saw, the road would take her to the house they'd met the old man in yesterday, who'd mistaken her son for his sister.

Poor Robert!

But he was *so happy* to think he'd seen her, Charlotte said last night at supper.

They ate in a wooden-walled restaurant in the hotel. There were candles. It was very nice, actually.

Just overjoyed at the notion that he'd somehow

seen her, Charlotte said. It didn't put him up or down that Robert wasn't her.

I'm not a girl, her son said. I don't look like a girl.

But something about you. The person you are. It gave that man a great deal of pleasure, Charlotte said. Something about *you* hit home for *him*. It's not about whether you're a girl.

But I don't, he said. Look like a girl.

There's nothing wrong with a boy looking like a girl, Charlotte said. In fact it's generally accepted that it's a core quality of true beauty, a bit of symbiosis between the genders.

A bit of what? her son said.

Symbiosis, Arthur said.

Like in biology? her son said.

The old man they'd met was a hundred and four years old. A hundred and four! They talked about that over supper. They talked about how amazing it was that the woman looking after him wasn't related to him, they were just friends, he was living on her grace, or her family's, in these latter years of his life, just because they'd been neighbours when she was a child. They talked about her telling them how it was the first time since she'd known him that the old man had ever said anything about *having* a sister.

And he was just full of happiness, Charlotte said. His sister, there in front of him. Even though she wasn't.

Is *that* symbiosis? her son said.

Like meeting history personified, meeting him, Grace said. What a story. Alive since the First World War. Interned in the Second World War.

That's patronizing, her son said. He's a person. He's not history.

We have a war story too, her daughter said. Our dad's mother. I'm named after her. Her name was Sacha Albert. Have you ever heard of her? She was a concert violinist.

Jeff insisted, Grace said. I wanted to call her my own mother's name.

Thank God she didn't, her daughter said. Or you'd all be talking right now to someone called Sybil.

Laughter round the table.

Grace didn't laugh.

Her daughter cast a guilt-stricken look at Grace. Her daughter knew it was a delicate matter.

But Grace was out for a meal with some people who were nice, kind, if still virtual strangers, so she decided to be gracious, nodded to her daughter that it was all right to talk about her father's side of the family.

Her daughter gave her a grateful glance back and went on talking about Jeff's family.

She was French, her daughter said. She died when I was ten.

I was seven, her son said.

And *her* mother'd died in the war when she was only three, her daughter said. And the people who brought our grandmother up, they knew she'd died because a girl came to see them in the war and told them what had happened. She said people had seen her be shot dead after she tried to help a lady in a market square stand up after a Nazi knocked her down.

We don't know if any of that old story of their father's is true, Grace said.

It *is* true, her daughter said. Gran told us.

That doesn't make it true, Grace said. Or any truer than most family lore. Anyway, their father insisted when she was born that she get called after his mother, and who was I to argue. It's a great story. Also it meant I got to choose Robert's name.

And I wasn't named after anybody, her son said.

That's because I wanted you free of inference, Grace said.

It's not just a story, her daughter said. It's true.

We've got all her violins, her son said. They're all just in a cupboard. Nobody plays them. Nobody knows how. There are five, in their violin cases. Like violin coffins. Nobody ever takes them out. Nobody even looks at them any more.

There's one really small one, her daughter said. We think it's the first one she had when she was a kid in the 1940s, it's called a quarter-size. It's only this big.

Smaller than that, her son said.

Grace changed the subject by teasing Arthur about the girl.

I thought you came all this way to meet a man who knew your mother. Not to meet girls, Grace said.

In the end, the old man hadn't seemed to remember about Arthur's mother. But he'd taken Arthur's hand and held it and wouldn't let it go and he fell asleep holding it and Arthur, Charlotte told them later, had stayed with him until about half an hour before they all met for supper which was hours later.

I didn't want to wake him, Arthur said.

You didn't want to leave that girl Elizabeth, Grace said.

Charlotte put an arm round his shoulder and kissed him on the cheek.

Too right, she said.

So it's a fact, Grace said. You really *don't* mind him looking at another woman like that. You two really *aren't* together then.

No they aren't, her son said.

Been there, done that, Arthur said. Much better now.

Not that I'd mind who he looked at even if we *were* together, Charlotte said. Love happens.

Yes, her son said. It does.

You can't deny it, Charlotte said. And you probably shouldn't.

Wish I was young again, Grace said.

Anyway, Art's like my brother now, Charlotte said.

Poor you, her daughter said.

It's true, she's like a sister to me, Arthur said.

Poor you, her son said.

Time is short, Grace said. Prime is short. Good for you. I envy you. All your lives ahead of you like that. You've got to use every moment. Because in the blink of an eye it's past you, and you never get your time again.

Forgive me, Grace, Charlotte said smiling, but I think that's rubbish. I believe we meet our times with our full and ready selves at whatever ages we are when the times happen to us. That's what it's all about.

Ah, Grace said. So naive. I was young once too and believed such things.

You're not old now, Grace, Charlotte said.

But Grace was finding Charlotte, who kept saying her name in that annoying way, a bit patronizing now.

And who knew that people were interned in England in the last war? she said instead.

I did, her son said.

You did not, her daughter said.

I did, her son said. I *did* know.

I suppose if he was a German, Grace said, they had to. For everybody's safety.

Dad's got stamps in his war collection, her son said. Isle of Man.

What's wrong with your supper, Robert? Grace said.

I'm just not very hungry, he said.

What do you need instead? Charlotte said. Can we get it for you?

Charlotte's hand was in the air for the waiter.

I need symbiosis, her son said.

I don't think they have that on the menu, her daughter said.

Grace, walking through town next day, smiles. Her clever daughter.

Her clever daughter had noticed how the stone in that corner of the old man's room was really remarkably like the stone Arthur was carrying around with him. And when Arthur opened the bag and got the stone out to give to the old man, told him his mother had asked him to do this in her will and put it on the bed, the old man saw it and said the weird thing,

the stone is a child –, Grace said at dinner last night. What a strange thing to –

No, her daughter interrupted. That's not what he said. He said *you've brought back the child*.

The woman called Elizabeth had asked Arthur to hand her the stone. She'd placed it in the curve of the piece of sculpture the man had in his bedroom.

It looks really good there, her daughter said.

The piece of sculpture was a real piece, the woman told them when the old man was dozing, by the artist Barbara Hepworth. Grace had thought it unlikely. What kind of old man's got a Barbara Hepworth sculpture just lying around?

But when she'd gone to bed she couldn't get the thought of that piece of stone out of her head. Well, that's what art is, maybe. Something that impresses mysteriously on you and you don't know why. They did look good together, the two stones, the curved one with the hole in it, the perfectly spherical one.

Walking along a pavement now, the front of her head filled with an image.

The image was her own mother's face, but as if made into a mask. A death mask or a life mask? Neither. A mask of her mother's face beyond both life and death, beyond happy and sad, alive and dead at once – no, not at all dead, nothing dead about it, not in any way. It was clean, and pure in the bone structure, the outline. It had skin the colour of life, hair scraped back off the forehead in repose, and it was made of stone. Next to it a smaller stone mask was the face of Grace's fourteen year old self, the age she was the year her mother died and the face she was wearing the moment she set fire to an armchair in the front room of their house, her just-dead mother's armchair. In her head as she walked along pavement the two faces sat blank-eyed next to each other.

Grace shook her head, shook herself back into a story of herself she could take some control of.

She was on her way to find a churchyard. She'd visited it one summer.

She passed a building with a film poster outside it.

Paths of Glory.

It caught her eye because the building was an old cinema. It was *the* old cinema –

and this was the point at which a memory, one she didn't even know she had, cracked open inside her head like the green of a seed cracking through the husk around it –

backstage in the little town cinema,

quaint little place ain't it quaint and dainty

(that's Claire Dunn singy-speaking like she's in a Sondheim show),

1989,

summer of discontent,

they're doing a two-night run here, Shakespeare tonight, Dickens tomorrow. It's hardly a theatre, darling, rearrange your expectations, Frank said when they arrived, and he's right. They're performing the play in front of a bright white cinema screen because there are no drapes or curtain of any kind, terrible lighting deck, no stage to speak of, just a narrow platform, and there isn't any backstage as such, just a box room stuffed full of the whole cast right now, fourteen people all

trying to remember their lines and no mirror to do
the make-up in.

Which is why Grace is sitting outside by herself
on the concrete steps that lead down out of the back
door. She's finished her first acts. Her character's
dead and gone now till her cue, that sky up there is
an early evening blue, the birds high, the ones her
mother used to say the thing about when they
arrived, well Grace, that's the summer here. And
when they were gone, well Grace, that's the summer
gone –

and then someone hisses behind her,
Graceforfucksake,you'reon,you'relate,you'reon–
Shit!

and she ups and races back in, up the stairs,
through the bendy corridor, and belts at speed right
out on to the platform to take up her Act 5 pose as
the dead queen's statue.

And then she sees Gerry and Nige are still on,
still telling the audience all the amazing things
that've happened offstage.

Which makes it still scene 2.

She's not due on for several pages.

Ah.

Uh oh.

So she just sort of stands there, middle of the
platform, frozen in mid-run, doesn't know what to
do with her hands, and now the whole audience
(and the place is packed out tonight for such a little

out-of-the-way town) has seen, running like a girl, a queen who's meant to be dead – which is the whole point, she has to be dead then come alive at the right moment for the play to work.

She takes three steps back.

She's now standing roughly where the curtain that's meant to hide her is meant to be.

She straightens her back, raises her hand, takes up her statue pose.

One or two people in the audience laugh uncertainly.

The boys are looking at her in confusion.

Then Gerry starts his lines again. They say their lines like she's not on the stage. Nige goes off and Ralph and Ed come on to say theirs. Ralph stares at her in a panic. He has a hard enough time remembering lines as it is. Stalwart Ed keeps going in his reedy voice. They get through the scene, then Frank and Joy and Jen and Tim and Tony and Tom etc troop on for scene 3 and they see her there and all stand back aghast.

Especially Joy, who's wheeling the curtain frame on that Grace is supposed to be hidden behind, and who's got so many lines about how they're all going to see something amazing which is hidden from them behind this very curtain right now.

Grace holds her pose.

She holds her hand just so. She looks straight through Joy. Joy finally gets it, stops wheeling the curtain aimlessly up and down the platform like a hospital nurse, and positions it in front of Grace.

Whew.

They start the scene.

The people in the audience who know the story already have been guffawing for the last several minutes. The people who don't, well, God help *them*. Now that she's behind the curtain she shakes her arm to get rid of the pins and needles. She's got twenty five lines till *behold and say tis well*. Then the curtain gets wheeled away and she has to hold the statue pose while they all look at her, first as a statue, then as a living body, and 120 lines before her cue to speak: *turn good lady our Perdita is found*. She gets her lines ready in her head.

You gods look down
and from your sacred vials
pour your graces
upon my daughter's head.
You gods look down
and from your sacred –
But –
ah.

Frank said a West End casting agent on holiday in the area is in tonight.

Grace behind the curtain breaks into a cold sweat.

It was Claire Dunn who cued her.

Was it? It was.

She's 99% sure.

Claire Dunn has sabotaged Grace's only chance so far at anything West End.

You gods look down

Did she do it on purpose?

Did she know what she was doing?

You gods look down

Next day the female members of STD (Sublime Tension Drama) (don't bother making the jokes, everyone in STD has heard them all before) are meeting in the cinema – which is like a pot with its lid on it on a lit gas ring in this heat – to rehearse a sticky bit of The World As It Rolled. The male members (har-har), except for Ed who's directing The World, are in the local hotel's very nice garden having beer and a pub lunch. They are lucky sods.

Ed gets them all to sit round on the platform in front of the cinema screen. He says he's got an exercise for them to do. He tells them he wants them to think about the word meander.

Me, he says. Ander.

They all look blank.

In other words, make myself other, Ed says. Make *yourself* someone *else*. Take a wander through the concept of multiple selfhood. Because this is the very beating heart of the story of David Copperfield. Think of all those different names he gets called all through his life, Trot, Trotwood,

Daisy, Davy. And yet he's still the same person. Isn't he? So I want us all to do an exercise where we literally *become* someone else in front of all our eyes. Yet we still remain ourselves. Let's go anticlockwise. Joy. You start.

Do what anticlockwise? Joy says.

Joy is Frank's sister who's been drafted in at the last minute, because someone else dropped out, to play Paulina in his Winter's Tale. She isn't really a drama type though her Paulina is really impressive for someone who's not a bona fide actor of serious intent; she usually works in an estate agent's, has taken the summer off to do this because Frank is directing the Shakespeare and asked her to, so is only here on sufferance and can never be arsed to play along with what she calls all the workshop shite.

I want you to other yourself, Ed says.

Anticlockwise? Joy says.

I want you to take the line: *The clock began to strike, and I began to cry simultaneously*, Ed says. And before you say it, I want you to go right back to the moment of birth of someone who's *in* you, but is *other* than yourself.

Yeah but I'll be doing that anyway when I'm acting, Joy says. Won't I? So why bother?

Ed looks personally hurt.

He is a sweet chap, gay. He's sleeping with Nige, everybody knows, though they're all acting like it's a really big secret. Grace has her own couple of secrets. She's sleeping with both Tom *and* Jen (Florizel *and* Perdita) and neither Tom nor Jen knows about the other. *Nobody* in the whole group knows, which takes some organizing, but so far she's pulling it off. Jen and Tom both think she's committed to each of them, at least for the summer. At the same time she's made it clear to both that she's not really available and can't commit for longer; she's told them about Gordon Stone, her longterm boyfriend at home.

(In reality there's no home and there's no such person. Gordonstoun is the name of a posh school in Scotland that her mother used to work at before she met her father. Prince Charles went there.)

An argument breaks out before any other inner selves have been accessed by any of the cast.

The argument is the same one they keep having. It is getting tiresome. It's about why Leontes in The Winter's Tale wigs out quite soon after the start of the play.

The argument is about feminism. Again.

Grace sighs.

But it's not *about* gender, she says. It's just a *blight*. A blight comes down on him, on his mind and on his country from nowhere. It's irrational. It *has* no source. It just happens. Like things do, they just suddenly change, and it's to teach us that everything is fragile and that what happiness we

think we've got and imagine will be forever ours
can be taken away from us in the blink of an eye.
You're bringing 1989 politics to a 1623 play.

1611, Ed says.

Okay, Grace says, but the point still stands. Give
or take a decade in the 1600s.

Yeah but you can't know that, Grace, unless
you're an expert in history between 1611 and 1623,
Ginette says.

For fuck sake, Grace says.

They bring up all the lines again about women's
utterance, women's tongues, the jealousy Leontes is
feeling because his wife is better with language than
he is.

Yeah but this is all just, like, notes in the margin,
Grace says. What's really happened is as random as,
I don't know, a plague. Like frost on flowers. A
blight. It comes from absolutely nowhere.
Shakespeare has Leontes say it. His brain's infected.

Yeah but an infection still comes from something
or somewhere, Ginette says.

And other themes in the play signal that the thing
that needs to be cured is the relations between the
genders, Jen says.

Even Jen, with whom she's secretly sleeping, is
siding against her.

Grace shakes her head.

They know nothing about real loss. None
of them.

It's *just what happens*, she says. A sad tale's best for winter. So Shakespeare injects sadness, like a device, a playwright's device, he infects things with winter precisely so that he can *have* a summer, make a merry tale come out of a sad one.

Ed puts on his teacher voice.

Let's look for a moment, shall we, at the very start, he says. The very first scene. What Camillo says is *it is a gallant child that physics the subject*.

Grace can't be bothered to argue any more.

Physics was never my subject, she says.

No, Grace, Ed says. Physic doesn't mean *physics* here.

Give me a break, Grace says.

It means something that makes people well, Ed says. And *subject* here means a citizen, the subjects, the people in the kingdom. It's about what makes the people in the kingdom ill or well.

And that's whether the person in charge is a misogynistic tyrannous bad leader, a bigoted useless king or governor who tells everybody that unless they toe his line they're traitors and betrayers, Ginette says.

Yeah and that's all tied in with the gender dichotomy in the play. Can't deny it, Grace, someone else says.

Then Claire says:

If only Tom was here too, eh Grace? Then we could all talk openly about Shakespeare's intentions in his use of the words infection and affection and what happens when people aren't as transparent with other people as they should be being.

What you on about, Clairey? Jen says.

I'm on about which of us in the company are getting a *surplus of Grace*, Claire says.

I've certainly had a surplus of this, Grace says. I'm off for a smoke.

Claire winks at her.

Come back a *new Grace*, yeah? Claire says.

It's, wow, like you know the whole play, Claire. All the places the word grace gets used. It's amazing how much of it you know off by heart, Ed says.

Photographic memory, Claire is saying. Come back soon, Grace. Jen and Tom'll be waiting, we all will. Hoping for a *better Grace*.

I don't see how anyone can play Hermione properly yet be so dead to the text, someone says behind Grace as she pushes the firedoors open.

Why d'you keep bringing Tom into it? Grace hears Jen say as the doors swing shut behind her.

Relief.

Blazing light after the dark.

Hot out here in the full sun. Grace, cold to the core, shivers. She stands for a minute, lights a cigarette.

She walks to the corner, looks out over the flat expanse of land beyond the town. There's a heat

haze off the tarmac at the edge where the
houses stop.

This summer, they've been saying in the papers,
is the finest summer of this whole century, even
better than the one in 1976. 1940. 1914.

She drops the cigarette half smoked, grinds it into
the pavement.

Fuck them and their themes.

She simply sets off.

She doesn't care where she's going, she's going
somewhere, anywhere away from the world as it
rolls, away from the envy with its own mini heat
haze coming off Claire, who's possibly after Tom or
maybe Jen, but above all has clearly seen the truly
amazing effect on every audience a statue that
comes to life can have when the people watching
don't expect it, and so, wants Grace's part.

Or maybe she just likes causing trouble.

A lot of people find that kind of thing
stimulating.

Grace shrugs as she walks along.

The sex with Tom is kind of what you'd expect,
does the job. The sex with Jen is pretty good, Jen is
unexpectedly heady and determined. There's a bit
of having to listen to Jen's emotional turmoil about
her brother who's a drug addict. But Grace has the
patience and the right facial (or facile) expression;
she's an actor. Anyway it's worth it to give herself
the space from Tom, who can't quite believe his

luck at getting to fuck someone who's got such a main role in the show and last time they did it told her he loves her and how in love he is, which always makes Grace literally want to throw up.

She walks past a house where some neighbours are having an altercation. A woman is standing on the pavement with her arm round the shoulder of a shamefaced boy. Her son? His mother? The woman has the boy in the grip of a loving vice and is shouting at a substantially bosomed woman in the doorway of the house, and what she's shouting is,

it's a brothel, it's nothing but a brothel you're keeping.

The woman in the doorway has a smile going up one side of her face while the other side is straight, which makes her face look a bit like a torturer. She says in a calm voice full of passive aggression, which, when Grace hears it, she decides to remember as a good example of someone like this should she ever have to act someone like it,

the boy's just enjoying himself, Mrs Mallard. He's just having a good time.

He's *twelve years old*, the woman on the pavement shouts back.

He's not doing anything to hurt anyone, Mrs Mallard, the smug woman in the doorway says as Grace walks past.

As she passes the boy casts a glance at Grace. She winks at him. He looks away.

He's got a mother.

He doesn't know how fucking lucky he is.

She crosses a parched marsh with its yellow burnt grasses and its noise of insects. She takes a single track road that opens up off to her right because it looks so nice. It's a road clearly not much used by anybody. There's a grassline running up the centre of it, and tree branches meeting over it, bramble bush tentacles reaching out towards each other from either side.

It's beautiful, she thinks.

She waves away some midges.

A tiny bird – a wren? flies across her path. Hello, bird.

Hedgerow.

Greenness.

Verge and leaf and grass, long seed-headed grasses.

The light gold, dark gold of the fields spreading back away from the sea, and the green of everything, green, dark green, the trees ahead down the road throwing long English shadows, like if you imagine a summer.

The patches of sunlight that come through them in the distance down the road, shining on its surface like a road shines after rain when the sun hits it.

Her inner grammar comes apart. Sentences don't have to comply. It's nice.

The swaying fullness of those trees.

Look what's happened to her in just twenty minutes roaming about under an English summer sun.

She's come over all thoughtful.

But that's summer for you. Summer's like walking down a road just like this one, heading towards both light and dark. Because summer isn't just a merry tale. Because there's no merry tale without the darkness.

And summer's surely really all about an imagined end. We head for it instinctually like it must mean something. We're always looking for it, looking to it, heading towards it all year, the way a horizon holds the promise of a sunset. We're always looking for the full open leaf, the open warmth, the promise that we'll one day soon surely be able to lie back and have summer done to us; one day soon we'll be treated well by the world. Like there really is a kinder finale and it's not just possible but assured, there's a natural harmony that'll be spread at your feet, unrolled like a sunlit landscape just for you. As if what it was always all about, your time on earth, was the full happy stretch of all the muscles of the body on a warmed patch of grass, one long sweet stem of that grass in the mouth.

Care free.

What a thought.

Summer.

The Summer's Tale.

There's no such play, Grace.

Don't be fooled.

The briefest and slipperiest of the seasons, the one that won't be held to account – because summer won't be held *at all*, except in bits, fragments, moments, flashes of memory of so-called or imagined perfect summers, summers that never existed.

Not even this one she's *in* exists. Even though it's apparently the best summer so far of the century. Not even when she's quite literally walking down a road as beautiful and archetypal as this through an actual perfect summer afternoon.

So we mourn it while we're in it.

Look at me walking down a road in summer thinking about the transience of summer.

Even while I'm right at the heart of it I just can't get to the heart of it.

Ten minutes later the road comes to an end in a tree glade with a couple of spaces for cars. To one side there's an old church, a small stone one with a graveyard settling round it, leafy, its stones skewy under old trees. Its gate is open. Its door is open at the end of its path. Music is coming out of its open door.

Who's playing Nick Drake in a church? Bryter Layter, pretty flute, very 1970s.

What trendy vicar thinks Nick Drake is good church music?

He's right. Hymn to timeless melancholy. Hymn to English summer.

The graveyard is overgrown, full of bees and flowers. Grace goes up the path between the flowers' nodding heads. She stands outside the door.

Someone inside the church is whistling along with the tune. There's a light scraping noise. The noise stops. It starts again. It stops. That explains the workman's van in the parking space.

There's a light coloured stone in the wall above her head. The words carved into it say:

THE NIGHT IS FAR SPENT
THE DAY IS AT HAND
LET US THEREFORE CAST OFF
THE WORKS OF DARKNESS
AND LET US PUT ON
THE ARMOUR OF LIGHT
ST PAUL : ROMANS
13 : 12
1   8   7   9

In days of old, she thinks. When knights were bold. And women weren't invented. They wrapped their arms around a tree. And had to be contented.

That old rhyme. She didn't even know she still

had it in her head. Her mother and father, her father was running the new car in, a Sunday afternoon, she sat on the back seat eight years old and laughed because they were laughing and it was funny and lovely.

You had to think up something that didn't exist in the times when knights were bold, and then make it rhyme. Her father was very good at thinking up rhymes though mainly the rhymes were about men doing things to women, things Grace didn't really understand but knew were meant to be funny.

In days of old when knights were bold and bras were not for burning. They took them off the girls at night to help them with the churning.

Laughter.

In days of old when knights were bold and women didn't work.

Her mother finished that one with the word berserk.

In days of old when knights were bold and girls were never blunt.

Don't, her mother said laughing. Don't dare.

What? I was only going to say *take a punt*, her father said.

Laughter.

Grace had laughed too, in the back. They both turned and looked at her laughing, exchanged a look with each other and laughed again but in a different way.

In days of old when knights were bold and women said don't dare. They pulled the ones they wanted into bedrooms by the hair.

Laughter, laughter.

Long ago laughter.

Were knights ever bold? Grace, twenty two, feels a chill at her back from the stone church wall she's leaning against.

A man in the church is bending to one of the long bench seats. He seems to be scraping it. Maybe he's cleaning it. He hears someone behind him and he stops, looks up, sees her in the doorway reading the stone.

He switches his cassette machine off.

Hi, he says.

Oh hi, she says.

He's about thirty, quite good-looking, a bit like James Taylor on the front of Sweet Baby James but with his hair tied back in a ponytail.

Don't let me disturb you, she says.

I was just about to say the same, he says. I'm sorry I was playing music, I didn't expect anyone to come in. Generally nobody does.

He puts the sander down, gestures to the little chapel behind him.

Please. Stay as long as you like, he says.

No, it's okay, I don't need to, she says, I'm not here because it's a church or anything.

Ah, he says. Okay.

293

I was just walking past, she says, and the door was open and I heard the music, I like Nick Drake.

You're a person of taste, he says.

What are you making? she says.

I'm restoring this pew, he says.

He tells her he's been replacing a piece of snapped-off seat and is cleaning and sanding the place where the new piece joins the old. He wipes away some little shreds of sanded wood. There's a slot in the seat where the wood is a different shade from the rest of the seat.

You can't even see a join, she says. Except for the colour difference. That's really good.

Not seeing the join, that's the whole point, he says.

How do you get it to look the same as the rest of the seat? she says. Or do you just leave it like that and it'll weather with time?

Little miracle, he says.

He holds up a tin of woodstain.

He puts it down, takes a cigarette from behind his ear and offers it to her.

That's okay. It's your only one, she says.

I've a tobacconist's shop right here in my pocket, he says.

He opens a tin, starts rolling another one then and there.

Oh. Okay then. Thanks, she says. What a great

thing it must be, to be able to make a seat like that look so good.

The best thing is, it'll last, he says. Decades. Simple pleasures.

Simple pleasures, she says. I was just walking along thinking about them. Well, about how I tend to wish pleasures were a lot simpler than they end up being.

He laughs.

He licks the cigarette paper along its edge.

Uh huh? he says.

Oh, you know, she says. How even when things are lovely it's like we can't help blocking them from ourselves. What a lovely summer it is and how, it's like, no matter what we do, we can't get near its loveliness.

He gestures to her to come over to the open door where he lights their roll-ups.

They stand in the cool stone shade.

Summer, he says.

Summer, she says.

You know it's also what the lintel in a building gets called? he says.

What is? she says.

Summer. The most important beam, structurally, he says. Holds up a floor, a ceiling, both. There's one, there, look.

He points behind them at a little balcony hanging as if in mid air.

Now that's what I call a lovely summer, he says.

Usually with such a good-looking man Grace'd just be looking at him and pretending to listen and thinking her own thoughts. But she is surprised to find herself quite interested in what he just said.

I never knew that, she says.

It can take a great weight, a summer, he says. It's why they also call horses that carry a great weight summers too.

Really? she says.

He raises his eyebrows, shrugs.

Are you making that up? she says. Take the piss out of a townie?

Nope, he says. I'm a townie myself.

Funny, she says leaning against an unexpected warm place in the stone on the threshold of the church and liking the feel of it on her arm. Like, how we overload summer most out of all the seasons, I mean with our expectations of it.

Nah, he says and nips the end of his rollie with a finger and thumb till it's out. Summers can take it. That's why they're called summers.

He tucks his smoke back behind his ear, smiles at her.

Is it out? he says. More than once I've set fire to myself.

It's out, she says. I think.

Want a coffee? he says. There's Nescaff in the back, and a kettle.

All right, she says.

I'm John, he says.

Grace, she says.

Meet me at the old tomb shaped like a table, Grace. There's just one like it, can't miss it, round the back there, he says.

Okay, she says.

It's got a skull on it, he says, but it's quite friendly-looking. Just warning you. Case you're squeamish.

I ain't fraid of no skull, she says.

See you there, then, he says.

His name's John Mison. He's a joiner and specialist carpenter. That's what it says on the side of the van parked at the gate; she can read it from here. She goes round the corner, walks between the curves in the grass, sits beneath the leaf dapple on the old flat-topped tomb.

He comes out carrying two mugs in one hand. He does have very nice hands. Workman hands. She takes the mug he gives her, turns it in her own hand. It's a red straw design, a Humphrey mug. *Drink it quick. Humphreys are slick.* He sees her turning it and reading it.

Gave you the best mug, he says. Hope no sugar's okay.

No sugar's fine, she says.

Good, he says.

A butterfly goes past, a white one. Then another.

It's a very preserve of butterflies out here, she says.

Sorry, a what? he says.

A very preserve of butterflies, she says. They only live a day. At least, that's what my mum used to say about them.

A very preserve, he says.

That's a line from a play I'm in, she says.

Pretty clever, that, to be preserved *and* only live a day both at once, he says.

That's Charles Dickens for you, she says. His words, not mine. His very preserve of butterflies has preserved the butterflies in his book David Copperfield for, uh, a hundred and forty years or so.

That what you do? he says. Student?

Graduated, she says. I'm a bona fide actress.

Sorry, a what kind? he says.

She tells him she's touring the region.

By yourself? he says.

She laughs.

I wish, she says. No, in a company. With a company.

He sits down in the grass with his back against the tomb, squints up at her.

Nice, to have company, he says.

Sometimes, yeah, she says.

Plays like what? he says.

She tells him about the Copperfield and the Shakespeare.

And in the Shakespeare I'm a queen whose husband goes mad and is convinced I'm having an affair with his childhood friend when I'm not, and because he's a king he banishes his friend, puts me in prison, throws his baby daughter away, inadvertently kills a son with his bitterness, and then I die too, she says.

God almighty, he says.

And at the end, sixteen years later, I get wheeled out as a statue of myself, and lo and behold I come alive and I'm not dead after all, she says.

What about the dead kids? he says. Do they come back too?

Only one of them, she says. It's a very uneasy play, really. Pretending to be a comedy.

So, were you alive all along then, and just faking being dead? he says.

That's not completely clear from the text, she says. It's possible. But it's also supposed to be possible that a wonder of wonders is happening and a statue that's been carved to look like me in later life comes to life, and *is* me in later life, though I've been dead for all those years. More magic than deception.

More magic than deception, he says. I like that.

Me too, she says. It feels pretty fine to act it. It's powerful.

Like that story about the man who makes clay models, brings them alive, gives them knowledge and art and all that, teaches them how to use law, how to be fair with each other, he says.

I don't know that story, she says.

Yeah, he's kind of a flash trickster, he makes humans out of clay, then steals the powers of the powers that be to give to his clay people. Then the powers that be get angry with him giving their powers to his mere creations, so they chain him to a rock and every day he gets pecked by the beak of an eagle, here, he says.

He touches his side.

Or maybe here, he says.

He touches his other side.

Which side's your liver on? he says.

Not sure, she says.

Both sides, to be safe, he says.

I'm getting pecked on both sides now, she sings. From up and down and still somehow.

They laugh.

Good voice, he says.

Thanks, she says.

I thought the Shakespeare play for the summertime was meant to be the one about fairies. Midsummer dream, he says.

Oh, the fairies, she says. The Winter's Tale's all about summer, really. It's like it says, don't worry, another world is possible. When you're stuck in the world at its worst, that's important. To be able to say that. At least to tend towards comedy.

He opens his arms wide to the leaves and the sky. Can't even imagine a winter right now, he says.

I bloody can, she says. Every second night I age years, winter summer winter summer. By the time I've finished this tour I'll be a bloody hundred years old.

My dad swears that if you don't wear your jacket inside out at midsummer out of respect to the fairies, the fairies'll cause you mischief all year, he says.

Uh huh, she says. Right.

He does it every year, says his dad did it and his dad did it, and his dad before them, and that we have to respect the lore, he says.

See, that's what I don't get about old customs and the like, she says. Because, why would fairies *want* anyone to wear a jacket inside out? What'd be the point?

So they can steal your wallet more easily, he says. He's got a market stall in town, my old dad. Fruit and veg. And if anyone comes to buy from him, and they've a bicycle, and they lean their bicycle up against his stall, well, he used to say to me, *nip under there John when you see anybody doing it and give the bike a push so it falls over.* Then he'd say to the person, *now then, that's the fairies telling you not to lean your bike up against my stall.* His mate does it for him now, crawls under the tarp from the back of the boxes and gives the bike a push. Over it goes. *The fairies*. His mate's seventy.

An old fairy, she says.

He laughs.

They can have my wallet if they want it, the fairies, he says. I don't care.

Don't you? she says.

Everybody's on about money these days, he says.

He shakes his head.

And all you want from life is to make new wood look like old, she says. You're a saint. Or a fool.

Neither, he says. Money always comes. Money isn't what matters.

Very unfashionable, she says. A man out of time.

I know all I need to know about time, me, he says.

He points upwards.

What? she says.

Listen, he says.

Right then the bell in the church tower tolls three times.

How did you do that? she says.

Inner clock, he says.

He starts singing, to an old tune she recognizes:

There will be sunshine. And lots of sunshine. The polar icecaps. Are melting down.

She laughs.

That's quite good, she says.

Get sun tan lotion, he sings. Here comes the ocean. We won't have to go to Spain to get brown.

You could join our theatre group, she says.

No thanks, he says. I like being me, me.

He stretches out on the grass next to the old tomb with his head on the humped part.

Hope whoever's under here won't mind, he says. Hope they had a few good summers, whoever they are. Too poor for a stone. Or just didn't need one, maybe. In the old days people didn't. Because, who's going to forget where your beloved's buried? Nobody, not while it matters. You know, back in your, what's his name, Dickens. Back in his time, there was a summer, middle of the 1800s, that was every bit as lovely as this one. But because it was just after they put the sewage system in, in London town I mean, and people all had toilets in their houses for the first time, water closets they called them, and the system took all the sewage straight into the river, and it poisoned the river, thousands and thousands of people, well, died.

They both laugh.

They hold themselves and laugh.

They laugh like anything, till they cry with laughter.

They get their breath back. She stretches herself out all along the top of the tomb. She knocks on it with her fist.

Sorry for laughing, she says as if to the person in it. Couldn't help it.

Don't know why it was so funny. But it was, he says.

Who looks after this place? she says. The roses smell amazing.

No idea, he says. Lovely here, though. Have to say it's nice working here.

Then lying in the grass John Mison simply says what sounds at first like a poem or an incantation but is just a list of the names of flowers. Flower after flower. Plant after plant.

Ragwort. Ramsons. Meadow buttercup. Chickweed. Stitchwort. Cranesbill. Vetch. Nettle. Dove's foot cranesbill. Ivy. Sweet Robert. Sweet violet. Meadowsweet. Willowherb. Cow parsley. Cowslip. Primrose. Goosegrass. Forget-me-not. Yellow archangel. Speedwell. Valerian. Daisies. Mayweed. Lords and Ladies. Groundsel. Dandelion. Not forgetting dandelion clock.

Yellow archangel, she says. Pretty. Sweet Robert.

The archangel's over there at the wall, he says. Flowers in spring, just looks like nettles now. But it won't sting you. They call it aluminium, and artillery. Because of its silver colour. The Robert's there too. Pretty little flowers, red, pink, cranesbill. It's a healer. Good for skins and wounds, good apparently for where there's been radiation, they should plant it round Chernobyl, sweet Robert, helps clean out the soil, good for oxygen. Smells horrible though. Which is why

its other names are things like stinking bob.
Crow's foot.

You know a lot about flowers, she says.

I like them, he says.

Then they stop talking.

They lie there for a while, her up on the tomb,
him down on the ground.

Collared doves occasionally flurry and call in the
trees above them.

She closes her eyes.

They say nothing for whole minutes, several
complete minutes.

She has never been as happy as she is right now.

Then she hears him roll over and get up.

Hey, he says. Come with me. I found the grandest
little thing day before yesterday, on an old stone,
when I was having my break.

She follows him round to the back of the church
where he bends to the ground.

In among the bramble bushes right at the back of
the plots there's an eaten-away stone. It's got words
written on it.

They both have to get quite low to the ground to
read the words, which are greened and yellowed
with moss.

Listen to this, John Mison says.

The tree in me shall never die. Be I ashes be I
dust. That is the tree that joins the sky. To earth
and us. The tree in me shall never die. No lovers

sleeping breath compare. With her shy music in the sky. Of leaves and air.

They both sit back on their haunches.

How pretty, she says.

Shy music, he says.

What a lovely poem, she says. Someone really loved someone. Is there a name? A date?

Just the words, he says. Who needs a name or a date when you can be remembered by something like that? Hope I will, when I go.

You can't go. You can't go anywhere, she says. It's not allowed.

He laughs.

I won't if you don't, he says.

He leaps to his feet.

I've to finish that pew, he says. You can put the stain on for me, if you want. Then we'll both have changed the course of history.

They walk back round, collecting the coffee mugs up off the top of the tomb-table as they pass it.

It's a self sacrifice, this, by the way, he says. My favourite part of the whole job. Putting the woodstain on.

I'm honoured, she says.

You are, he says.

What Grace remembered three decades later was that there was a fine summer's day back when she

was in her twenties and on the Winter's Tale /
World As It Rolled eastern counties tour when she'd
gone on a walk, found a church with a man
working in it, had a nice uncomplicated afternoon
in a summer that'd become way too complicated,
one when she'd made matters worse for herself by
sleeping with too many people, not eating enough
and not looking after herself well enough, and that
she'd left that churchyard feeling more free, more
herself, more hopeful than she'd felt for a long time.

Here are some of the things she didn't remember
from that time:

She didn't remember that after it she'd walked
back to the cinema.

Rehearsal was over. Nobody was there.

She'd had to go and find them all in the pub
garden, where she ate a baked potato with beans
and cheese in it without it being complicated, being
anything but delicious, which was, for her, at this
point in her life, when it came to food, quite a feat.
The World As It Rolled cast was angry with her for
not turning up. She'd laughed at their anger and
hugged every one of them, Jen and Tom and Ed and
whoever. She'd even hugged Claire Dunn, they'd all
looked a bit stunned when she did. Life's too short,
she'd said to Claire. Stop it. Life's too short, she'd
said to Jen and Tom together too. If you want me,
you've both got me, for now anyway, and that'll have
to be enough. If it's too unsimple for you, then tough.

Jen and Tom both disappeared from her life after that summer. Possibly even together.

It had been something of a relief.

She also didn't remember how that evening in the cinema she'd stood at the front of the stage and said the lines about remembering a mother's face in a way that made the whole show pivot on those lines, lending The World As It Rolled a real depth it hadn't yet acquired. The audience had given them a standing ovation, and afterwards the whole group, pretty much, approached her with their eyes shining, and hugged her, because something real had happened, and the next day strangers, people from the town, or holidaying in the town, had stopped her in the street over and over again to say thank you, and their eyes shone like the group's eyes had shone at her the night before.

It's like you literally *were* another person, Ed had said that night.

But thirty years later? she'd forgotten being that other person for ever. She'd forgotten, too, that one of the people who stopped her in the street the next day was a West End casting agent who took her by the hand and said, you were so good about mothers tonight, and you were so good as the mother in The Winter's Tale, and I've got a role that'd suit you down to the ground in an upcoming commercial if you'd like to call me on this number and arrange a screen test.

Walking along in the future looking for an old English church she visited once three decades ago and vaguely remembered as a special place, what she came to instead was a massive wire fence that seemed to block off most of the common.

The fence was a double fence. In between the two was a newly tarmacked road. A notice on the outer fence said:

THESE PREMISES PROUDLY
PROTECTED AND PATROLLED
24 HOURS A DAY BY
SA4A
CAUTION
THIS FENCE IS ELECTRIFIED
ALARM SYSTEM
CCTV RECORDING
IS IN OPERATION
FOR THE PREVENTION AND
DETECTION
OF TRESPASS AND CRIME

She walked alongside these fences for a while hoping she was going in the right direction.

When she met a woman out walking a scruffy little dog she asked her if there was a church anywhere near here with an old graveyard round it.

The woman shook her head.

Then she said,

oh, maybe you mean the Armour?

Very possibly, Grace said.

It's disused, I mean it's a discontinued church, what's the word? the woman said. Disestablished. You can't get through this way any more. You used to be able to.

Why so high? Grace said. Is it a prison?

It's a government place for people who don't belong in this country, the woman said. But you can get to the churchyard if you double back. Take the road at the end there, go down the cul de sac and up the pedestrian lane, cross the field when it ends and follow the cliff walk.

Grace asked the woman, who was bending to pick up dogshit in a bag, how long it'd take her to get there.

Half an hour at the most, the woman said.

Then the woman threw the bag with the shit in it as if to get it up over the fence. The bag caught in the razorwire on the outer fence and hung there torn open.

Bullseye, the woman said.

Grace looked at her in astonishment.

She thought about asking the woman why she'd just done that.

She decided she'd rather not – better not – get into it.

She turned and walked back the way she'd come.

She headed towards the coast.

Britain was a confusing place these days.

Was Bullseye the name of the woman's dog, maybe?

Or did she mean she'd hit a bullseye by throwing the dogshit on to the razorwire? Like kids did with each other's trainers on power lines?

So did she do it because she didn't like immigrants?

Or didn't like SA4A?

Did she do it for fun? for no reason at all?

She'd looked like a respectable person.

Let it go.

Grace did.

Look at her now, walking along the eroding edge of eastern England, in the future and the present and the past all at once. She was keeping to the new footpath and away from the dangerous edge like all the signs told her to. As she walked, more pieces of the Dickens show they toured back then came fully formed up from wherever they'd got buried inside her head.

Can I say of her face – altered as I have reason to remember it, perished as I know it is – that it is gone, when here it comes before me at this instant, as distinct as any face that I may choose to look on in a crowded street?

Grace had no memory, none at all, of herself on the cinema platform standing in the dark and the light saying these words David Copperfield says about his dead mother.

But that night back then, with such a channelling of her own mother's long-gone face entering her in the moment she said these lines, it so happened that several people in the audience burst into tears, were pierced by the brightness, the vividness, of the return inside *them* of what they'd thought they'd lost and forgotten.

She didn't remember.

She was thinking, instead, as the lines from the past fell away and she walked along, about what it was, the commerce between people.

What was it that people wanted from each other?

What had her mother and father wanted that had gone so wrong?

What had she wanted from Jeff?

What did he ever want from her, or for her?

What did Ashley give him that Grace hadn't or couldn't?

What had they all wanted from each other in that vote, say, the one that had split the country, split her own family as if with a cheesewire, sliced right through the everyday to a bitterness nobody knew what to do with, one so many people used to hurt people with, whichever way they'd voted, a vote that could now be so anathema to one of her own kids and so like a permission to be foul to others for the other, so important to her, but so much old hat to a bright young person like that girl Charlotte that she could call it *a fly on a corpse*?

And if it were all to be taken away from us, she thought. Say Sacha and her apocalyptic instinct, the thing that wakes everyone in both houses in the middle of the night because Sacha is shouting so loudly in her sleep again, the vision of the world on fire, blight on her daughter's mind – say it really was real after all.

Well, don't be stupid. It wasn't.

Nothing like that was really ever going to happen.

Nothing really disruptive to life as they knew it.

The blight was all in the mind, not in the world.

But say, just say it was. Say it did.

Then what would have been the point of it all?

What were we here *for*?

To make as much money as possible?

To have all those people shouting your name at you, or even a name that's *not* yours, like famous Claire Dunn faking it on the TV?

Was being on this earth really all about who owned a tree in a garden? About whether it gave you satisfaction and pleasure and fulfilment when you looked at a tree *because it was yours*, but when you thought it *wasn't* yours you longed to remove that tree?

She saw a church tower, off to the left.

She turned inland. She slid herself down a

dog-path between bushes towards the bare trees round that tower.

But when she got there she didn't recognize the place as anywhere she'd ever been before.

Was this it?

She was a bit disappointed.

Well, it was a long time ago.

Summer, then.

Church of the Armour of Light. What a strange name.

In days of old, when knights were bold.

Her mother turning to look at her, laughing, but with a hurt look on her face.

The churchyard gate was locked. So she climbed over the little stone wall. She crossed the graves in the winter sun and sent a scatter of birds from branches. It was beautiful here, even though it wasn't anything like she remembered. So it had been worth coming for that, very pretty, even in winter, even though there was nothing here but a lot of old graves and dead leaves.

She tried the church's door.

Locked.

She stood on one of those metal boxes that has electricity stuff inside it. She peered through the bottom of a latticed window.

There was nothing at all inside the church. It was just an empty stone space.

I wonder where the seats went, she thought.

As she did, it came vividly into her head that she had, of all things, actually helped mend a church seat in there.

So I did!

He'd replaced a bit of wood in the seat, the man, and he let me paint it for him.

(She stepped down off the metal box.

She was smiling at the thought.)

He was restoring it. He let me paint it so it'd be the same colour as the rest of the wood it was made of.

She leaned against the side of the church and looked round her at all the sunken stones, the bared structures of the trees.

There was a grave that was a kind of box shape, wasn't there? I sat on it, or lay down on it.

Did I even fall asleep on it in the warm?

She pushed herself off the side of the church and went round to the side of the graveyard. More graves, more bushes and grass. But there *was* one of those box graves there under the branches, as big as a table or a high single bed.

She went over to it and read the words on it.

It was the tomb of Thomas Lummis, and of his wife, Anna, and other members of the Lummis family including a baby, Marjorie Lummis, who only lived eight months.

Dates. A skull relief, with what looked like draped veils, theatre curtains, above it.

She didn't remember any of that.

But wasn't there a poem?

She walked all the way round the stone slabs.

No, there was no poem here.

She leaned on the tomb and she put her hands over her eyes.

A small beautiful stone, with a poem on it. Somewhere round the back, by a compost heap. Was that right?

But the back of the Armour of Light church was all fenced off.

The wire was broken open, though, at dog height, fox height. She pushed herself through the gap. She poked a hand through some overgrowth. She could feel something deep inside it. She snapped some of the twiggy stuff away. She pushed the rest back. It sprang back at her in turn.

But there definitely was a stone, back then, with a poem carved into it. And an incredibly nice man, I met him for, what, two or three hours, he was a joiner, I can't remember his name. James? John? and we talked, we just talked, about nothing much, and we did nothing much, we just hung out, lay about in the graveyard like friends though we didn't know each other, we'd only just met, and we never even thought about keeping in touch, and he let me help him paint a church seat he was mending so it looked, well, not good as new. Good as old. He showed me an old gravestone he'd found with no name on it, no date, obviously a hundred, couple of hundred years old. And we both got right down on the ground to be able to read it.

That's what she remembered.

Here was the stone. Still here. It was old and curved, eaten into by weather and plants. She pulled the growth away from its front. She got as close to the ground as she could to read its poem. She followed the words on it with her finger.

Such a pretty verse.

She held her phone down low and took a photo of it to show the kids.

She stood back up. She was late.

There was a train to catch. In ten minutes there'd be two irate kids standing on a pavement.

She got herself back through the hole in the fence. She got a move on.

It wasn't till she was halfway back to town on the cliff path, walking in the sea air with the sky so wide all round her, that she looked at the photo she'd taken and saw that though it was still a beautiful picture you couldn't see any of the words on the stone to read them, and all she'd actually got a record of was a blur of twigs, a surface of old stone, some bright lichen.

So, Art says, this is how we're going to get through this time.

It's nearing the end of the month of March. Charlotte and Art are on different coastlines of the same country. He's east, she's west.

They haven't been this far apart, and for so long, for a couple of years now so are both finding it odd.

Or maybe it's just her who's finding it odd.

Given that what Art's found is love, and so on. *Partner.* Art doesn't like the words girlfriend and boyfriend. Art and Charlotte have been *not-partners* for more than three years now. Deciding to be *not-partners* is one of the best things they ever did.

But it's still weird, to Charlotte anyway. A bunch of strangers he only met last month have magicked themselves into becoming his family. Equally weird, *she's* now living with *his* aged aunt at *his* dead mother's old house in Cornwall, a house so huge that it feels pointless. What also feels a mixture of too-meaningful and pointless is how he's not here but most of his stuff is. His books, notebooks, are scattered round the house splayed open page-down as if he just left the room for a minute. The mug he likes best is still upside down on the kitchen draining board. A T-shirt that smells of him is still on the back of that chair here in her bedroom. In his own bedroom that old plastic water bottle he always keeps next to the bed to drink from if he wakes up in the middle of the night has water in it from the last time he filled it. His bed still has the dip in the pillow where his head last was, covers folded back like he got out of it ten minutes ago, because the last time he was in this room he didn't think for a moment he'd be anything other than back in that bed a couple of days after they'd done their Worthing work and gone to Suffolk to meet the old man.

Things can change fast. They just do.

The whole world's learning that lesson simultaneously right now, one way or the other.

One of the things that has changed is that this is the first day they've spoken for about a fortnight.

Charlotte is trying not to feel resentful. But it was *so* love at first sight that since that moment of first sight he hasn't come home. He spent the first weeks away travelling into London and staying there with his new love, when university teachers were still going to work, then travelling back with her to her mother's at the weekends. When lockdown happened he'd made his choice.

You listening? he says.

We're speaking on the phone, Charlotte says. What does that tell you about whether I'm listening or not?

Actually not that much, Art says. Though since you're on your stupid James Bond phone that's about all you *can* do, so I suppose you must be.

Art is irate because at the turn of the year Charlotte reverted to a Sony C902 from 2008, a phone that came with a special set of decade-old Quantum of Solace tie-ins ready-installed, some preview stills, screensavers, a ringtone she's never listened to. Charlotte bought it before Christmas so the net would neither own her nor succeed in its mission to become her new phantom limb or brain.

You *can* access the web on it.

But she told Art you can't, that it's too old.

Charlotte's non-web, Art said when she told him this.

If you'd a smartphone, he says now, we'd be able to see each other. I'd be able to see where you are. Where are you?

Sitting on the stairs, she says.

It's a lie.

If you had a smartphone I'd be able to see which stairs you're on right now, he says.

And why would you want to? she says.

(It cost you more than *my* phone, Art said when the box arrived from eBay and she unwrapped it and set it up and first phoned him on it.

She was in the bedroom looking out at the garden. He was in the piece of garden they've turned into an allotment. They waved at each other while they spoke.

I can't believe you paid that much for a phone that *won't* do things, he said.

Negative capability, she said. I don't want all those old shed-skin selves following me everywhere putting their footprints all through the good clean new-fallen snow of my life.

More proof of how cold you are, Art had said.

I think you mean cool, Charlotte said.

No, I definitely mean cold, he said.

Then he told her it was a particularly dyspeptic thing for an internet artist, writer and publisher to do.

Dyspeptic? she said.

Ornery, he said.

Or – ? she said.

Irascible, he said. Waspish.

Are you looking up adjectives on your phone while we're having this conversation? she said.

Maybe, he said.

See? she said. *That's* why.)

Anyway, he says. I'm phoning because listening and communicating and staying in touch with each other is how we're going to get through this time for sure.

Not that *this time*'s going to be over for any of us very soon, she says. I have a feeling this time's here to stay, one way and another.

She sits on her bed, stares in the little light there is at the chair shoved up against the door of her room.

No, Art says. Times do pass. They do. But we have to choose to live through our times as mindfully as we can.

Pff, Charlotte says.

Which is why I had this idea about the structure of our day that I wanted to talk to you about, he says.

Our day, Charlotte says.

Well, your day, Art says. And mine. And to some extent, yes, everybody's.

If this, Charlotte says, is going to be you telling me what to do even though you're four hundred miles away and officially someone else's boyfriend –

Partner, Art says.

Instructing me, Charlotte says, about me structuring my days with regular mealtimes and being up by 8am and not letting my day lose its shape and doing exercise etc. Well I know all that stuff already inside out. Being just as self employed as you. Isolation's what our everyday life is like. No?

She hopes she sounds blithe enough.

But I don't mean just you and me. I mean *all* of us, Art says. You know. All of humanity.

You want to talk to the whole of humanity about the structuring of its day? she says. Ambitious.

We're all in the same boat now, he says.

Yeah, albeit with an awful lot of humanity still stuck in, you know, steerage, she says.

So, he says. One of the ways we can get through this is every day for you and me to just say hello. Like we are right now, I mean personally, intimately, on the phone.

Us phoning each other, she says. That's your eureka?

Calling each other expressly every single day, he says, just for a few minutes, no pressure. But also, get this. We make it an aesthetic practice. We tell each other expressly, consciously, something we've happened to see or experience that day.

Expressly, Charlotte says.

Yes, Art says.

How else would we tell each other? she says. By *not* saying it?

Uh, Art says.

And if that's what you're saying, Charlotte says. Does your Elisabeth know about you phoning me right now asking me to be personal and intimate every day with you?

That's not what –, Art says.

How is Elisabeth, by the way? Charlotte says.

She's fine. And that's not what I mean, and you know it isn't, Art says.

And how's the old man? she says.

He's fine, Art says. Thank God. Thank God he's here, because the care home he was in this time last year has a lot of people very sick in it. Nobody's been tested there. His carer told us. His carer comes in every day, she sees quite a few people in the course of a day, not just him.

Has she got masks and gloves? Charlotte says. Nobody seems to.

She bought herself some masks on Amazon, Art says. She has to put them on secretly at the front door because her work bans the carers it employs from using anything since nobody's been given it officially and their line manager's been told to avoid accusations of inequality and not to report shortages.

Christ, Charlotte says. Christ almighty.

I know, Art says. For some reason the government wants them all equally in danger. Plus the people they visit and care for.

How's Elisabeth's family? Charlotte says.

Everybody's fine, Art says, Elisabeth's mother's fine. And her partner, she's fine. But it's quite a small house now for all of us. So Elisabeth and I have converted the front room into a bedroom. I best not stay on the phone too long. Anyway. I was saying. We could, I mean you and me, Art and Charlotte, do this every day, just as a token, a little door open into each other's day.

I hear you, she says. You're saying I'm token.

No I'm not, Art says.

You're asking me if it'll be okay by me if you phone me or I phone you every day, she says. Yes?

Yes, Art says. But. Then we listen to the thing each of us tells the other, and we go away and *write up* the thing the other person's told us. I tell *you* something I've thought or seen or whatever, then you tell *me* something you've thought or seen or whatever. Then *I* go away and write what I remember or took from what you told me, and *you* do the same with what I told you. Then we put it online, and people, anyone, can join in with their own comments or thoughts if they want. Like giving a gift out to the rest of the world from our own isolation every day. To keep the days going. To help mark them, for you and me, *and* not just for you and me.

Charlotte looks at the line of light coming in at the edge of the blind.

Charlotte? Art says. You there? Hello?

So what gift are you going to give me from your isolation today, then? Charlotte says.

Okay. For instance, he says. I just saw a pigeon fly past the window and it had a long piece of twig in its mouth, and it was so long, the twig, it was so much bigger than the bird, that it was sort of unwieldy for it to fly with it. But the pigeon still did. It kept having to correct its balance, adjust to being pulled lopsided. But it did.

Silence.

Then:

is that *it*? Charlotte says.

Uh, Art says.

The sum total vision of your day? Charlotte says. The pressing thing you saw and wanted to tell me?

Yes, Art says. But. Obviously. Because, because from seeing this, I knew, I know, don't I, that that pigeon'll be making a nest with that twig. And that's really meaningful right now in this world where everything is so surreal and seems to be coming apart at the seams for so many people, especially people who are stuck at home. Whereas, in nature, creatures are rushing to *make* themselves homes. It *is* meaningful. It is. It's hopeful, and natural. You can't deny it.

Right, Charlotte says. And you think this is worth telling the lockdown world about, *because*?

Why are you blocking my benign analysis of what I've experienced and my determination to connect through it with others and let them connect with me and you? Art says.

I'm not, Charlotte says.

You're being quite chippy, Art says. I'd forgotten how unromantic you are.

Unromantic's better than being a clichéd and stupefied-by-love romantic any day, Charlotte says.

Are you jealous? Art says.

No, Charlotte says.

I feel a bit better, Art says. It's quite like bodily being with you, you being this grouchy. Anyway. Now. You tell me something you thought or saw. And then we go away and write down our take on each other's moment, and then we post both versions, our own and the other person's. And then – do you think we should post it online via the Art in Nature site?

Charlotte winds the drawstring on her pyjama trousers round and round her finger really tightly till her finger starts to pulse. Then she whips it off again very fast.

I've been thinking, she says. I'm not sure I want to keep going on our Art in Nature platform much longer.

Silence.

I've been meaning to say, she says.

Right, he says. Okay. Well. Yes. You're right. It has to change. It has to meet the new situation head on. So. Would, would we maybe call it something else, something new? How about Art in Nurture?

How about Art Inertia? Charlotte says.

Ah, Art says. I see.

What I'm saying is, I don't want to do the Art in Nature project at all any more, she says.

You mean you're leaving the project? he says.

(He sounds hurt now.

Good.)

And anyway, she says. If we *were* to do what you're suggesting, what we're doing wouldn't exactly be art. Would it? Not what you're proposing.

How do you mean? Art says.

It's just not what art, lower case a, is about, she says.

Charlotte sitting in the dark picks at the already red raw side of a fingernail with her thumbnail.

How about you tell me again one more time in our lives, like I'm not allowed to know for myself or decide, and you're the only authority, what art lower case a *is* about, then? Art says.

Art lower case a, she says, is, is, it's uh about the moment you're met by and so changed by something you encounter that it uh takes you both into and beyond yourself, gives you back your senses. It's a, a shock that brings us back to ourselves.

If that were true there's enough shock happening all across the world to make the whole of the world right now the biggest ever art project there's ever fucking been, he says.

Well, she says, well. Well, art lower case a always

was about our getting to grips with concepts like mortality, and randomness –

And are we really going to have a lockdown argument about art? Right now? he says.

Randomness, she says, and contingency, and –

She picks again at the place on her finger, which now seems to be bleeding.

Uh huh, he says. Okay. You keep finding the big words for what's happening to us all so that you won't have to think about what's happening to us all, yeah? And I'll sit and contemplate how my pigeon with a twig just wasn't striking enough to count, and how here I was, thinking wrongly all along that art lower case a was something to do with coming to terms with and understanding all the things we can't say or explain or articulate with help from something which we know will help us feel and think then articulate those things, even at times like this when feeling and thinking and saying anything about anything are under impossible pressure.

Except, she says. That art lower case a isn't ever about helping anyone.

Oh really? he says. Who amputated your ethos?

What art *does* is, it exists, Charlotte says. And then because we encounter it, we remember we exist too. And that one day we won't.

At the other end of the phone Art yawns.

He has a tendency to yawn, she knows from her

years of living with him, when he's particularly angry.

Then Charlotte yawns too.

I just caught your yawn, she says. So much for isolation.

Yeah, he says. Tell you what. I'm feeling a bit rattled now. Maybe we'll talk about this another day.

Okay, she says.

Okay, he says.

And thanks for phoning, she says. And forgive me for being a bit, you know.

I'll forgive you if we finish this phonecall with you telling me something you saw or heard, he says.

I can't, she says. I've got to go. I want to uh go and help Iris with the rooms. Or she'll do it all herself.

I was just about to ask, Art says. How's she doing?

Great, Charlotte says.

(She hasn't actually seen Iris for three days.)

She's amazing, she says. She's been cycling to town and back, delivering bags of food and things to people thirty years younger than she is, and yelling hello at everyone she passes, asking them if they need anything or if she can help. I couldn't, can't, persuade her not to go out. I tried. There's no stopping her.

Can't tell old Iris what to do, he says. Nobody can. You're so alike.

Charlotte's heart sort of folds in two. It hurts inside her.

I came in from the garden and caught her dragging one of the mattresses up to the third floor, you know, up the spiral staircase, she says. I said, can I help you with the others? and she said, no, darling, this is the last one. Which means she'd already got the six other mattresses up there. By herself. On her own steam. Without even telling me. She's actually in great form.

Great form, Art says. Now *there's* a good name for a web page like the one I'm talking about. Talk tomorrow? When do the people all arrive?

This is the precise point at which Charlotte takes the phone away from her ear and presses the hang-up button.

She puts the phone in her pyjama jacket pocket.

She is close to tears.

Why is she nearly crying?

Because of something quite unexpected. The bright sides of graffitied trains and the smudges on the insides of train and bus windows where people have pressed their noses.

She is now crying because she is missing these things so much.

Just thinking about it. Thinking about a

pigeon. And Art seeing it with a twig in its beak, and about a smudge on a window on a train they were on not that long ago, though in truth it's a different life ago. And some orange-jacketed workmen in the sidings of a station they passed through. She fills with love for everything and everybody, every single human being, young, old, all of them, who's ever thought about or not thought about seeing a pigeon fly past, or ever left an oily nose or mouth or finger smudge on a public transport window.

The feeling fills her so full that it has to come out at the eyes. There's nowhere else for it to go.

She cries with love for Art.

She cries for their intrepid selves, for their travelling around, Art sitting next to her on a train, on a bus, for them both slamming the doors on the new car and heading off out into the world, her in the driver's seat, Art lying flat out on the back seat, which he likes doing because it reminds him of when he was a kid.

The level of love has blocked her nose now.

She sits in the bedclothes, breathes through her mouth and misses her mother, who died in 2012, and her father, who went the year after.

Dear God.

She is now completely without family.

She is living in the house of someone else's family, not hers.

She puts her hands over her face and cries soundlessly into her hands.

Come on.

Get a grip.

Thank God they're dead now and they missed this and you're not sitting here worrying about them.

Get up. Go downstairs.

Help Iris.

She doesn't move.

Outside the day is happening regardless, full of birds doing things in the air etc.

Charlotte sits in the dark.

She looks at the side of her finger but it's too dark to see what's bleeding and what isn't.

She looks at the line of light still getting in at the edge of the blind.

If she had some gaffer tape she could stick the blind to the window frame and stop that light getting in.

There will be gaffer tape downstairs.

But that would mean going downstairs.

Okay. There are two chairs. One is jammed up against the door. She could use the other one, balance a pillow on the back of it and let it rest against the blind so the blind presses back against the window. Then that line of light will disappear.

She gets up, takes Art's Pussy Grabs Back T-shirt off the back of the chair, throws it into a corner of the room. She picks the chair up. She moves it over to the window. She takes a pillow, positions it.

The light lessens.

Charlotte. Yes. *Charlotte.*

Who used to think herself quite revolutionary.

Everything's got to change. Everything.

Now? Everything has.

Though Iris isn't so sure.

Christ but there's <u>so much</u> you should be blogging about, Iris had taken to saying every time she saw Charlotte anywhere near one of the computers.

Charlotte had sent the three other people in the Art in Nature team home before the lockdown.

Why did you do that? Iris said.

They've got families to be with, Charlotte said. And anyway, we shouldn't be cohabiting with so many people.

We need them, Iris said. Can they work from home? You should all be writing about the PPE shortage. About a too-late response from a useless and distracted government who never thought for a minute they'd end up governing anything. Whose only thought about state was how to dismantle it as fast as possible. Who thought it was all going to be such a *blast*, being in power, making lots of money for themselves and their pals.

Uh huh, Charlotte said.

You should be writing about how many people have died and are going to die in this country because of this government's rank carelessness, Iris said. They're saying twenty thousand deaths will be good. Good!

(Iris has friends in Italy who've kept them in touch with the speed of catastrophe.)

Get on to the team, Iris said. Get them writing. About how the hedgefunders have made billions already out of what's happening. Billions going into their accounts from other people's losses, while nurses and doctors and cleaners have to wear binliners. Binliners. A government treating them like rubbish. The NHS is *not* happy to let people die. That's the difference between them and this government, happy to count the heads of their so-called herd, like we're cattle, like they think they own us and have the right to send thousands of us to slaughter to keep the money coming in. Peevish. Too focused on their infantile Brexit obsession to accept offers of help and equipment from our neighbours. I bet you anything they're getting their data scientist pals and advisers and their friends at Google to *model pandemic data* while they talk a lot of Dunkirk spirit shit to a public they're selling down the river.

Uh huh, Charlotte said.

Write about how the people who've never been properly valued are all holding this country together, Iris said. The health workers and the everydayers, the deliverers, the postmen and women, the people working the factories, the supermarkets, the ones holding all our lives in their hands. Write about that. The mighty Etonians brought low one more time and the meek revealed as the real might after all. Because believe me, it can go either way from here, we need to think about it, and fast, and we need to get united just as fast, because in my experience the mighty don't like it when the meek get elevated.

United in what, though?

In isolation?

Charlotte shook her head.

Imagine. She used to call herself an online activist, Charlotte, who knew now she was never anything but a revolutio-lite, a sort of Good Life Bless This House sitcom revolutionary, a nostalgia-revolutionary. Who, even though she was born two decades after the 1970s happened, and even though that decade, as she knows from reading countless books and watching countless films, was one of the most fiercely politicized and prescient and fragmented in history, had focused at length, in her dissertation about culture and the 1970s, on why Gilbert O'Sullivan, though he was a grown adult, had chosen to wear 1940s schoolboy clothes to launch his first songs into popular culture and what this had meant for his subsequent lyrics, chart positioning and cultural legacy.

Charlotte. Nothing more than an alone again naturally no matter how I try why oh why oh why sort of revolutionary.

For instance, the only word she'd really heard, really recognized, in that typical Iris outpouring was the word *blast*. She recognized the word because just then it was a bit like there'd been a bomb blast very near her head, one that had knocked her senses and all her cognitives sideways, leaving her lopsided, strangely deaf, nothing to say.

I'm so sorry, Iris, she said. I'm feeling very much at a disconnect right now.

Nothing's not connected, Iris said.

Iris is Art's aunt. Charlotte's not related to her. She's a seasoned lefty activist. She won't tell Charlotte how old she is, but she must be in her eighties. Greenham, Porton Down; she apparently also used to help run a sort of commune in this very house, years ago. Then someone chucked the commune out and left the house uninhabited and rotting.

Then Art's business-minded mother, Iris's sister, who'd liked it here, bought the empty falling-down house for herself and renovated it. Iris is always exclaiming about walking into walls that didn't exist when she first lived here.

Then Art's mother died, left the house and

contents to Art with the proviso that Iris can live here till she dies.

Then Art and Charlotte moved their Art in Nature team down here to live here too. Free lodgings.

Now that everything's changed she and someone else's aunt are the only people living in this cavernous house. They each have a floor of it to themselves. The floor Charlotte's room is on has six other bedrooms on it. Charlotte hasn't seen anything else of the house, or of this floor, except this room and the bathroom next door to it, for three days now. *I'll be back in a minute*, Charlotte had said to Iris. That was three days ago.

Every night Iris knocks on the door and leaves a plate of food and a jug of water outside.

The first night she said,

are you running a temperature?

No, Charlotte said from the other side of the door.

A cough? Iris said.

No, I'm fine, Charlotte said. I really am. I'm not ill.

So this isn't a case of you isolating because you're feeling ill? Iris said.

No, Charlotte said. It's a case of me isolating because I very much want to be an isolate.

Okie doke, Iris said. Tell me if you feel ill or have any of those symptoms. Or any symptoms at all. Or if you need anything. I'll check in on you every day, if that's okay. Take your time.

Charlotte thinks Iris looks a bit like what a hedgerow would look like if an animator for a film made up a character who was meant to be a hedgerow. Her hair is wild. She looks out through it with the bright eyes of a bird. She partly brought Art up, from what Charlotte can gather.

She never talks about herself. She says things like this instead:

Yes, it's surreal for us here right now. But it's never not a state of emergency somewhere. We're naive if we think life normally isn't as surreal as fuck for most people scraping a living on this earth.

Charlotte can't take it right now.

Also, when an old person swears like that it's actually sort of shocking. It has revealed her own prurience to Charlotte, who'd also, till now, always thought herself an activist. Until she met the real thing, that is.

Call me Ire. My name's the only ire left in me. I'm way beyond anger now.

Is it something about how equipped, how practical, how sorted Iris is that has defeated, stunned stone dead, the calm-hearted activist in Charlotte?

Charlotte, when she first got back here from Suffolk, had told Iris about Art falling in love.

She and Iris had both laughed, both fond. Like they were like each other.

Then she'd told Iris – foolishly, her selfish self knows now – about Art and herself going to visit the detainees in the SA4A Immigration Removal Centre and how a clever and thoughtful young virologist being held indefinitely there had taken pains to explain to them, and this was back in early February when nobody much was taking the virus seriously in England, about the dangerous-sounding virus that was beginning to take hold in various countries and had reached England via the airport right next to the Immigration Removal Centre they were sitting in now, from which the planes that took off over their heads made the room they were sitting in literally shake every few minutes, and the virus was apparently now also present in the city just down the road from here where they were about to go and stay for the night.

He told them that if the virus happened to get into this centre he was being held in then all the detainees would catch it because the windows are made of a combination of perspex and metal bars, none of them openable to the outside world, the only air in there the recycled old air filtering through the place's ventilation system.

Iris's eyes had lit up.

They'll quietly let them out, she said. They won't want detained people dying and becoming a bad publicity story.

Then a week ago a news story broke about the

government release of a few hundred illegal immigrants thought to be most medically vulnerable to such an outbreak.

They won't be the only ones, Iris said. That's just the iceberg's tip. And released to where? To what? Where will they go?

I don't know, Charlotte said.

A lot of vulnerable innocent people will be homeless soon, Iris said, with no money and no family, and they'll desperately need somewhere to stay.

I guess so, Charlotte had said.

We have thirteen empty bedrooms now your Art in Natures have gone, Iris said, and three large public rooms. That's a possible sixteen separate rooms for people. I'll ask Artie if it's okay with him. I'll ask him if we can use his room too. That's seventeen.

(It was in the first days of Art being away elsewhere with other people.)

Ask him if you can use his room for what? Charlotte said.

The only two things we'd have to sort out, Iris said, before people arrive I mean.

What people? Charlotte said.

Because I think we'll have enough food for everyone for a couple of months, Iris said.

(Iris still works three times a week at a wholesale local healthfood place and the barn is already full of sacks of things like lentils and rice, Iris being generally of a state of emergency mindset.)

No, the real problem, Iris said, will be the increased load of shit, what to do with it.

Shit? Charlotte said.

Sewage is something Chei Bres has always had a problem with, Iris said, when there's more than a few people living here.

What's Chei Bres? Charlotte said.

(She thought it was maybe the name of the revolutionary group Iris lived with here in the 1970s and 80s.)

Chei Bres is this house's old name, Iris said. It's Cornish for house of thought, house where gestation takes place. House of the mind *and* house of the uterus. And when my sister renovated it what she forgot to renovate was the sewage system. Not that I'm speaking ill of my beloved dead. But for all her brilliance she could never be bothered to go deeper into anything than she had to. Including this house's foundational infrastructure. We had overcrowding sewage problems when just *two* of us lived here. So. First thing we'll need is a septic tank bigger than the one we've got.

Charlotte had nodded calmly at everything Iris was saying. Simultaneously she saw herself driving as fast as she could down to the Asda in town and packing the back of the car with tins of anything she could get and as much toilet paper as she could buy then phoning her old landlord to see if she could rent her flat back again and, even if she couldn't, driving at over the limit speeds back to London to find somewhere like it as fast as possible.

Why toilet paper?

Because it's what everybody in Australia had panic-bought.

So, logically, it'd be the thing that would run out first.

You'd always need toilet paper.

And why her old flat or something like it?

Because her old flat was a one-person flat and there wasn't room in there for anyone else. Or their shit.

She stood up and stretched.

Back in a minute, she'd said as if she were merely going through to the toilet.

She'd nipped upstairs to get her jacket and her wallet and her laptop and her toothbrush etc.

She'd slipped quietly out the back door.

She'd come round the side of the barn where nobody from the house can see you, and she'd opened the car door.

She'd sat in the driver's seat with the door still open.

But instead she'd opened her laptop and typed in *septic tank suppliers cornwall.*

Then she'd gone back into the house and given Iris a number to ring for someone to come with a digger.

At least she'd done *that*.

There'd still been some life in her *then*.

That's the thing about Iris. She's always unfailingly dauntingly right.

I wish they'd stop using war language, war imagery. This isn't a war. The opposite of a war is happening. The pandemic is making walls and borders and passports as meaningless as nature knows they are.

That evening, as they'd watched half an hour of the endless newsfeed,

Iris, Charlotte said. You're the endangered age. You have to isolate.

That'll be the day, Iris said. Isolation spells d, e, a, t and h to me. But don't worry, I've no intention of dying any time soon. And there's no such thing as the endangered age. We're all the endangered age now.

You're being stupid, Charlotte said. Your good intentions mean nothing. Not up against a virus.

Grant me some common sense, Iris said. We're all walking the line now, the line between one era and another. And you know how the old song goes, don't you?

Which old song is that, then? Charlotte said.

The one people ceremoniously sing, all across the world, when we're passing from one time to another? Iris said.

She sang a little of the song people sing at New

Year when they're all holding other people's hands with their arms crossed over themselves.

And there's a hand, my trusty fiere, she sang. And gie's a hand o thine.

My trusty fear? Charlotte said.

It doesn't mean fear. It means a friend, that word, Iris said. And I know, I know full well that we can't *literally* give a hand. What we have to do is work out how to give as much of a hand as we can in all the other possible ways.

My trusty fear.

A friend.

Charlotte went out of the room with the television in it. She sat on the stairs with something inside her as numb and dead as a, a what?

A toilet roll.

She hit herself hard with her own hand, with her fist, in the chest.

It hurt.

Good.

She did it again.

How do you jolt a dead self back to life?

She heard Iris coming through. Iris touched her lightly and affectionately on the head as she passed; she was carrying a lot of laundry under one arm and she had a screwdriver in her mouth.

She dropped the laundry in the hall, went to the front doors and started doing something to the lock on the inside door.

What Iris was doing, Charlotte saw, was taking the lock off.

She slid the Yale apparatus out of its slot and let it fall on to the floor. Then she went to work on the outer door too.

Are you replacing them? Charlotte said.

There'll be no locking anyone in here, not in any lockdown of ours, Iris said. Not for people who've been locked up for so long.

Charlotte's inner toilet roll blanched even whiter.

Shall I put that laundry in the annexe for you? she said.

It's clean, Iris said. But if you want to be really helpful you can bring me all the T-shirts you can find in the house.

Why? Charlotte said.

Masks, Iris said. I've twelve of my own here. We'll need between thirty six and forty. Thirty six at the least, two each so everybody's got a spare. Including you and me. Bring the kitchen scissors. I'll show you.

Charlotte went upstairs like a person going upstairs to look for T-shirts.

Back in a minute, she said.

She went into her room.

This was three days ago.

She'd shut the door.

She'd got one of the chairs and wedged its back right under the handle so nobody could open it from the outside.

She pulled down the blind.

Then she went and sat on her bed.

She got into the bed.

She pulled the covers right up over her head because a line of light was still getting in at the edge of the blind.

She put her own arms round herself.

A text arrives on Charlotte's non-web phone.

It's from Art.

It's later on the same day that he finally phoned and they argued.

It says:

Forgot to tell you this tale. Remember the Greenlaws from Brighton who we took with us to Suffolk? Today a parcel arrived addressed to Daniel. There was a very small violin case in the parcel and inside the violin case there was a very small violin.

Remember the kids? The boy who was really infatuated with you?

He sent a note. Dear Mr Gluck, thought you might like a small present from the past. Best wishes from your sister, Robert Greenlaw. The little violin is really beautiful. Daniel can't remember what it's about but he likes the violin a lot, it has delighted him. He has it on the bed next to him. But I bet the boy's mother and father don't know he sent it. Have you got an email or an address? We need to check with them.

Charlotte reads it again.

Best wishes from your sister, Robert Greenlaw.

She smiles.

She reaches and puts on a light next to the bed.

Here's some of what she remembers from the time she drove that family to the hotel they all stayed in, just after the visit to Mr Gluck.

The boy: Why did he call the stone a child?

Their mother: He's old. Old people get very addled.

The boy: I don't think he seemed at all addled.

Their mother: He was so addled he thought you were a girl.

The girl: *You* look like a *girl*.

The boy: He just thought for a minute I was someone he knew, that's all. It wasn't about being a girl or boy. He wasn't addled when we talked about Einstein.

Charlotte: When did you talk about Einstein with him?

The boy: He knew loads about Einstein. He knew about how Einstein played a violin when he was a child and he knew how much Einstein liked Mozart. And he told me what Einstein means in German. It's not just a name, it's two words. It means, literally, one stone, or a stone. So then we talked about Einstein's stone theory and he knew about that too.

Charlotte: What's Einstein's stone theory?

The boy: It's about how reality isn't what we see or what it seems, and you can prove it, and how susceptible the mind is and how we make stuff up all the time about reality, by lining up different coloured stones in a geometric shape and counting them. Then you add some more stones, yeah? But when you count them again it's like you didn't add *anything* because the number seems to add up to the same as it was before.

Their mother: Now I'm the one that's addled.

The boy: And we also talked about how particles meet, I mean when two meet each *other*, and how something changes in both of them. And after that, even if the particles are nowhere near each other, if one changes, the other does too.

The girl: Yeah, like when Arthur met Elisabeth. Oh my God. Did anyone else see?

Their mother: Oh, I saw.

The girl: Charlotte, did you see?

In that room that afternoon with the old man in the bed, a bright and charming old man who didn't seem to remember Art's mother but who took Art's hand in his and wouldn't let it go, Charlotte had seen the woman called Elisabeth see Art.

She had seen Art see the woman back.

Well, Art said in bed that night in Suffolk. Because we've, we've a lot in common.

It wasn't an answer to a question she'd asked. Charlotte hadn't said anything. He'd simply begun to try to explain or articulate something out loud, to himself really more than to her. But she sensed, she knew, that she was meant to ask, meant to engage with his engaging. So she did.

Like what? she'd said.

Well, for one thing. We both grew up with absent fathers, he said.

Charlotte lay on her back and looked at the plaster decoration round the light fitting in the ceiling. Fruits and flowers round the source of light.

How does it feel? she said.

It just, feels, well, right, he said.

Right, Charlotte said.

Like a very long view has opened in front of my eyes with a sky that goes on for miles across a sort of summer landscape, he said.

Uh huh, she said. Right.

It's like, I just, know, he said.

You just know what? Charlotte said.

I'm supposed to be with her, Art said.

Like you used to say you knew about me? Charlotte said.

Aw, Art said. I always knew, we always both knew, that I was pushing it when I told myself that about us.

True, Charlotte said.

I'm not pushing it when it's about her, he said. It feels quite different. It's amazing. It's shocking. It's lovely. It just, well, is. Where are you going? It's half eleven. Why are you getting dressed?

I just feel like going for a walk or something, she said.

You want me to come too? he said.

No, no, it's fine, she said. I just feel like getting some air.

Are you taking the car key? he said.

I might go for a drive, she said.

Will you be long? he said.

No, she said.

When she'd got back after driving around, the bed was empty. It was still warm from him when she got into it.

He'd left a note on her bag.

Am over at Elisabeth's. You take the car tomorrow. I'll get myself home when I've worked out where I am and what I'm doing.

Charlotte sits in the pool of light six weeks later, a lifetime later, and reads the text about the violin again.

She laughs out loud remembering.

The boy. The boy who stuck glass to his sister's hand so she'd break it and cut herself.

She remembers him saying, when they drove past a lighthouse on their way to the hotel, that Albert Einstein had once had an idea that a spell of enforced solitude – like lighthouse keepers had to endure as their everyday job – would be a good thing for young people who had a scientific or mathematical bent, because it would give them the chance to be uninterruptedly creative.

Don't believe anything he says, his sister, Sacha, said.

It's true, the boy said. Einstein *did* say it. He made a speech at the Royal Albert Hall and he said it then.

Yeah, sure he did, his sister said. *Char*lotte, Robert wants to tell you all about *Ein*stein.

In October 1933, the boy said. I can prove it. I can. It's in a book. I have the book with me.

She remembers he did have the book with him. In fact he had the book with him and nothing else.

His mother told them that night in the hotel pub when they were eating supper that her son had packed an overnight bag with no pyjamas in it, no toothbrush. All that was in it was a book about Albert Einstein.

Yeah because he's travelling light, his sister said. I mean literally, at the speed of.

At which point the two kids, who'd been fiercely arguing about everything, both fell about laughing at the joke with a pleasure, an infectious delight, the kind that made everyone in that restaurant turn towards their table, not in a way that meant they wished they'd be quieter or were finding something intrusive, but in that way where something warm happening will unite a room of strangers.

Charlotte sits up.

She gets up.

She takes the pillow off the chair by the window and leaves it on the floor. She takes the chair over to the desk. She puts on another light.

God, this room could do with a clean and an air.

She goes back over to the window and opens it.

Better.

She picks up Art's T-shirt. She puts it back over the back of the chair. She sits down.

At the desk she starts composing a text back to Art on her James Bond phone.

Was thinking about that time we were walking around north of kings cross not long after we first met, summer afternoon, and we saw the things arranged on the wall outside that block of flats with the sale sign next to them and you bought the ceramic dog, it said £3.50 on it do you remember, and you gave the man a fiver and told him to keep the change.

What she'd thought at the time was, *this man is a fool*. He was buying rubbish. Someone either very young or very useless had made it, white and yellow baked clay, body bent in the middle, shapeless paws and a dog head you could see thumbmarks in on both ears.

Over time she'd come to love that ceramic dog.

Not that she'd ever have admitted it to Art.

I think you buying that was the point at which I,

too, knew we weren't really meant as lovers but that I did love you anyway, she thinks.

She doesn't write that down. She deletes the bit of text she's already composed.

I'm terrified. Plus I'm having weird dreams. I had a dream where pain all over my body turned into paint all over my body.

She writes none of that.

What she writes instead is this:

I've an email for the greenlaws somewhere. I'll look it out. I wonder if ashley started speaking again or not. More than ever i want to send her a link to that lorenza mazzetti film. I will now.

Thank you for pigeon story. I will write about it and send you the piece i write tomorrow. Anyway my story for you about what i saw today is that i went online and looked at some photos of some of the places we've been in our time, all in lockdown, all looking you know as if a hand has come out of the sky in each place and gathered everybody up and away or like the living people have just been photoshopped out and it struck me it was like how in very early days of photography anything that was moving used to disappear because camera exposure took so long, like horses or traffic or people walking along. They became evanescent and vanished altogether or turned into a ghosty blur. Then i found some lockdown pictures of that street we stayed in in paris in montmartre do you remember the bed creaked so neither of us got any sleep so we sat up instead and watched the new day come up? Anyway i gasped out loud when i saw the street because the street has been being used as a location for a film set in the 1940s and when the lockdown came in they stopped filming there and just left it all done up like occupied paris all the fronts of the buildings with brown facades. The very few people in the photos looked like ghosts from modernity visiting the past wearing puffa jackets and facemasks and the occasional 21st century couple walking a little paris dog. So then i looked up the film that's been stopped by the lockdown. It's called adieu m. haffmann and seems to be a story of a jewish jeweller who has to hide to survive so hands his shop over to a younger assistant. The assistant asks the jeweller to help him and his beloved have a child. Stage play first, acclaimed in france and when i looked it up too voila this coincidence. The stage play was written by a man called jean-philippe daguerre. So. I began to wonder if the contemp playwright daguerre is maybe related to louis daguerre inventor of daguerreotype the man who took some of the earliest photographic images ever in many of which that vanishing effect happened. One of his most famous photos is of boulevard du temple late 1830s taken at busy time of day and almost every moving or living thing is gone except a man standing

*having his shoes shined. Everyone else
disappeared! It says online that's the very first
living person ever photographed. All because he
stood still. Yeah i thought but all the other gone
people are still there too. We just can't see them.
That is the thing from today that i wanted to tell
you. You know how people keep saying about this
time we're in now, oh well, we are where we are.
It's more like <u>we are where we aren't</u>.*

It has taken her an hour to write that text on her
Quantum of Solace phone.

She presses send.

Her phone in her hand goes blank and switches
itself off.

What?

What the fuck?

She switches it on again.

The text has disappeared.

It hasn't been saved.

She checks in the sent folder.

It's not there either.

She laughs out loud.

It is where it isn't!

She starts all over again.

*Just tried to text you a really long text but james
bond phone confiscated it. Here's a shorter one
instead. Got an email *somewhere* for greenlaws.
Let's also contact ashley who wrote the letterbox
thing and ask her to let us use her writing. We*

*could start an imprint. Art inertia. Ha ha. I mean
real books as well as online. We can use it to report
on what language was and is doing to us, what it
did in the run-up to now, and what it's doing in the
process of what's happening now to us all. *Good
to talk. I've been freaking out for a couple of days
but i'm back now.* Thank you for pigeon with
unwieldy twig and the urge to put things together.
I'll send my thoughts on it tomorrow and maybe
also on the boy sending the violin. It is a lovely
story. Plus i wd like to write a piece or two about
mazzetti the filmmaker and post online, what do
you think. Also we must start to lobby. Iris says a
german artist she knows told her he looked in his
bank account and found €9,000. €9,000! Where
did it come from? From the german government to
all that country's artists and arts workers no
strings attached. Piece on art in nature about that
too i think.*

There.

She presses send.

It goes.

It seems to have gone safely.

It's in the sent folder.

She takes the T-shirt off the back of the chair and
puts it over her nose. It smells of Art, of wood
shavings, vinegar.

She smiles.

Best wishes from your sister.

Imagine opening a parcel and inside it there's a violin case, but a very small one. Like the child of a violin case. Inside that, a small violin, like the child of a violin. It'd have that soft cushion stuff lining it over the fitted shape for holding and protecting the violin. It'd all smell of rosin, and wood, and of those two things coming together.

She gets up off the bed.

She takes the chair away from the door. She opens the door. She looks down.

Soup in a bowl at her feet.

Iris left it there, must be two hours ago.

But there's still a modicum of warmth in it.

She sits down in the threshold.

It does taste fine.

When she got downstairs in the hotel that night, no idea what to do with herself, no idea where she was off to or where she'd end up, only knowing she had to start out on a path for herself or there'd be no path, she saw that the Greenlaw family was still sitting in the pub part of the restaurant.

Grace was texting somebody or reading something on her phone. The kids were, yes, arguing.

Virtue signalling, the boy said.

Better than corruption signalling any day, the girl said back. And I want and need as many languages as I have selves. So should you.

I only need English, the boy said. Needing or knowing anything more is unpatriotic.

Stooge, the girl said. That's you all over.

What's me all over? the boy said. You're a stooge. You're a scrooge. You're a humbug. Shut up.

Retarded, the girl said. By what you think is your own initiative and which you imagine is keeping you safe. Oh, hi Charlotte.

Oh, the boy said. Hi.

Charlotte sat down at the table. Grace nodded to her and then to the half empty bottle.

Help yourself, she said.

She'll drink the whole bottle if you don't, the girl said.

I'm on holiday, Grace said. It's what adults do.

Yeah *some* adults, the girl said.

I won't, but thank you, Charlotte said.

She shakes the car key.

Are you going? the boy said.

Maybe, Charlotte said. Depends. What are you two fighting about?

We weren't fighting about anything, the boy said.

We were, the girl said. First he made me feel like I was going to throw up by telling me about how maggots can jump in the air.

They can, the boy said. They can do somersaults into the air thirty times their own bodylength. They are like little acrobats.

Then he said there was no point in learning different languages from other countries any more, the girl said.

What, like French and German? Charlotte said.

Or even from our own country, the girl said. Like Welsh. Like Ashley speaks.

Languages, Charlotte said, don't exist singly. They're like family. They all feed into each other all the time. There's no such thing as an isolated language.

The boy went red.

Oh I was just devil's advocating, he said. I don't really think it. In exactitude I think other languages are cool. I just didn't want her to think she had the monopoly on, on,

On what? the girl said.

On me, he said.

He stared at the car key on the pub table.

We're off really early tomorrow morning, Charlotte said. Before you're up. 6am or so.

Definitely before we're up, Grace said.

Oh, the boy said.

So I was about to go to bed, Charlotte said, but it struck me. We still haven't been, Robert, to where you said you wanted to go.

The Einstein place? Robert said. Really?

Depending, Charlotte said. On one or two things. The first, whether your mother says it's okay for you two to come, because it's ten past ten now, quite late to go anywhere. The second, on how far it actually is from here.

You're going to pander to him? Sacha said.

If it's not far, Charlotte said. Whoever'd like to come.

Robert leapt up almost sending his chair over. He ran out of the pub and they heard him clattering up the wooden stairs towards the rooms.

I'm not coming, Grace said. Count me out. I'm fully committed to communing with Val here.

Friend on your phone? Charlotte said.

Val Policella, Grace said. How's your hand, Sacha?

Same as it was the last time you asked, Sacha said.

We changed the bandage, Grace said. It was getting grubby.

Sacha held her hand out so Charlotte could see.

Is it painful? Charlotte said.

Only when Robert asks me if it is, Sacha said. Then it's really really painful.

He can go if you go with him, Grace said.

There's no way I'm going, Sacha said.

Robert burst back into the room waving an open book. He slammed the book down on the table sending the wine bottle rocking.

Roughton Heath, Charlotte said. Am I pronouncing it right?

Ruffton, Sacha said. Rowton. Pity nobody at this table speaks English.

But we don't need to know how to *say* it to *go* there. Do we? Robert said.

You can't go unless I go too, mum says, and there's no way I'm going, Sacha said.

Robert, you know it's a heath, Grace said. You know there'll be nothing to see. It'll be dark. It'll be a lot of bushes and trees in the dark.

Still, Charlotte said. You can say you've been.

But only if I say I'm going, Sacha said. And I'm not.

You know my little brother is totally infatuated with you? she said from behind Charlotte in the driver's seat half an hour later, when they stopped on a verge, its grass silver in the headlights, to let Robert empty his bladder into a hedge.

Her voice was serious.

He's really easily hurt, she said.

Charlotte switched the little light above the rear mirror on and turned to look at Sacha.

When I was a bit younger than you, Charlotte said, I had an American cousin who came to stay. I still have her, I suppose, somewhere in the world, but I don't know where, I've never seen her since. She came to stay with us for a summer, she was seven years older than me, I was ten. And I thought she was the best thing since sliced everything, the best most exciting person I'd ever met. And she knew I did. And she was kind to me.

My father and mother afterwards always remembered her visit as this terrible time, and my cousin as scandalous, as trouble, coming home at four in the morning covered in lovebites from the nightclub in town, a wild child they were scared to have to be so responsible for. For years I'd hear them talking about someone and a terrible time that this someone gave them, and I'd no idea they meant my cousin. It's only later in my life I realized that's who they were talking about when they said those things. My glamorous kind funny cousin. I think now that the fact that she was kind to me changed my life dramatically.

Uh huh, Sacha said as if saying *I'm listening.*

If people think you like them, Charlotte said, well, it can go either way. There's a lot of powerplay in liking and being liked. Such a powerful connection, it's a chance to make the world bigger for someone else. Or smaller. That's always the choice we've got.

Uh huh, Sacha said.

That's why we're on the Einstein trail at eleven o clock on a Friday night, Charlotte said.

My brother's had a lot of trouble with online bullying, Sacha said.

Ah, Charlotte said.

It's pathetic, really, Sacha said. Some thug at his school found out he won prizes for singing when he was a little kid. He did, he had a really amazingly high singing voice and it made him a kind of local celebrity. When they found out, they started to make fun of him about it. Then they started taking the piss out of how clever he is then all these kids on social media and a bunch of people who trolled into the thread kept telling him to commit suicide.

Christ, Charlotte said.

So they moved him to a new school, Sacha said.

Thank goodness, Charlotte said.

But someone at the first school wrote to someone at the new school, Sacha said, and then it all started happening there too.

Tell you what, Charlotte said. I wish I had a sister like you.

What've you got? Sacha said. Have you got brothers?

Charlotte laughed.

I've got Arthur, she said.

You're not related to him though, Sacha said. He's not your actual family.

Do you think you have to be related, to be family? Charlotte said.

I think it helps, Sacha said. And hinders.

Robert got back in the car.

What? he said. What are you talking about? Are you talking about me?

Tell Charlotte about when you did the Facial Rec project, Sacha said.

No, Robert said.

Go on, Sacha said. It was really good. He did this project called F-ART, where he made a poster-screenprint series at school by mapping facial recognition technique faceprints like stars across a night sky, only he made them look like the linked-up drawings of constellations, you know, the ones where lines go between the stars to try to make pictures so you can see it's a bear or a plough or Orion. Except, his constellations were all faces, he did one for me, one for our mother, one for our father, he wrote our names underneath each pattern –

But not Ashley, Robert said.

– then across the bottom of the pictures he wrote the slogan, CHANGE FRT TO ART, Sacha said.

That's fantastic, Charlotte said. Why not for Ashley? I thought you were friends with Ashley.

Yeah, that's right. Big friends with Ashley, Sacha said.

Ashley and I weren't speaking to each other on friendly terms at this point in the trajectory of our very recent friendship, Robert said.

Anyway, the point is, he got into trouble from the school, Sacha said. They said he was only doing the screenprint series to get a rude word pinned up repeatedly on the walls of the art classroom. But I'm telling you. They were really beautiful. Revolutionary. I think that's why they wouldn't put them up.

Charlotte told the kids she once had an idea that she'd like to hack Facebook and replace everybody's faces and bodies in their photographs with the faces and bodies of Pokémons. They both laughed out loud at that, leaning forward, hanging off the front seats from the back seat like much smaller children. Sacha said that her own revolutionary plan in Christmas week was to smash the glass doors of office buildings all round the city so homeless people would have somewhere warm and sheltered to stay in.

That's because she's got the hots for a homeless guy in town, and he's a really old guy, in his thirties or forties, Robert said. OW.

It's not the hots, Sacha said.

Just the warms? Charlotte said.

She wants to warm his heart, Robert said. Or his something. OW. She definitely gives him more than money. OUCH.

What about you, Robert? Charlotte said. Any plans to change the world?

I'm a realist, Robert said.

What does that mean? Charlotte said.

It's a thing that can't be done, Robert said.

Defeatist, Sacha said.

Yeah and you with your *the day will come when we'll all be wearing leaves instead of clothes* vision of the world, Robert said.

It will, Sacha said. We'll have to change everything. And leaves really matter. They're how we get oxygen.

Overweening pride, Robert said.

What is? Charlotte said.

To think an individual can change the world, Robert said.

That's an overweening kind of a thing to say on an Einstein-themed roadtrip, Charlotte said.

Yeah, but that was, I mean, he was Albert Einstein, Robert said.

And you're Robert Greenlaw, Charlotte said.

Here lies Robert Greenlaw, Brother of the great Sacha Greenlaw, Sacha said.

Yeah, cause that's what it'll actually say on my gravestone, Robert said. Robert Greenlaw. Pity him. He was once somebody's brother.

Robert Greenlaw, Sacha said. He was once somebody's brother. Pity her.

Robert Greenlaw, Robert said. Renowned for making a fortoon. And his sister, Sacha Greenlaw. Renowned for spending a fortoon giving it to homeless people to buy boots.

I *told* you, he had his boots *stolen*, Sacha said.

That's your excuse, Robert said.

People always steal homeless people's shoes, Sacha said. It's one of the cruel things that happens to homeless people quite often.

Or it's the thing homeless people say to get you to give them more money, Robert said.

What's a fortoon? Charlotte said.

A cartoon-sized fortune, Robert said. Are we here?

Charlotte has stopped the car in the dark in the middle of nowhere.

Look, she said.

She pointed to the satnav.

Off to the left of the cursor that meant their car the screen had the words ROUGHTON HEATH on it.

She switched the headlights off.

They all got out.

They stood around.

The moon was bright.

What they could see in the moonlight was a spread of undifferentiated darkness.

Why did he come here again? Sacha said.

It says in the book, Robert said, that the Nazis were distributing posters with his picture on them and the words Not Yet Hanged underneath. And he was in Belgium and someone told him the Nazis knew where he was and were coming for him. So he took up an offer of a hut on this heath from an upper class English guy in politics who'd started off being very right wing and thinking Hitler was a good thing, then changed his mind and invited Einstein to stay with him and live in a hut on the heath. So Einstein did, for, like, a month, and gamekeepers guarded him, and he spent the time in solitude and worked on theories, and then a month or two later he went to America. And that month when he was living here he used to go to the post office in the village and buy sweets. Can we go to that post office?

They got back in the car.

They drove to where the satnav told them Roughton Post Office was.

They peered at it through the car windows.

Do you think it's the same one as it was in 1933? Robert said.

Hard to say, Charlotte said.

They drove up the road a little further and stopped next to a shut pub.

Look, Charlotte said. Robert.

She said it quietly because Sacha was asleep, curled into herself with her bandaged hand at an angle away from herself.

Near the shut front door of the New Inn there was a circular plaque, like a blue plaque. It had Einstein's name on it.

She got out of the car. Robert did too. They both left the doors a little open so as not to wake Sacha.

ALBERT EINSTEIN
fleeing Nazi persecution stopped off en route
for America to live in a hut on Roughton Heath,
September 1933

Underneath, it said the plaque had been made by the Eastern Daily Press and the Norwich School of Art & Design.

Art and design and the fourth estate, Charlotte said. Here's to them.

Do you think he came to this place? For a beer? Robert said.

I've a feeling that if he did, Charlotte said, then this pub would have a sign up saying Albert Einstein fleeing Nazi persecution stopped off en route for America at this pub for a beer, September 1933.

But he could've, Robert said. It says in the book nobody in the village knew who he was. He could've come here for a beer and people might just not have known it was him.

That's possible, yes, Charlotte said.

Possible, Robert said. Possible possible possible.

He walked purposefully about back and fore in front of the front door of the shut pub saying the word possible.

Do you think I'm traversing some of the same ground he did? he said.

Why do you like Einstein so much? Charlotte said.

Apart from that he was one of the most brilliant minds that ever thought about anything on this planet? Robert said. Because he has a face like a lamb.

Ah, Charlotte said.

Because he was truly in love with the universe, Robert said.

Yes, Charlotte said.

Because he wanted to understand the architecture of light, Robert said.

The architecture of light, Charlotte said. I like that. That's like the name of a poem.

Is it? Robert said.

Yes, Charlotte said. Did you think that up?

I don't know, Robert said, I might've read it somewhere. It doesn't sound like me. And if you and me, I mean I, were standing on the edge of a black hole. Which we're not. But if we *were* to stand on the edge of a black hole. And say you happened to be standing closer to its edge than me.

Okay, Charlotte said.

And then we both came back down to earth, Robert said. Then I would've got older faster than you would've, because I was standing further away from it, and by the time we got back to earth we might've been able to catch up on an age difference.

That's very interesting. Thank you for telling me, Charlotte said.

They decided to walk as far round the outside of the building as they could to maximize the possibility of walking where Einstein possibly once walked.

While they did, Robert told Charlotte about the day he saw a man, not an old man, he was quite a young man, stumble when he came out of a Wetherspoons, because he was so pissed, and fall flat on the pavement then crawl on all fours all the way to the seafront with his trousers and underpants down around his ankles.

And it wasn't even a Friday, or a Thursday, Robert said. It was only a Monday. He wasn't even with any other drunk friends or having a good time. He was just pissed. And you could, you could, everybody could, see all of him.

Ah, Charlotte said.

Primal, Robert said.

Good word for it, Charlotte said.

I don't want to live in a world like that, Robert said.

We're certainly living in one where the primal and the public have been getting more and more fused together, Charlotte said.

Yeah, Robert said.

He said it sadly.

But if we don't attend to the primal stuff inside us all, Charlotte said, where will it go?

I don't know, Robert said. Into our bones?

I think it surfaces so we have to decide what to do about it, Charlotte said. So, there's that man you saw. And then there's, well – you said it. There's also the people who study all their lives to understand the structure of a shaft of sunlight.

But what if you're a mix of *all* of the things. And it's not possible to be just *one* of them? Robert said. What does that make you?

Human? Charlotte said. Like, you know. Someone who'd stick a glass thing to his sister's hand? With superglue?

It wasn't just glass, Robert said. It was so much more than just a *glass thing*.

What was it, then? Charlotte said.

It was time, Robert said.

Time, Charlotte said. Is that the gift we get to give to others, then?

Robert shrugged.

Don't know, he said.

Me neither, Charlotte said. What would Einstein say?

He'd say, Robert said, that the human species got our best intellectual tools from looking at the stars. But that this doesn't make the stars responsible for what we do with our intellects.

Wow, Charlotte said. Robert. What a great thing to say.

Is it? Robert said.

Pleasedness radiated off him.

But I didn't say it, he said. Einstein did.

But you said it *now*, Charlotte said. You said it *for* now. You said it like, I don't know, like you hit the target. Knockout punch. Perfect timing. Hole in one.

Black hole in one, Robert said.

They stood under a night sky in a car park where Einstein himself perhaps maybe possibly once stood and looked up at the lit pinpoints in the dark that meant the ancient and original and already dead stars, till Robert's sister, waking up and seeing them wave to her, pulled her coat round her shoulders, got out of the car and came over to where they were standing in the cold and they all looked up together to point out which constellations they knew the names for and to guess at the ones they didn't.

1 July 2020

Dear Sacha Greenlaw,

Thank you very much for writing to me. It was very kind of you.

Thank you for telling me many things about the bird.

I write to you today because I have seen this bird and its family in my sky. I want very much to tell you.

Our friends Charlotte and Arthur gave me your two letters. I really enjoyed them very much. Thank you for telling me stories of your life. Thank you for imagining my life. Thank you for allowing me to imagine your life. Thank you for telling me legends of the hero name. Thank you for the funny poem.

My name in Vietnamese English is ANH KIET.
I cannot do a thing I need to do on the computer
keyboard for the E in KIET to be correct, which
requires a hat above it like a roof and also a small
dot like a full stop beneath. In Vietnamese my name
is like a picture of a figure with wide shoulders, or a
house with two wide strong roofs, with one roof
placed on top of the other roof. The words of my
name when they are separate mean

ANH: brother / you

KIET: masterpiece

When they are together they make a meaning like
the English word hero. I am not a hero! I am not a
masterpiece! But I am a brother.

I am living now in a house with 15 other released
people and our mutual friend Charlotte and
her Aunt Iris. They are very, very kind. The
immigration removal centre unlocked its doors and
placed us out on to the road in a dark night. It was
raining heavily so we went to the airport and slept
on seats in Departures. We called on a phone to a
friend. We are lucky. They came to find us. Friends
drove us here in three trucks that sell coffee, very
handy for the long trip!

My small medical abilities help a little if people
get sick. One man to the hospital and died. But now
everybody here at the house is well. I also help keep
neat and flourishing the flowers in the summer
garden. I am a good gardener. I did not know it

about me! I am a new man. The garden is very beautiful here. In one place in it they are hundreds of older roses. They make me very happy.

Your letters make me very happy. Thank you for the bird messages. Bird of all nations. It looks like something created with only the ash after a fire, like a delicate gesture of ash. But truly it is as strong as the anchor that holds a boat in the sea.

I hope with my heart you and your family are well at this time.

I agree there is more summer to come and there will be more weeks of your bird in my sky. This makes me very happy.

The bird that I see in the sky, the bird of your kindness in your letters to me, will fly to you in your sky in the shape of members of its family. They will bring with them my very best and warmest good wishes. Health and luck for you and your family and your friends and your loved ones,

to my friend Sacha Greenlaw

from your friend and brother

ANH KIET / Hero

Acknowledgements and thanks

A number of online and textual resources concerning
World War 1 and World War 2 internment in the UK
have helped in the writing of this book,
especially texts by Ronald Stent
and by the great Fred Uhlman.
The book that Robert Greenlaw refers to throughout
is Einstein on the Run by Andrew Robinson (Yale).
Of the many resources I went to for swift life,
by far the most inspiring was Swifts in a Tower
by David Lack (Unicorn).

Thank you, Simon.
Thank you, Anna.
thank you, Hannah, Lesley L, Lesley B, Sarah,
Richard, Emma, Alice, and everyone
at Hamish Hamilton and Penguin.

Thank you, Andrew,
thank you, Tracy,
and everyone at Wylie's.

Thank you to my anonymous friend who
tells me about everyday life in this country's
Immigration Removal Centres.

Huge thank you to Brighid Lowe and Henry Miller –
an especially emphatic thank you to Brighid,
and to Robert Osborne at Zidane Press.
thank you to Robin Baker at the BFI,
Gaby Smith, Olivia Smith and
Donald Smith at the SFI,
thank you, Jeremy Spandler and the Feminist Library,
and to the Word and Image Department at the V&A.

Thank you, Kate Thomson,
thank you, Lizzie, Dan, Nel and Béa.

Special thank you to Isla Casson
and to Anna-Maria Hartmann.

Very special thank you
to Batia Nathan and Idit Elia Nathan
and to the memory of Rachel Rosner
for the kind of family life story
that puts the life into everything

and to Gillian Beer
for her immortal Winter's Tale tale.

Thank you, Mary.

Thank you, Xandra.

Thank you, Sarah.

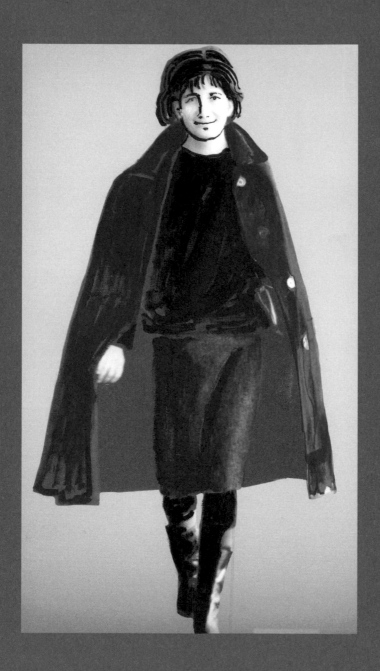